OUR NUN

OUR NUN

A NOVEL
BY ROB LAUGHNER

MELVILLE HOUSE PUBLISHING
HOBOKEN, NEW JERSEY

MELVILLE HOUSE PUBLISHING
P.O. BOX 3278
HOBOKEN, NJ 07030

BOOK DESIGN: DAVID KONOPKA

ISBN: 0-9718659-6-5
FIRST EDITION | OCTOBER 2003

LIBRARY OF CONGRESS CATALOGING-IN-PUBLICATION DATA

Laughner, Rob, 1958-
Our nun / Rob Laughner.— 1st ed.
p. cm.
ISBN 0-9718659-6-5
1. Boys—Fiction. 2. Farm life—Fiction. 3. Pennsylvania—Fiction.
4. Male friendship—Fiction. I. Title.
PS3612.A943O97 2003
813'.6—dc22

2003017222

To my mother,
Francis Knox Laughner
and in memory of my father,
John William Laughner

OUR NUN

CHAPTER 1

He was down in the oldest part of the cemetery lying on Cress Wells' grave, just lying there, on the ground, on somebody's *grave*. You weren't supposed to even *step* on somebody's grave if you could at all help it... but there he was—about the last place you'd expect to see our Sunday School teacher. Especially now when everybody was supposed to be inside for Opening Exercises. That was that little aerobic interval between church and Sunday School class when the Sunday School Superintendent—Murray Glenn at that time—said a prayer, talked a little bit about something pertinent and then led us through a song before breaking us up into our individual classes. To tell the truth, Stan, Ben, Charlie and I usually skipped Opening Exercises and wandered around outside instead. It was the end of May and already very hot inside. But Bobby Morgan who was an actual adult never skipped as far as we knew so that's why it was surprising to see him down there. More surprising because he was down there in his good clothes, in the grass... right on a person's *grave*, for Pete's sake. But the *most* surprising thing was that he had been beheaded.

And I don't mean just a little bit. This wasn't one of your vague, half-hearted beheadings. This was the kind that took your literal breath away. Ours anyway. It did.

He had on his good brown suit, kind of a cowbird head-brown, white shirt with a green plaid tie, wingtips. If you hadn't recognized the suit, the wingtips you would have. Bobby Morgan was still in his 20s but he was a nut about wingtips and his were all nubs and shine. He was lying face-up—or, you know... There were definitely stains on his shirt and tie but I'd say he might've even looked neater than normal because if there was ever going to be anything messed up about Bobby it was his hair (that wiry hair that won't go right each and every day).

Well, walking along away from the church between two rows of head stones towards the woods and the edge of the cemetery, our first sight of him, our very first glimpse was only the lower half of Bobby Morgan. Naturally, we stopped right then talking about how we were going to skip Sunday School class, too. Then we finally got to him, I mean, to all that was left of him.

Stan emitted a long, low, whispered: Hohhh-*ewww*-ohhh-lee-*cow*!

Ben, astute as ever, added, "He looks *dead*," and no one said anything more.

We failed to make fun of Ben or to even look around for Bobby's head or to dwell on anything like emotions about our former Sunday School teacher resting there before us. Stanley crushed what was left of the cigarette, a loaner he had borrowed from his father on the sole of a penny loafer and we started quickly back to the church.

When we came through the back door into the sanctuary they were singing, due to Mr. Glenn's pathological weakness for Christmas carols, *O Come Emmanuel*. Janie Graham... she was playing the piano.

He stood, Mr. Glenn did, up there between the two front rows of pews, facing the back of the church where everyone had piled up, but his eyes were on the frayed, green, cloth-covered hymnal spread across his right hand and he didn't see us at first. We looked at each other nervously for about two "O comes". Charlie's eyes were big, round rings, his face whiter even than his towheaded noggin.

Then without warning, Stan yelled out over the warbling, "There's a dead body in the cemetery!"

That was what he actually said. The news came as a surprise to no one of course but a shout, a real and true, if not completely top-of-the-lungs, shout, in our church did. The place went silent in what was the closest I ever heard our congregation come to unison and there was a great pinkening in our direction as the back of every head turned into a face.

I avoided my parents' stare by focusing on Mrs. Morgan. Stanley had been ambiguous for a reason. It wasn't always easy to believe but he could be a pretty considerate kid when it was really called for. Mrs. Morgan's square but not harsh face and unlipsticked lips quickly became too much to handle, too, though, and I locked onto Rev. Stone who had stood up just in front of Mr. Glenn. Our hearts pounded out a short moment of awkward silence until the Rev. spoke.

"Boys? What are you up to?" he asked.

Stanley responded. "Up to? Nothing! Rev. Stone, our Sunday Sch—there's a—we need to talk to you," he said, his composure disintegrating. He took off up the left side of the church walking fast, really fast, trotting.

Ben, Charlie and I stayed put and let the attention shift away with our brave friend to the side doors of the sanctuary where he converged with the Rev. coming from the opposite direction. They talked. You couldn't make out any single words, just their hash and rustle.

Stan had his back to the congregation and his ears were the color of sour cherries. Pie cherries. They were shining. Rev. Stone listened intently, brows furrowing and face becoming waxy. Then, quickly, even as Stan's head still bobbed, some magical religious training took hold and the Rev.'s face regained a measure of calm and color.

He looked out past Stan to the pews and said, "Friends, something untoward seems to've taken place in the cemetery. Timothy and Charles, Ralph, would you mind coming with us please. I would ask that everyone else please stay inside until we check this out. Please. We'll be right back."

Timothy Robison, he was my Dad (still is), got up, as did Charles Glenn and Ralph Alexander—they were the current elders of the church who were there that morning—and headed for the doors, the side doors where Stan and Rev. Stone were standing. Those doors marked the divide between the threadbare carpet of the sanctuary and the rutted linoleum of the vestibule beyond and they swung both ways like saloon doors in movies. As Dad and the others went clicking across the harder floor to the church's main doors and the outdoors, Mom and I shared a split second of frightened, suspicious eye contact—frightened for me, frightened and suspicious for her. Then we three hustled back through the back doors figuring the Rev.'s request could not logically apply to us.

Outside we took a dead sprint down the west side of the church. I mean, we were *sprinting*, and, still, we barely beat the rest of the congregation into the cemetery. Our old Sunday School teacher, in spite of himself, still managed to teach us something important that day: Presbyterians do not take orders too good.

When Dad and the others got to Bobby Morgan they immediately set into a shuffling circuit around him. Their expressions were grim but not animated in any other way. Except for Mr. Glenn's. He looked not only grim but also really mad, his hands—thick as catcher's mitts from a whole life of milking cows, the first half of which without benefit of milking machines—away from his sides, and in front a little bit, like he was about to hurt somebody. We—Stan, Ben, Charlie, me—stood right at the edge of the woods and tingled, weirdly, with both guilt and pride, guilt over causing this disturbance and a simple, bizarre, dog-like pride of discovery.

And, tingling, we watched everyone else come down through the rows of gray and brown stones.

Some of the women picked their feet straight up, marching sort of, like carefully browsing chickens, because the grass was still dewy and their little Sunday shoes were not great in the wetness. As the first ones got close enough to see the whole picture there was a fluttering chain reaction of gasps and hands flying up to mouths and finally, suddenly, after a certain critical mass of shock and awareness had coalesced, some frantic hen dancing and a great herding of the little kids back out of the cemetery to the church, the shoes thoroughly bedewed.

I only caught a glimpse of Janie Graham helping get the little ones away. I don't know what her first reaction was like.

My sister Isabelle—Izzy—and her friends kept their distance and went to shoo-ing, too. My older brother Cambell wasn't home from college yet and my seven-year-old brother, Jacob... he somehow broke away from the flock and ran a zigzag between headstones and folks and got close enough to get a glimpse before being roped in by Izzy who pushed him in Mom's direction.

The ghastliness, in its full, of what had happened to Bobby Morgan was only now truly sinking in to me. There he was, neat as ever to behold, but his head was not. His head had been hacked off. Bobby Morgan had been hacked to death. Our Sunday School teacher. An accountant, of all the things. This was bad.

Dad knelt down and lifted the right lapel of Bobby's suit coat. Ben elbowed me but I did not look at him. I thought

8

he would say something idiotic. With his left hand Dad reached into Bobby's inside pocket, found nothing, and then, strangely, I thought, gave Bobby a pat on the chest. It was a gentle, there-there, you'll-be-okay pat. He looked up at us. The widow's peak of his crew cut appeared sharper and more severe than usual but his face was composed in a faintly amused dumbfoundedness that your face gets when you need to pretend you're shocked at some unpleasant thing that you actually aren't shocked at and don't find unpleasant. Dad wasn't faking though.

He looked over to Rev. Stone, who held the tattered green hymnal he had carted outside tightly to his chest, and said, "This is a woman."

As Dad said this—which, truthfully, struck me as kind of a rude thing to say—the really old people of the congregation had finally made their way over. Mrs. Morgan was among them and I don't know if she actually heard what Dad had said or what but when she peered over old Mrs. McHenry's shoulder and saw the body, the clothes, she tipped over sideways, her face disappearing for a moment behind Mrs. McHenry before reappearing on Mrs. McHenry's other side. Luckily, Mr. Kendall caught her, saying, "*Whoa, whoa!*" while propping her up on her feet. She was woozy, not completely out, and assisted in her own recovery.

At that very moment, however, a car pulled into the parking area on the east side of the church. You couldn't see it but you could hear the tires crunching the gravel and then the choky rattle of an off engine running on. Seconds later who should stumble into view, bobbing down through the newer part of the cemetery in his normal skewed manner, but Bobby Morgan, the living specimen, a man.

This sight knocked many, many, more than a few, off their kilter. Mrs. Morgan drooped back into Mr. Kendall's grasp with all her weight now; Mrs. McHenry, in front of her, went all the way to the ground, instantaneously, *instantaneously*, like a load of rocks. She was *not* a small woman. Rocks, like the latch had been tripped on the front-end loader and out they fell all at once. *Woomp*! One instant she was standing and had her recognizable shape and the next she was a formless pile of polyester and bulges.

Most, it turned out, had not heard my Dad's discovery. So having two Bobby Morgans, one dead and headless, and another fully alive and walking towards us, head and all, was slightly supernatural. Even there in broad daylight. For his part, Bobby must've initially thought he'd not only shown up late for church but had wandered into a bizarre, impromptu graveside memorial service. Accordingly, and understandably, the closer he got to us the slower and more cautiously he approached. His hair, not going right, of course, dented and bent on one side and kind of puffy on the other, combined with the way he moved and his confused expression, due probably increasingly to the looks he was getting from us the closer he got rather than to the oddness of the big gathering out here, made him look kind of pathetic and even stupid in a way.

He reached us, a ghost and his gallery, and stopped, just shy of Mr. Alexander and Mr. Glenn. He did not see "his" body right away.

"Bobby," Mr. Alexander said—or something about as simple as that—and then stepped back a little, turning sideways as if to introduce the two. Bobby to the body, body to Bobby.

Now he saw it. His mouth, which had been hanging open, went closed, his jaws tightening, the knotty joints lifting on either side of his face. His eyes squinted.

Ben elbowed me again and this time I looked over at him. He was fixed on Dad who had a piece of gold jewelry in his hand. It was attached to a fine chain that disappeared between the second and third buttons of the body's shirt, a necklace. Not just a necklace, though. A cross. And not just a cross. It was a crucifix.

The limit of how weird and impossible things could ever get on any given morning at Perth Hill United Presbyterian Church had thus been reached. A body. Murdered. Headless. Female. In Bobby Morgan's clothes. And... *Catholic*.

CHAPTER II

Well, we were assuming it, the body—she—had been those
things, murdered, Catholic. There were other possibilities, I
guess, but they seemed slim: accident, suicide, Jew,
Protestant, etc. To tell you the truth, I didn't know the
cross was a crucifix until Izzy talked about it on the way
home. I don't think I'd ever seen one before. At the time I
just thought it was some fancy cross or something with extra
decoration or something, maybe a strand of golden thorns
wrapped around it as a symbol or something. I hadn't gotten a close enough look to tell it was actually supposed to be
Jesus Christ right there on it, nailed, crucified and all, as per
the Bible and Easter and everything.

Rev. Stone said we'd better call the police and Gorty,
older than my parents but one of God's least complex

beings, was off running back to the phone in the church shouting as he ran that he would do it before the Rev. had finished saying it. Volunteering for things was about Gorty's favorite activity.

Folks started whispering and gawking closer and milling around the gravestones and settling into groups of a couple to several to talk the situation over. Bobby Morgan didn't know who it was. He had given those clothes, if they were in fact his, to the City Rescue Mission. They weren't worn out, just didn't fit anymore since he'd gained weight.

Mr. Glenn shook his head as if nothing made sense to him, particularly giving away perfectly good clothes, saying, "We should keep things as they are until McDonough gets here."

John McDonough was our constable, for our township, Fox Township, and that was probably what the Rev. meant when he said 'police'. The seriousness and incredibility of all this must have made the word 'constable' seem not quite up to the requirements. Whichever, the notion that some kind of outside authority would be here soon now occurred to me for the first time and that unseemly pride I'd been feeling vanished.

A question throttled me: Had I held that stupid thing with my fingertips? Or just between my fingers?

Gorty came back running and yelling. "They're coming! They're coming!" You could tell from that 'they' that Paul Revere had gone beyond the call of duty, that more than just old McDonut would be showing up.

Minutes later the first soft sneer of sirens started to range in over the hills and woods and plowed fields from, it seemed, halfway round the planet. I moved away from the woods behind Wells' headstone and Wm. Mawson's right next to it and the body and went slowly down the edge of the old cemetery toward the church hoping Charlie would get away from his mother and sisters, which he did.

"What about the bush?" I asked.

"What about it?" Charlie said, shrugging. His coat was tight. It was his next older brother's. Too small already because Charlie got most of the plumpness in his family. All the Lane kids had white hair, though. Charlie's face had color again.

"Part of the crime scene," I panted.

The bush, a shrub, was where Stan had stuffed that cigarette butt. It was where we always put them.

Ben—Benjamin Dudley Graham—came over just then, saying, "Maybe this isn't a crime scene."

Charlie blinked at him. "Is that a joke?"

Ben held his hands out in front of himself like he was a reasonable person. One whose zipper was up. And one who was about to explain an obvious fact to us. "Maybe it didn't happen here. It could've happened anywhere. D'joo hear the Bad Ones last night? I did. They were loud. It could'eh happened down by us. Maybe it did."

"You think dogs did this?" said Charlie.

"Nooo, well... something had them riled up."

I had heard the Bad Ones, too. And we didn't live close to Ben. We lived close to the church. They were getting around, a bunch of strays that got themselves together for the sport of killing sheep, kind of like a demented fox hunt.

Sorry thing about sheep, they expire when they get chased too much. Their little bleating hearts just quit, simple as that. The Bad Ones, every reincarnation of them, never *ate* the sheep. They were in it just for the chasing and the killing. Lots of fun. It would end badly, of course, for the Bad Ones, as it always did, and pretty directly.

Charlie's patience was usually pretty thin with old Ben. "So every time you hear a dog there's a murder?" He snorted. "It's a crime scene, Ben. Even if it didn't happen here, y're still not allowed to just dump dead bodies off."

"Even in cemeteries," I added.

"Thank you, Boyd. Right. That has to be illegal. Even if it isn't the only crime scene."

Ben gave in. "Okay. I did hear the Bad Ones though. That's what I meant."

"Y're even a crime scene, Dudley," said Charlie. "Check yer barn door, would'jeh?"

Ben peered down, then yanked his zipper two-thirds of the way up. Benjamin wasn't usually so docile, not because he was too big for his age or anything, which he wasn't, just because that's how he was, like a paper cut. Not big or dangerous, just annoying.

"Do fingerprints show up on paper?" I asked nervously, trying to recall how I'd held that stupid cigarette.

"Probbly," said Charlie brightly. "Especially yers and Ben's. Why are you so paranoid? We'll stick up for yeh, Red. We know you killed her in self-defense."

"Very funny. Hilarious... that's not what I'm worried about."

"I know. Don't worry about it." Charlie sounded calmer than I figured he was. "Nobody's going to find out," he continued. "We'd just blame it on Stanley anyways. He made us."

"Oh yeaaaaah... He'll go along with that."

"Sure, Red. He has a big heart. He'd like being the fall guy for you degenerates."

"US degenerates... weasel."

Behind us a voice, Jimmy Alexander's, said, "This place is full of... *degenderates* this morning." and hesitated as we turned around. "Get it? De-GENDER-ates?"

He laughed silently, his head dipping up and down. Jimmy had black hair and a slight, angular build. He had an angelic, kind way about him, which was good cover for the way he could really be at times, that being kind of evil, in a playful way, of course. His mind could cook up some pretty dirty things. About girls and other stuff. *They* didn't know that of course. *They* thought he was sweet and cute and could play the piano without looking at his fingers. All true but he was way more interesting than that. He and Ben were cousins. You wouldn't know that though unless you just knew it.

"Don't talk about Ben like that, Jimmy," Charlie said with a laugh, somehow happy and at ease with our parents finding out we'd been smoking and then killing us. "You'll hurt his feelings."

Ben hit him in the small of his back.

"Ow! See! I told you."

"Did you see the look on Bobby's face?" Jimmy said. Then shaking his head, "The one time I go to Opening Exercises... beheaded. Can you believe that? You guys thought it was Bobby? You didn't touch it or anything?" He turned back in the direction of the body, squinting. "This is sick. Where's the head?"

"At the other crime scene," offered the Paper Cut, insistent on salvaging some fly speck of his theory and ignorant pride.

"Yeah," said Charlie, "She probbly ran around for a while. Like a chicken. Ended up here."

We choked on guilty chuckles. Charlie kept his thin lips pressed tightly shut and shook his head gravely.

"Jimmy, how often do you guys clean the church and mow out here and everything," I asked quietly. The Alexanders were the church custodians.

"Once a week." He eyed me suspiciously. "Why?"

"You know the bush... have you ever actually cleaned it... of all the you-know-whats, the... loaners from Stan's Dad?"

His jaw dropped as his head went up. "The burning bush! Stan got a loaner? I thought his Dad quit smoking! Oh man! You bastards didn't tell me—"

"You should be happy about that. We didn't know till he pulled it out of his pocket."

Charlie slapped Ben on the upper arm with the back of his hand. "They're bad for you anyways. Right, Ben? He should be happy."

"I like things that're bad for me. Remember? This hurts."

"I'm sorry. I hope you get cancer, Jimmy, really. And end up a shut-in. A one-lunged wheezer. A big widower. Really."

"Y're just saying that."

The sirens had grown very loud and now became deafening. Two big, shining cars blasted into the east side parking lot. One was a chocolate brown Crown Victoria that had no writing on it and the other was the regular sheriff's car that you saw once in a blue moon if you were in town or close to it, a white Crown Victoria with lights on top and 'Craig County Sheriff' arced across the doors in brown block letters.

They braked to a stop right behind the Orr's car, Tom and Beth's, and ours, blocking us completely without seeming to notice it. Not that we were going anyplace in a hurry anyway, I guess. Strangely, a tall, fairly young guy in a brown uniform got out of the unmarked car and a shorter, older guy in a suit but no tie got out of the regular sheriff's car and was the one who turned out to be the main sheriff.

They walked down together rather calmly, compared to how they had driven in, and came to the body without saying anything. The older guy, the sheriff, nodded to my Dad and Mr. Glenn but that was it until they had looked at the body. Bent over at the waist, they pulled their heads this way and that kind of sizing up the situation the way you might a map scratched in the dirt with a stick. Then they looked into the woods, then across the cemetery where all of us were and beyond to the church. They didn't exactly look like they had all the answers.

After the sheriff cars had pulled in there had remained, a ways in the distance, a siren that we hadn't had time to ponder until it arrived in the form of an ambulance. Gorty had *really* come through. The 'uniform' went off to meet it.

The sheriff finally started talking to the Rev. and Dad and the others. Mr. Alexander pointed in our direction and Dad waved us over. Stan was already heading that way and we met him there at the end of the second row of tombstones and stood on the church side of the corpse, the corpse formerly known as Bobby Morgan, and faced the men on the other side and the woods behind them. We would all have been standing on an actual grave, the first grave of the second row, except that the woods jogged in there a little and there was no first grave, so we were okay.

Rev. Stone introduced us sort of. "Sheriff, these are the boys who found this... her. Here. Boys, Sheriff Donrett."

We said hi.

How old were we gents?

We said fourteen.

He had a pretty good belly on him and some hair was spilling over the open top of his shirt like shredded packing material. There was, in fact, a kind of overstuffed living room chair look about him in general. He wasn't ugly or anything but he did look like he came from somewhere else, not from around here. Which of course he did not. He was from New Sterling.

"So you found the body. Just like this?"

We nodded.

"Did you touch it, or disturb anything around here?"

We shook our heads.

"You didn't see anybody else I suppose?"

We shook our heads.

"What were you doing down here?"

There was a very brief, unnerving pause, and then Charlie and Stan spoke at the same time. It came out about like, "*We were out just looking skipping the old gravestones Opening Exercises.*"

We stared, scared, as Charlie and Stan looked at each other out of the corners of their own eyes. Quickly, Stan said, with a nice level of certainty, "We were looking over the old markers. And kind of skipping Opening Exercises. It was too hot inside."

I kept focused on Stan, then the sheriff, avoiding my Dad. Opening Exercises weren't mandatory, I didn't think. But it was, as I'd been previously informed, impolite not to go. And as illustrated to us now it opened you up to questions about what you did with that time instead.

"I see," said the sheriff, smiling.

Stan added, unnecessarily, I thought, "My grandma was a Mawson." He raised his hand toward the weathered sandstone marker next to Cress Wells'. One of 'Bobby's' feet was pointed towards there. "He was her great-grandfather. I think. She knows."

Again the sheriff smiled and nodded. "Well, your family knows how to stay in one place, don't they?" He paused. "I'd wager William Mawson skipped Opening Exercises once or twice in his day, too."

I doubted that. Nice of him to say, though. We were dismissed and resumed observing from a distance. While we were being interrogated, the local constable, Mr. McDonough, roused out of church over at Grangefield via a series of passed messages touched off by our Gorty, had finally pulled in. Grangefield was another Presbyterian church in the township, still rural but pocked with acre-ettes. It was about three miles away, closer to Mt. Air.

The sheriff had come twice as far and got here in half the time but that didn't mean our constable hadn't also hurried right over. He had, but at a rate that took into account what the sheriff had just noted about Stanley's people. Probably at a little quicker rate than his normal instincts actually dictated even—getting yanked out of church, right there, meant the situation was a little out of the everyday. And you could tell he was getting a fuller appreciation for just *how* far out of the everyday as he wandered down through the grass and stones and folks exchanging a word or two along the way.

When he came to the body his face plainly revealed that what we had here was indeed something brand new for the old resume. McDonut's experience heretofore had derived primarily from the petty Halloween vandalisms and thieveries—"pumpkin crimes"—and sporadic outbreaks of truancy, keg parties in the quarries, etc. And most of that thanks to the towns of Mt. Air and Quarry and to a lesser extent the castaway settlement of Lost Acres. These are *small* towns, too. No-post-office-type towns, nothing like New Sterling.

He conversed for a few moments with the sheriff. They both pointed down the two grassless tracks of the dirt lane that rimmed the cemetery, first the sheriff, then McDonough. This was the constable's turf but from the way they were with each other you could tell who the boss was going to be. After a bit they got around to chatting with Bobby Morgan about his clothes and all, I suppose. And they got a list from the Rev. of all the members of Perth Hill and where they lived. And that was more or less it. Some murder experts from the state were supposedly on the way but there was no need for us to be there for that.

Eventually the little kids were released from the church basement along with their keepers, the older girls and women. Jacob walked between Mom and Izzy in invisible handcuffs straining and stretching his neck around and around for a view of the newcomers until they got to the temporary distraction of the sheriff's car. Mom let him give it a once over while Tom Orr went to ask the deputy about moving their cars.

I watched as the paramedics turned away from the body and ambled back toward the parking lot. They seemed to be laughing, or rather, trying to keep from laughing.

CHAPTER III

Aaron Birr was out messing around in that one garden next to the barn where his sheep pen used to be and we all gave him a wave. His arm raised like a railroad crossing gate, his hand coming up big and open from the ground as he sat back on his haunches. I wondered if he already knew what the sirens had been all about. Figured he did.

Past Birr's the dust hung above MacRae's lane. Stan had probably badgered his Dad into letting him drive down it. He wasn't worried in the least way about the bush. That was Stanley for you. But I... I prayed for it to be consumed.

Mom and Dad talked a little on the way home. Dad had both hands on the wheel and a thinking list to his head. They didn't say anything too notable until Isabelle's comment.

"Linda MacRae said there was a crucifix. Did you see it, Dad?"

"Bigger than life," he answered, nodding slightly.

Mom, whispering almost and looking out her open window, said, "This probably wasn't her first choice as a final resting place."

"Safe bet," replied Dad. "Didn't look as if she had much say in it."

I leaned forward. "What are you talking about? I mean, what is a crucifix exactly?"

"Was he born in a cave, Mom?" Izzy asked.

I flicked her on the back of her head. "At least I was *born*. You came from a petri dish."

"What's a petri dish?" Jake asked.

Iz: "It's something cultures are grown in. Cultures a hundred times more sophisticated than your brother."

I flicked her again. I hated that "'your brother'" stuff, like she was Mom or something or not related, which in a perfect world she wouldn't've been. Dad stopped us.

"That's enough of that."

"A crucifix," Mom said, "Is a cross Catholics wear. But it has, well, it has..." she hesitated, then in a hushed, hybrid tone of reverence and embarrassment, said, "Jesus still on it. Crucified."

"Hence, crucifix," said the girl genius in front, exhaling dramatically at the end.

"Oh... that's all I wanted, a simple explanation. Thank you... Mom."

I leaned back trying to picture it again in Dad's hand. Jacob looked over at me.

"What is a Catholic anyway?"

I had to think for a second, then whispered, "You know how there are Methodists. And Baptists and... whatever else like that?" He nodded. "Catholics are like that sort of, kind of another branch of church. Sort of like us sort of... only... gorier... I guess. They're not Jewish or Moslem or anything."

"I know," he whispered back.

"Sure you do. Mr. Birr's a Catholic."

Jake squinted. "They don't have to go to *church*?" He sounded hopeful, interested, a potential convert.

"They go to church. Sometimes on Saturday, though."

"Saturday? Why?"

"I don't know. You could ask the expert up there next to Mom. But I wouldn't recommend it. She'll bite your head off."

I was surprised by Jake's questions and tried to be careful with the answers. I had no memory of anyone actually telling *me* what a Catholic was. It was something you just knew. Sort of knew. Mom and Dad talked about them hardly at all, just a brief comment here and there few and far between, just enough so you knew that they weren't bad, just kind of mixed up. And it wasn't their fault. They just grew up that way. This wasn't Northern Ireland or anything. But there were never any discussions about it so I was trying not to say anything wrong without really knowing what I was talking about.

"Crucifix," Jacob said after a moment, softly. "Cruci-FIX? Because he still needs fixed?"

"I don't know, Jake. Maybe because he's *in* a fix."

Iz couldn't take it anymore. "Mom, can we make them stop? They're giving me a headache."

After changing out of our church clothes and gathering the eggs, we ate. Dinner. Dinner was what lunch was called on Sunday, except with food that was all new and supper-y not lunch-y. It was very, very good because my Mom was a very, very good cook (still is). An excellent cook. Cooking must be like coordination, either you're born with it or you're not. I know this because once in a while she lets Iz try.

Not today though. The smell of roast pork, sharpened with sage, had been hanging lightly over the stone steps to the back porch when we got home from church. Through the doors and inside it became overpowering and filled your whole head and made you almost forget what you were doing.

"Ohhh-wuh," Mom said, hurrying in to the stove, "It's going to be dry as a bone."

It wasn't.

There wasn't much talk about what had happened beyond, "How awful," and, "Who would *do* such a thing?" and, "Poor Mrs. Morgan! I can't *imagine* how she felt."

At one point, though, Mom tried to turn it into a lesson. "You boys should've been at Opening Exercises."

"Mom, we didn't kill her," I said.

"I hope not, Boyd. I meant someday you might be the Sunday School Superintendent and you won't think it's very nice if no one shows up."

Izzy laughed at the thought. "Heaven help us."

"That would be weird, wouldn't it?" I had to admit.

"More really like scary."

"You'd make a good Superintendent—" Mom stopped and looked at Jake who had been abnormally quiet. He didn't notice her stare. One hand was moving his fork around the plate in a rather poor simulation of a person eating but his head was pointed down, way down. Mom reached over and pulled a National Geographic from his lap.

"Jacob, eat. This isn't a library."

He looked at his carrots and decided it was worth arguing. "Dad reads at lunch sometimes," he said.

"Your father is not the last word on manners."

"I am the foremost authority on manners. Eat your carrots, young man. They're especially good."

"I hate—I mean, I don't care for carrots."

"You'll learn to care for them," Dad said. It was less prediction than command.

Jake stabbed one and chewed it, mouth closed, with rapid little jaw movements, never chomping clear down, trying to keep it away from his taste buds while preparing his throat to accept it more or less whole.

Sympathetically, Dad diverted our attention. "It's a shame more folks don't wander through that part of the cemetery. Hugh's Ben Franklin trees have gotten some real size and those fancy yews he put in... it's the fanciest area of the whole place. Isn't it, Boyd?"

"Yeah. It is nice."

"Poor Hugh Wilson," Mom said. "Poor old Bushy."

Dad sighed in agreement, shaking his head. "He's in a bad way."

Mr. Wilson had gotten cancer in the spring. He was, in fact, ancient but he had never gotten grumpy. He was happy, very big on young folks, very big on planting bushes and trees for them and their future.

I wondered if *the* bush was a yew.

Our beloved Z—Izzy, that is, the most dangerous of complications: our sister and a girl, the kind of multiplied being too weird for just one name—brought up the subject again while we cleared the table for dessert, which was a lemon meringue pie we had started the day before. (Mom apologized for having the leftovers so soon and for the meringue's posture but she said it goes 'foo-ie' too fast to wait. It was excellent.) She was in the kitchen, Z was, and she didn't think Jacob and Dad and I would hear her but we did.

"Mom, that person might not be Catholic. She could've been wearing that like jewelry. She could be an atheist for all we know."

"Jewelry? That sounds like sacrilege to me."

"It is," Iz said firmly.

Dad had picked part of Friday's paper up off the washing machine and leafed through it.

"Was it gold, Dad?" Jake asked.

"Was what gold?"

"That cross-y thing."

"It was gold colored. I'd guess it was gold plated."

"Would it still be good luck if it wasn't real gold?" Jake knew instinctively what its purpose had to've been.

"I'd say her luck was pretty frightful either way."

"Who was she?"

"Nobody knows. Likely a homeless person who got into very bad trouble."

"What did she look like?"

I answered this. "You saw as much as anybody, Jake. You ran right by her."

"Her face, I mean."

"Nobody knows," I told him.

"Where's her head?"

"Nobody—"

"That'll be a plenty sufficiency of that," Dad interrupted. "The sheriff and other experts will figure it all out. Your mother's lemon pie is too good to dwell on that anymore right now."

"That's true."

"Can I read during dessert?"

CHAPTER IV

To make it clear, early on, I am not—NOT—a necrophiliac.
No matter what Charlie Lane might say. So don't worry
about that.

Charlie had his learner's permit, you know, quote,
unquote, Perth Hill's local version, not anything real official,
the kind of invisible type of permit by which farmer kids, if
they could reach the pedals and their parents allowed, could
drive farm vehicles—loosely defined—from one field to the
next—also loosely defined—without McDonut caring. So
Charlie came and got me after dinner to go over to Stan
MacRae's to play football. This was the standard thing to do
on Sunday afternoons. No matter what time of year it was we
played football because, mostly, because... because that's
just what we did. Maybe because the field and equipment
requirements were minimal. Flat place, one ball.

On this day the usual band of idiots showed up plus Tom Orr who came every once in a while. He was the oldest one— by a long shot—actually married and had kids (the twins) and everything, the whole ball of wax, otherwise he was okay. Ken's cousin, Ken Orr. The other guys, juniors and seniors etc., they were too important to show up. Had better stuff to do, I suppose.

When we pulled in Stan was putting rocks out to mark each corner of the field. We were laughing before we even got out of the car.

Charlie yelled, "Hey, there's a... *DEAD BODY IN THE CEMETERY!* No *SHIT*, Sherlock!"

Stan came over quickly. "You better pray my Mom didn't hear that," he said, his big ears looking huge. They were the first thing you'd notice about him due to their redness, the angle of their attachment to his head—nearly perpendicular—and the shortness of his hair. But he was bigger than most *seniors* and enjoyed confrontation so there was no way you'd make fun of them. "What the hell're you doing screaming something like that?"

"Sorry. I was excited to see you, that's all."

Glen Wallace was also laughing. It wasn't even June yet and he had already molted once or twice and all his freckles had joined up leaving his face a mottled, glowing orange brown—except for the hole on his head where for some reason no freckles joined up or even grew at all. This part of him was over his left eye and nearly round, size of a nickel, very distinct in the summer, kind of like a vaccination mark, kind of like a little space dish, one that could catch a few frequencies from out there, not *way*, way out there, but out there a ways. It was slightly phenomenal and so was Glen, kind of, in that he could wonder way down deeply about almost anything. Laughing, he said, "That was crazy, you have to admit, Stan."

"Hey, a man's got'eh do what'eh man's got'eh do. These panty-wastes were like a buncha deaf mutants."

"As far as anyone knows," Tom Orr said, "that's the first time anybody ever actually yelled in that church. You gave all the old ladies a coronary."

Stan relaxed, grinned. "I did, huh? I didn't mean to do that. It just came out."

"Got the job done."

Jimmy, the one the girls find so sweet and charming, held his slender hand up, "Wait. *Wait.* Is a panty-waste someone who's, like, you know, a dump inside a diaper or... w-a-*I*-s-t-e, the elastic around a pair of panties?"

"Or a homo?" added Ben, intellectually.

"Take your pick," Stan said.

"No. I'm not kidding. I need to know." While we're on faces—we all had them—Jimmy's was the exact opposite of Glen's. It was always pale, his whole face, anytime of year.

Tom laughed. "It's 200 years old. The church. You, Stan, were the first to yell."

"Also the first to ever see a dead corpse on top of a grave," Stan noted.

"You didn't see it first. I did," Ben said.

"You did not see it first," I said. I had.

"See," Stan said. "Thanks, Boyd."

"Uh, yeah, no problem. Has anyone ever seen a live corpse?"

"Lycanthropologists have," stated Jimmy incomprehensibly.

We stared at his wispy, bloodless form for a second. Then I asked, "D'joo guys hear if those were really Bobby's clothes or not?"

"If they are this'll be the strangest miracle of all time showing up in our cemetery," said Glen, his little space dish receiving a signal.

Charlie nodded. "The *strangest* miracle would be his clothes ever getting that close to a *girl*... speaking of panty-wastes."

We chuckled, cruelly, but not without a tiny note of disapproval of Charlie for saying it. Tom tried to stand up for Bobby.

"Yeah, but who could hold a candle to a bunch of lady's men like you'ns? Come on, really."

"Good point," said Glen. "Are we going to play some ball or not?"

It was four on four and rough as always. Something about those dairy farmers that made their muscles knotty and rocky and their joints sharp. Stan, and Ken Orr (face: *some* freckles), in particular, you'd prefer not to have to tackle. It wouldn't've even helped to perfect some kind of fake tackle because they just stomped right through you. They didn't evade or juke or go sideways at all unless they absolutely had to to run over you. In fact, that was the fun part for them, running into people, and they were very fast, so you'd have to have a pretty special level of both cowardice *and* speed to ever save yourself. Plus, none of us except for

Charlie even ever played for school and none of us except for Glen was coordinated.

Somehow Stan and Ben (face: stupid) and Charlie and I ended up on the same team and we became known as The Degenderates. Jimmy was still thinking that was very funny. We called them—Tom, Glen, Ken, Jimmy—The Weeners because nothing better came to mind.

Needless to say, The Degenderates played with great heart and fierce determination, not to mention a singularly generous spirit. As far as I remember we only played defense and even that was debatable.

Here's how it worked. Charlie and I manned the trenches. The Paper Cut moseyed around back behind us somewhere in the middle distance. And Stanley hung way back there in 'prevent' land. *Prevent*. Good one!

So, The Weeners would score. Then they'd kickoff. Then they'd recover our fumble—this was basically our primary offensive weapon, fumbling, and we were *not* afraid to use it. Then The Weeners would score again. Our heads weren't exactly in the game, I guess, not exactly a new development, but church, that particular Sunday's church, really did pre-occupy us.

"I don't care what your Dad says," Stan jabbered as we readied for another assault, "I still say that body—HE'S THROWING! HE'S THROW—OHHHhhhhh-too bad—was Bobby Morgan."

Tom had slipped and Ben accidentally fell on him. The tide had shifted! They huddled up, nervous as heck, and we bided our time prowling around back near Stanley.

"Stan, you should tell the sheriff it's Bobby. Maybe he'll hire you," I suggested.

"He should, Boyd," he agreed with confusing seriousness. "Charlie, you play back here this time. Tom's going to throw it again. I'm sick of running around back here."

"Stanley," I pressed, "if it was Bobby Morgan who was that guy walking around with a head just like his?"

"Hey, I didn't say I had all the answers."

The next down ensued. Boyd C. Robison, dog tired but wild with the scent of blood, leapt off the line of scrimmage like an unbroke buck rabbit and lit into the Weener's QB.

Tom yelled, "*Oh-oh-oh! Good catch, Glen!*"

Then, patting the buck rabbit on his head, he continued, "That makes it... 42 to 2. Weeners ahead."

"Glen, you suck," said Stan. "Boyd, what were you doing?"

"Rushing."

"You were? To where?"

"Their right Weener was holding me."

"Was not," Jimmy said. "That's legal. Hey, I just figured out who did it."

"Who?" asked Ben excitedly.

"Mrs. McGeehon!"

"With her cane?" Tom laughed.

"She didn't do it. She has an alibi," said Charlie, "She was with Ben Dudley all last night. Right, Dud?"

"You're perverted," responded Ben. "And don't call me Dudley."

"You guys are the Degenderates," said Glen, with a high degree of accuracy.

"Y're ALL a bunch of perverts," Tom stated, with a higher degree.

"Who do you think did it, Tom?" I asked.

"They need to figure out who it is first.... but I'd say it'll all come down to vagrants from New Sterling and a trashed-out El Camino."

"Let me kick that thing—" Jimmy grabbed the ball from Ken.

"Not from there, Weener!" yelled Charlie. "You're on the 50, for crying out loud."

"Come on. I'm not very good."

Stanley threw small rocks at him, saying, "Back, back, back."

"You know, a head would make figuring out who it is easier—"

Jimmy, backing up, said, "They need to ask Fern Whiteside."

"This should be good."

"She gives—you know what!" he sang out and took the snap from Tom.

"Like you'd know!" bellowed Stan.

Jimmy gave the ball an anemic boot, yelping—

"UHHH! Wait! Wait!! Let me try again!"

"Y're right. Y're not very good."

At a point Ben stoved his fingers—all of them he said—and we stopped playing and planned to start again but we didn't. Tom left because he never hung around to shoot too much of the breeze; he always left saying, "This crowd's too rough for me." But he was probably on a schedule. Beth, his wife, is a Lane, cousin of Charlie's, and she's really something. A real loose cannon. When we were little, at this one tureen dinner, she brought a plate of these crunchy things nobody had seen before. They got talked about quite a bit at the time. We're all up to speed on tacos now and other international foods. Don't worry about that.

"There are NO cookies," Stan insisted. We had been bugging him while Ben played with his fingers. "If there were I sure wouldn't tell you bozos. I supplied the field. One of you'ns should've brought something to eat."

"That's not how it works," I said. "When the Indians show up at Pittsburgh do they have to bring their own hot dogs?"

Stan rolled his eyes. "The *Indians* never show up at Pittsburgh. They're not in the same league."

"Oh." I hesitated, then said, "In a world series they could. It's the principle."

"Do you want me to sell you some cookies? That I could do."

"How's yer hand, Ben?"

"Hurts."

"Tom throws a rocket. You should'eh just let Ken try to catch it."

"I would'eh caught it—"

"And run like the breaking wind—"

Beth Orr then commandeered my thoughts for a moment or two and I quit paying attention to the conversation.

CHAPTER V

That evening, Sunday evening, was actually pretty relaxed because the next day was the last day of school and we didn't have any homework. Why didn't they end it on Friday? Because teachers as a group are like sisters: mean. So after the chores, I looked for arrowheads in the cornfield between the lane and the back woods. Mom and Dad had actually said to steer clear of the woods for a while but I had already just about convinced myself that another lesson our Sunday School teacher had taught us that day was that donating your clothes to charity was dumb. Fortunately, it was only Bobby's clothes, and not Bobby, that had gotten mixed up in some very bad thing, a city thing, a city thing involving pathetic vagrants, driving, possibly, a trashed-out El Camino. Anything else was simply unimaginable.

Perth Hill was just a convenient dumping spot—we had the dogs and cats and half grown Easter peeps to prove it.

I hadn't intended to look for arrowheads. I was just wasting time, wandering around till it was time for 'party' (every Sunday evening: popcorn, pop, peanut butter, the occasional hot dog—took the place of supper, which we'd had at dinner) and drifted out to the pond, then across the road into the field and wound up idling along, up and down the not very straight rows with my head down looking for them. The rows weren't very straight because I had planted this field and I hadn't planted corn until this year and wasn't very good at it yet. Plus I probably wasn't concentrating as much as I should've been because I hadn't realized how obvious it would be what a crummy job you did when the corn came up. It was really obvious.

Cambell's rows were always perfect. But this was his first year in college so I had to help plant. People took pride in straight rows. I found that out. Anyway, it didn't make any difference for arrowhead looking.

The spring had been relatively dry, not too dry, but dry enough, early enough, so that we had gotten it in earlier than usual and it was coming along nicely, a few inches high, and the ground had settled between the rows. The conditions, in other words, were perfect for finding an arrowhead.

After going up a row or two and thinking about things, Beth Orr, the Bad Ones, the body, Dad's search for a wallet, the crucifix, how mostly everybody thought—and, therefore, so did I—she had been killed in New Sterling and just dumped out here and how I had never touched breasts with my hands but had brushed against Trudy Schuster's in the hall between classes recently with my upper arm, left arm, etc.—after going over that, I decided something. I decided that doing this was a nice peaceful thing to be doing after the type of day most of the day had been.

Nice and quiet and lonely, this was. I think people think living in the sticks is nothing but lonely but it isn't. It's the opposite. Mostly it's a constant agitated bee's nest of family and friends and relatives and neighbors and church people and all the family and friends and relatives and neighbors of all those people. Being on a tractor was *kind* of a reprieve but not quite because of all the noise. It was a true miracle if you were *ever* by yourself and it was quiet.

And it's a fun thing to find an arrowhead, a shaped thing, purposely shaped, a wrought shape, floating out on top of all the formless dirt. Something that was obvious and made sense of itself by simple contrast. That was kind of my view of Perth Hill, too, and, more or less, Fox Township. You know, compared to the city and all.

I stayed out tramping up and down until it was too dark to see and like most times I got skunked. When I got up into the yard I could hear a siren so far away it sounded pretty. New Sterling, of course. At the time I didn't know that my view of the worlds—Perth Hill's, New Sterling's—might not be a hundred percent perfectly accurate.

CHAPTER VI

Here was the deal with school: I didn't like it.

School consisted not mainly of farm kids but of kids from a couple of small towns and developments like Lost Acres. There were Italians and Poles and Germans and Finns—pretty much the typical European melting pot melted together in factories and quarries—and also a few blacks thrown in for fun. We, the farmers, were a minority but nothing compared to them, the black kids. I cannot for the life of me imagine what was going through their heads.

But they were probably as glad as I was that school was over for the year because up out of all the suburbanish kids, like an oil slick, had come a *cool* group of beings and it was just a relief to get away from them and from yourself trying to be like them.

There's no point really in any of that information. But I'm the one passing this sordid little tale along so I guess I can put in whatever I want. Maybe it's important to see that I'm not exactly an impartial observer here. The corpse formerly known as Bobby Morgan turned up in *my* cemetery after all. Not *mine*, mine, but you know what I mean.

My analysis of the situation was this: There were two worlds. Two and a half, actually. One was Perth Hill, the real world we will call it. Two was New Sterling, the type of place that was tugging on Jimmy Alexander's strangely turned heart, a place that had nothing to do with farming or normal, real life. And then there was the half, the zero point five, the in-between one. Like Lost Acres and Mt. Air and Quarry and the couple of other poor little half-baked towns, which, of course, was where the *cool* had bubbled up from.

On Monday, at school, the last day, the news of the body had spread like mumps. Stan, Ben, Charlie and I were kind of sought after commodities for a while. Come to think of it, it was kind of like being cool. Kids would rope us in between classes to see what we had to say about it. You got four minutes to get from one class to another and we were using them all by the end of the day. To keep the story fresh certain 'details' got added in as time wore on. *I* made an effort to maintain a fairly truthful and consistent story line, which was a whole lot more than I can say for Stanley or Ben.

After lunch, which was excellent—since it was the last day Mom let us pick what we wanted: I picked fried baloney; Jake, peanut butter and jelly sandwich made with *toast*;

Isabelle opted to buy lunch from the cafeteria—Ben and I were in Miss Raney's English class. She was trying to explain what Ninth Grade English was going to be like and I could hear him behind me going on and on and on: *blood was everywhere, the heart might'eh still been beating, it was all over, gravestones, grass, everywhere, it was gruesome, the legs moved once a little bit, like a twitch or something—have you ever butchered a pig?—the head was completely gone and cut off but it takes a while for all the nerves to find out 'specially down in the feet, the feet moved for sure, it was pretty neat, in a bad way I mean, and you know what? it was on one of my ancestor's graves, I'm not kidding you, I find it and there it is on Nathan Graham's grave, talk about coincidence, and...*

Meanwhile, Stanley was going on about how it was on Mawson's grave. It was on neither. It was on Cress Wells', Berylie McHenry's grandfather. Also, they hadn't seen it first. I had. None of *my* great old dearly dead and gones were in Perth Hill's graveyard but I had seen that body first. Let's try to remember that.

All of our stories, though, you want to know something? We never mentioned the crucifix part. I guess, to us, it didn't seem like such a big deal yet.

Janie and I saw each other in the hall a couple of times and we said 'hi'.

"Hi."

"Hi."

Nothing elaborate. We never really talked too much in school but I know she had to've been annoyed at how we were transporting ourselves to near popularity on the shoulders of a headless woman. A murdered woman. That's just how things panned out. We weren't doing it on purpose.

In any event, at the end of the day was the end of the year and the joy was making me lightheaded. It was simply the greatest feeling to say goodbye. The majority would be no more than five, ten miles away but we'd never run into each other. It would be the greatest.

CHAPTER VII

I waved to him and yelled, "Hi, Mr. Birr!" and went back to tying the gate shut with a piece of binder twine. We had chased a sow back in. She had gotten out, almost by mistake, I think, because she was just ambling along between the fence and road very calmly without looking guilty of anything. Dad and Aaron Birr talked quietly next to his vehicle. I heard Frank Stearns's name mentioned. When I got to them Dad said, "There's a good reason I am always pestering at you boys to set the brakes."

I blinked at them. "I *do* set the brakes."

"Frank Stearns is in the hospital. Run over by his own tractor."

"Oh..."

Mr. Birr pursed his lips and kicked a piece of gravel

under the car. I didn't know Mr. Stearns very well. He always waved though when I was on my bike or the tractor.

"How did...."

Dad looked at Mr. Birr. He was tall and seemed especially so right then because he was standing further up the barn bridge than we were. He put a foot on the bumper of his car.

"He was picking rocks. Myron Rantle found him. Looked like he had gotten off the tractor to throw one on and it rolled backwards over him. He's lucky to be alive... for now anyhow."

"Good old Perth Hill has been an unusually deadly place of late."

His head swaying with a brief, bewildered thought and a low humming, Dad said, "Can't argue that...."

The two then went into who would be taking care of Mr. Stearns' cows. There was a little snideness in the tone, as there always was when Mr. Stearns was the topic of conversation. He was a little amoral. Didn't go to church. And his farm was 250 acres or something, more than half of it tillable. It was well drained and had two springs on it. As Dad said, a real showplace. Mr. Birr's home place was sixty acres, dogleggedy and a little swampy.

Mr. Birr was our Justice of the Peace so he didn't really depend entirely on his place for a living but I think it perturbed him that someone like Mr. Stearns had inherited such a dandy place. He and Dad got off that subject eventually and moved on to theorizing about the dead lady.

"Aaron Birr, it was not jewelry. In spite of what you and my daughter might say. It was under her shirt. And maybe you can try to tell me what woman who is trying to dress up as a man would wear jewelry?"

"An unstable one for starters."

"I'll second that," Dad said, nodding his head, not smiling.

"She might've been Catholic. But lots of folks wear poorly chosen good luck charms. Perhaps it was simply that."

"Which would only prove she was Catholic."

Mr. Birr laughed.

Dad was always trying to convert Mr. Birr. I never paid any attention to it till now.

"Not everyone is able to think so easily in the abstract as you, Timothy. Some of us need a thing or two to keep our minds focused."

Finally Dad laughed. "Fair enough."

"We'll know who she is soon enough, I'd think." Mr. Birr paused. When he started again his voice had relaxed some. "Now... I've been in Perth Hill's cemetery but I know quite a number who could be convinced to step foot there only on the condition they were in the condition our anonymous visitor was in."

"Well, at least she made it."

"Huh! God help her. This young'n got himself a real surprise, didn't he?"

"I should say."

I laughed weirdly.

"George Burns said he was most impressed by how my neighbor's oldest boy brought yer discovery to everyone's attention."

"By yelling?" I guessed.

"I wouldn't expect anything different from a son of Lucy Wolfe," said Mr. Birr.

"Hoh! Y'r right there," agreed Dad. "The constable will keep you in the latest news on this, I imagine?"

"Up to a point. He—we're at the mercy of the sheriff and his crowd. But so far I already know more than I'd like."

"True for all of us, I'm afeard. Have they said how long she had been dead?"

"Not long. Saturday evening. They took Bobby Morgan through the ringer, I gathered. He was home with his mother that night but you can't blame the sheriff for giving him the once over, given the unusual, uh, coincidence."

"I reckon not. You can't condemn a man for donating his clothes to charity, though. He's always been an odd kid—" Dad paused, thinking, looking out to the sow we had put in. "But this whole affair is odder than even him."

"Odder than the whole tiny Morgan clan in gen'ral," added Mr. Birr, a sorrowful shift bending his words.

Just then Mom's voice turned our attention around from the front pasture to the driveway. "Aaron Birr, you're not keeping these gentlemen from their chores, are you?" She was carrying her garbage bucket down to the sows in the pasture below the barn.

"Uh-oh, felluhs, jig's up," Dad laughed. "The foreman."

"Guilty as charged, Rose. My apologies. My wife is probably wondering what happened to me and... hoping for the best, already went ahead with supper!" He laughed and straightened up. His crew cut, a taller, sharper, darker version of my father's, made a littler me pretend he was an Indian, a Mohawk Indian.

Mom laughed.

"The poor woman," she said, tipping the bucket over the fence. The pigs were waiting for her and, overly eager, betrayed us. "You two haven't even fed the sows out here yet!"

"I'm going."

"Don't fret, Rose, we'll be quick, won't we, Boyd? When's supper ready?"

Mom reached the barn bridge. "Fifteen minutes ago," she said flatly.

"These two can pass along the news about Frank Stearns," Mr. Birr said, his face serious again, before folding into his car.

"Mrs. Gorton informed me," my mother said. "On the phone." She hesitated. She was tall, thin with short dark hair parted on the side, pale skin. Her rough hands, stained reddish-brown with whatever she'd been working on, hung still by her side, the bucket, also stained, in one of them. Her eyes settled on me. "He is an unlucky man. You guys need to be more careful on the tractor. Boyd."

"I'm careful, Mom. Mr. Birr, whenever they catch who ever killed that lady, do, uh, do you get to be the judge?"

"This one I will shuffle on up. Gladly. Our office specializes in much lower-grade miscreants. Murder is a might beyond my purview. This hasn't kept the good constable out of harm's way, though, lately." He smiled at the thought.

Mom started toward the house, "And he's probably not out of harm's way yet. Bad things happen in threes."

"Ha! I'll be sure and tell him. He'll have something to look forward to." He stopped, then in a softer voice that Mom couldn't hear, "Speaking of charms and luck and the like, Mr. Robison? Bad things happen in threes, is it? Maybe a good, superstitious Catholic like myself could learn a thing or two from a Presbyterian after all!" He gave a good-natured laugh looking out the passenger window at us.

"It's that bad Irish blood. Isn't it, Boyd? It's a good thing these boys have one sensible parent."

I laughed, again, weirdly.

Backing onto the lane and hearing something prudently noncommittal in my weirdness, Mr. Birr said, to *me*, "Ha! Y'r the only sensible one of the whole bunch! Evening, gentlemen."

He got no further than the gingko tree, Mr. Wilson's, flanking the west end of the pasture gate and backed up even with the barn bridge. "Almost forgot my main reason for stopping. I think I'm going to have time to knock some hay down tomorrow and was wondering if I could borrow the crimper? Should be done by noon. Unless you had plans for it."

"No plans. It's at the far end of the chicken house."

"Thank you, sir."

"Not at all. So long, Aaron."

He drove away, his hand resting out the window in a static wave and we went to finish the chores.

Odder than the whole tiny clan... I drug that around for a while, starting right then as we quickly fed the pigs. The soft hollowness of Mr. Birr's tone had that backward, historical drift, and I got the feeling, not a completely new or unfamiliar one, that you should be careful about how you went about deciphering it. Like Murray Glenn's missing finger, which even Jake knew better than to bring up in front of anyone but me. Some things were too hideous to be decently talked about. So I drug it across my own mind at first, kind of reluctantly, but dutifully—little Bobby was my Sunday School teacher after all—and brought it out later for only a light pawing around with others, and chiefly only among my fellow knuckleheads.

CHAPTER VIII

Mr. Birr didn't get around to coming for the crimper until the evening of the following day. This was after supper while we were planting the last row of new strawberry plants in the garden. The berries on the old plants were already starting to blush. They would lead off what turned out to be the best berry year in my memory. Berries are good.

Jacob didn't necessarily think so. Before your legs got your little feet to the tractor pedals you, sadly, were sentenced to the garden and weeding, and to helping Mom candle and grade eggs. He could never bring himself to be very cheerful about this. Part of the problem was that he couldn't see the point of a garden, nor eggs for that matter. In his opinion, when it came to food, if it didn't try to get away it wasn't worth eating. Jacob had the heart of a small Neanderthal.

Oh, he actually did like berries okay but there were plenty of wild ones that made this garden business seem foolish.

Well, we, *everyone*, not just Jacob—everyone, that is, but Cambell who was getting home from school the next day—finished getting them in and soaking them good with an hour or so of daylight left. So I headed directly from the garden for the corn field to look for arrowheads again. My object was to find an arrowhead, or at least a pretty rock, not to wind up over on the Stearns place. That's the truth.

I followed an outer row around the notch in the back woods, looked up and realized I was only about a quarter mile from the edge of the place. Away I went with hardly a thought.

To get there I had to cross Gil Moore's field. Mr. Moore is mostly retired and the Olivers rent some of his land. This field looked like corn, too, at this stage, but turned out to be sorghum. I hurried across it and kept my head up, because I knew that if I saw an arrowhead, I'd take it. Mr. Moore wouldn't care; he was a fine old guy, but I didn't look anyway. Traipsing around somebody else's land made me feel goofy.

The air this same time of day was filled with bird calls, the birds having come back to life after the heat of the day for a short spell of activity before night fell. But when I got across Stearns Road and into the woods it was like stepping into an empty barn. This felt weird too: any woods did that wasn't your own. I'd been in here before, of course, but it'd been a year or so. We had come to understand, more or less instinctively, that we should steer clear of the place. No one said Mr. Stearns was a bad guy. But he didn't come to church.

Light, filtered by fully leafed-out oaks and maples and hickories, had smoothed out already into a deepening gray. *Dark*, in fact, was crowding in on things, quietly taking from them their steadfastness, their trustiness, and giving them plenty that wasn't theirs. Things that you knew couldn't move in the daylight... could, now. And they could combine. The quiet didn't fool me. It was summer and everything that *could* be alive *was* alive.

I came to a creek in a hundred yards and thought I remembered it. Crossing it, I went up a steep bank, stepped over a rotten log. A giant web of wild grape vines, spun down from the highest tree limbs, diverted my route. Some of the grape trunks were as large as my forearms. They were twined and twisted like dragline cable. In broad daylight I would have looked for one to swing from but that didn't cross my mind now.

Tim Gray was out here somewhere. But he was supposedly harmless enough, just an addled tramp who had perfectly normal relatives. And he could be in any woods in the area not these.

After working around the edge of the grape web to a point that I thought kept me on the straightest, shortest course through to the field, I came to the zigzagged remains of a split-rail fence. This I would've remembered because I like old split rails, the way they look, and their blatant absurdity. How could anything like that keep *anything* in?...

By magic supposedly and at this moment I was thinking most probably *black* magic.

I tried to think. What was I doing in here last time? Where did I go in? Come out? The angled joints of the fence became inseparable from the rest of the half-seen forms in either direction. Had I simply missed it last time?

I stepped over the tangled rails, took another step and another, saplings, and who knows, brushed my face and arms, a spider's web stretched across my forehead. I felt something moving on my head. Swiping a hand back behind my ear I tried to knock it off but it ran across my neck to the other side. I quickened the pace and swiped with my left hand now. It was gone.

The route became thicker and jumbled with fallen limbs and trees. Scrambling through and around them I tried to speed up. Again, the creep of tiny legs tickled my neck. It *wasn't* gone. No... it was.

Then it came back, under my collar, moving. I stopped dead up, hunched my shoulders forward and clawed at the front of my shirt pulling it tight. There followed a tiny, barely perceptible *pop*. I didn't hear it. I felt it against my skin.

For a moment longer I didn't move, frozen by the fleet but shocking thought of the lapels of Bobby Morgan's suit coat, and the neck, her neck.

I stumbled forward, needing to go. Any direction. My spontaneous trespassing, innocent though it was, was yielding, suddenly now, a panic. I crashed and bored through the woods. They worked me over good for ten or twenty strides, tripping me and tearing at my arms and clothes... and then brightening in front of me with rather embarrassing speed.

Out in the field, I was startled by how light it was still. I mean it wasn't hardly dark at all. My lungs inflated.

Down across the field, a field of last year's soybean stubble and this year's weeds and an unusual number of rocks, stood the house and barns. Very big. The barns were white. The house was brick, one of the oldest in the township, from before 1810 maybe, made from bricks fired right here on the place. It still looked like a showplace to me.

I looked up and down the field for any signs of the thing that had happened wondering how a field that had been tilled for almost two centuries still had so many rocks in it. People of Stearns' reputation (before Frank) weren't the kind of people to not pick rocks. And even Frank picked rocks. I moved generally away from the woods back towards the road and buildings. A hill lay ahead dropping away from the woods. Maybe that could be where it happened... As I approached the crest it became clear this was more of a hill than I first thought, and when I actually got to the drop of its downside it became clear that this was the one that had nearly killed him: The tractor and wagon were still there at the base of it.

I hesitated for a minute, a lump clogging up my throat. Mr. Stearns could not still be here, too, I knew, but it didn't matter. Walking down the hill slowly I looked for signs in the brown and brittle plants and the earth. He should've set the brakes. He thought maybe the tractor was safely beyond the rise and on flat ground. He should've set them anyway.

A John Deere 2020. Whatever they said about him he still had nice equipment. Several rocks were on the hay wagon, near its edge. The tractor and wagon were in a nice line headed uphill and it gave the situation a sort of life-like feeling, like the stage and props of a play, like Frank might come out from taking a leak in the woods any second and continue on picking his rocks. We both would've been pretty surprised if he had.

I left the tractor and angled toward the house. The cows weren't bellering.

The white paint on the wooden trim around the windows was peeling. People said he'd let the place go some. Mostly, if anyone said anything like that, they always made sure to also mention that his wife had died. Like Gorty, who put it this way: *Mr. Frank's wife died on him. He took it kind'uh personal.* I suppose that's true.

It wasn't something that happened every day around here, a woman dying before her husband. They usually get fairly old and move into a house trailer on that little spot poached from the closest hay field so that everybody can have a little privacy, her and whichever kid got the house. Poor Mrs. Stearns never herself got a chance to be downsized because she had died too early to even have kids.

It usually didn't work like that. Special case here and I found it kind of appropriate to get kind of sad walking along Stearns Road back toward home. There was only one of them left. Barely. There would be a Stearns Road and no Stearnses. That was sad to think about.

Seeing our house again and barn and pond chippered up the spirits considerably. And the best thing possible to end the evening was about to happen. It really was almost too dark to see the ground now, I mean to pick out any distinct smallish objects there, but my head had automatically defaulted downward as soon as I got back into our corn field anyway and when I got about even with the dam of the pond a thing suspicious enough to stop me appeared and got my heart going. My hand went to the earth.

It was lying loose on the surface, not covered at all. I picked it up. It was remarkable. Not the shape, which was beautifully perfect almost, but the color. Instead of the usual black or gray, it was golden, the actual color the sunset had been.

In the house, held up to the light, the little scallops of the razor-thin edge were nearly transparent, letting light pass through, glowing, a rock. It was not quite glassy but unlike any flint or chert we had seen. There was, in fact, one imperfection on the corner where the notches were. It was chipped slightly so that the two notches were not symmetrical. But this could easily have been done by the Indian who had made it, Dad said. Wouldn't affect how it worked in any way.

It was amazing how a field could be plowed and plowed and plowed and disced and disced and disced and run over back and forth for total centuries and still give up whole, unbroken, beautiful arrowheads. Good as new. If you were an Indian you could lash it onto a nice black gum shaft you made and use it just as if time had gotten stuck on something, in a dead furrow maybe, and we Robisons and MacRaes and Grahams and Alexanders and whoever had never showed up here. It would be just as perfectly good as ever at killing a nice buck, or a rabbit if you were really good, or even an enemy Indian who was trespassing on your happy hunting grounds. I loved arrowheads. Sometimes I thought it would be very satisfying to shoot something with a bow and arrow, something like, say, Benjamin Dudley Graham. That's a joke. I wouldn't shoot the old Paper Cut. I love arrowheads, though, I mean that.

Dad said the new one was a "beaut" and that he bet the Indian who lost it was probably beside himself because it was such a unique one. Even Izzy said it was pretty. Mom said it looked "lucky": and thus began its long journey riding around in one pants pocket after another, dutifully transferred each time I changed pants. It became my lucky arrowhead. I felt lucky just for finding it. Jacob offered to buy it from me but he didn't have enough money, or *any* money, and wondered if I'd take an IOU until his birthday when he was likely to be rich again. I wouldn't. It was my lucky arrowhead.

CHAPTER IX

Several days went by and "Bobby's" head was not turning up. And there was no word on who the woman was or who the killer might be. But our suppertime speculations and theories finally got a rest when Cambell got home all full of his own exotic college information.

Listening to his stories about certain professors and the dorms and various strange people, who were always from Philadelphia or Wilkes-Barre or had a name like Zangwill Rosenbaum, gave me an intense desire to go to college as soon as possible. For once, I sort of understood Jimmy, who hankered for college, or the city, or any fine terrain beyond parental supervision.

Life pretty much went on like normal except that for the evening meal Mom always made one of Cambell's favorite things, even though, if you ask me, he didn't need any special favors on the eating front—he'd gone slightly doughy around the equator. A year of dorm food and no work.

The most exciting thing, conversationally speaking-wise, was that Cambell had seen Tim Gray. Cambell had been on his way over to Burns's to borrow their Burdizzio's because we were pinching the bull calves that afternoon. I mentioned Tim Gray earlier. A Tim Gray sighting was notable because he didn't pop up very often, and also because he was on a bike.

"I'm gone for only a few short months and I hardly know the place anymore," Cambell said. "People are dropping like flies, getting beheaded, run over, and who knows what all. The place is going down the tubes. Except for Tim Gray. He's moving up in the world."

"Where d'joo see him?" I asked.

"Reed Road."

"Which way was he going?"

"Into the woods."

"The woods? On a bike? I mean, on a bike?"

Cambell laughed. "*On* a bike."

"Why would you try to ride your bike in the woods?"

"Why would you live in the woods?"

He was the closest thing we had to a leprechaun, Tim Gray was, not counting Mr. Bell who owned the sawmill and could wiggle *one* ear, and over the years I had alternated between thinking he was the best thing since toast and thinking he was a worthless deadbeat. When I was little, about like Jacob, I had this idea he got all his food from the woods, trapping and hunting and eating frogs and bugs like an Indian. It was depressing to find out Wally Fergus, a relative, just gave him food. Mom tried to cheer me up: *Oh, honey, I'm sure he gets most of his food like an Indian. Mr. and Mrs. Fergus just give him leftovers to be nice.*

Mmm-hmmm. Still, there was enough crazy about him to keep him a low-watt legend, a little scary and noteworthy. He'd been to Viet Nam but no one tried to pin anything on that. He hadn't been all that normal to begin with.

And speaking of scary behavior, now in regard to Cambell, what could possibly have happened to a person to make liver and onions one of their favorite meals? How could a person who liked something sensible like fried chicken be the very same person who requested liver and onions? *Requested.* More to the point how could a person like that inflict this sick thing on somebodies as nice as Jake and me? His own flesh and blood? It just goes to show you that no matter how great a guy might be in general he probably still has in him a little hidden pocket of cruelty or at least a bad little corner that's inscrutable and stupid.

Well, we fought our way through it, some a little more bravely than others—you just couldn't watch Jake. It made you feel helpless, like watching someone slowly die from an overdose of sheep dip—but there was a payout at the end: strawberry shortcake. The mercy, ultimately, of our mother and the first ripe strawberries of the season, repaired our temporarily hellish view of the world. Naturally, there was some vanilla ice cream to go along with the shortcake so actually, after Mom had taken the first bite and then we, our first bite, euphoria swept back through us. It was that kind of psychotic meal. Isabelle during this time gave us all the news from her Bible Study.

"Carla's Dad's going to be Bobby Morgan's lawyer," she said, referring to Carla Zahnhiser, her friend. They go to Perth Hill and Mr. Zahnhiser was one of the few like his new client who had strayed away from farming into a tie and wingtips job. At least Mr. Zahnhiser still had some cows of his own and actually did some work.

"You have to have a lawyer even if you didn't do anything, she said. Mom... this is sooooo good."

"It is, Mom," we all echoed, dutifully and honestly.

"Thank you, dear ones. Keep eating. Poor Bobby."

"His clothes did something," Jake said. Cambell took one of his soft, possomy, college hands and patted Jake on the head and they kept talking about Bobby, but my mind got distracted. There was a rumor floating around about Carla Zahnhiser, my sister's good friend, that she had partially webbed feet. You could guess this came from Ken Orr because he specialized in really oddball rumors like this, webbed feet, and even though he was in my grade and would have absolutely no way of knowing anything like this about Carla Zahnhiser, he always had a way of making you think it just could have possibly been true by adding one or two modest details that sort of soften the oddballedness of the rumor and diminish slightly the sensational nature of it. In this case her feet weren't all the way, full-out duck feet but only 'partially' webbed and it wasn't both feet, just her left foot, and it wasn't even her whole foot, it was just her little toe and the next two that were connected up by skin. After getting all the facts like this you really didn't have much choice in the matter. You'd be an idiot not to believe it. Next chance you got you were watching Carla to see if she walked funny or wore a special shoe or something. But in spite of this deformity, Carla Zahnhiser was quite a pretty one and I wondered sometimes, like right at this moment when everybody was going over little Bobby's problems, how it would be to kiss her. She had one of those angular Scandinavian-type faces that's almost a little bit Chinese— probably had some Finn in her—which I tended to like and she was thin. I didn't care if she did have that clubfoot and needed a crutch to get around. That was why she would like me and we would date and kiss because I didn't care what other people would say, I'd like her for her and that was all there was to it. It also might be nice to have the kind of girl-friend who had a father who was an attorney.

The table conversation gradually got relevant again the closer I got to the end of my strawberries and shortcake and ice cream because a body couldn't just jump in any old place interrupting and all just to ask for seconds. Frank Stearns and whisky and the Stearns family, that's what they were on. Not your everyday topics so I was glad Carla and I had broken up.

"Mom, can I please have some more shortcake please?" I asked, trying to look gaunt.

"Yes, you may, dear one. Help yourself."

"Anyone else, while I'm up?"

Everybody said again how good it was but there were no takers.

Cambell said, "Just you, big fellow. Y'r a marvel."

"Hah! Look who's talking. Big-GEST fellow. I'm just taking more to be nice."

"At least one of my children won't get rickets," Mom said. "You need more dessert. Liver isn't your favorite thing, is it, Boyd?"

"Not exactly." I retreated quickly to the kitchen.

"Well," Dad said, "I sympathize wholeheartedly with Aaron Birr's opinion of poor Frank. Word was that he started toasting each and every cow, not just the herd." He gave a spare, gristled laugh. "It was a pack of foolishness to begin with and this is exactly where it was bound to lead. He should've married that little Stewart gal after Patricia died. She would not've put up with that nonsense. To be handed a showplace like that and then..."

"It's just too bad," Mom said.

"What little Stewart girl?" I asked, excavating a second but actually smallish scoop of ice cream out of the container.

"Mrs. Kendall. Stewart and Debbie and Rhonda's Mom."

"Little?"

"Well, not now. She was, though. She's gotten pretty big. Poor girl."

"If Mr. Stearns married her Rhonda would be an orphanage," Jake reasoned, looking concerned.

"Jake, Rhonda would have a different Mom. Sort of. She wouldn't be an orphanage, or even in one probably," Z said.

"Really, Iz?" I knew she didn't have one clue what she was talking about. Mom saw where this was heading and interrupted, "Children, you are all excused. Shoo. Take your plates out first. Thank you."

"I have a Session meeting at eight," said Dad. "Would you gentlemen do me a huge favor and check those two closest sows for milk. They shouldn't be ready. But that's what I thought about that sow last week that had her litter out by the pond. Those young ones don't show much."

We complied, of course, all three of us. Actually, Jake and I followed Cambell around as he complied. With him home we naturally deferred to his expertise. And, simply, to our own selfless dedication to letting him do everything. It was the least we could do to help him overcome his guilt over being gone all year. He heaved the sack of feed onto his shoulder from the barn floor and headed out along the road to the low place in the woven wire fence where we crossed over to the feeding area.

As he made small piles of feed here and there on the bare ground, we called.

"Suh! Suh! Suh! Pig! Pig! Pig! Hog! Hog! Suh! Suh! Suh!..."

They were already running in from the creek and the pasture before we even started calling because this was later than usual to be feeding them and they had their eye out for someone with a big sack. When most of them were in and fully occupied eating and milling from pile to pile Cambell sidled calmly up on one with a plump udder and squeezed the hindmost teats. Nothing.

"This could be one, huh?" Cambell said, pointing to a small sow.

"Could be. This one over here, too." I tried to direct him and be helpful.

They were skittish, the young ones usually were, but we finally got a hand on them and found no milk. Which meant none would have to be moved into farrowing crates that evening. This was a relief to all of us, Cambell because he had a date, to Jake and me, as a matter of principle.

Cambell handed me the feed sack and hustled in to get ready. Jake wandered down to the creek in the pasture, the one the hogs had just crossed, and I walked back to the barn. I heard it coming, the car, coming from down below, from the East Francis Forge Road direction, but it came too fast and I was too full of shortcake and it was on me before I could make it into the barn to hide. I was not that shy but some people, if they saw you when they drove by, would stop and chat your physical ears off.

This turned out to be Aaron Birr and no call for alarm. We were all eager to speak to him these days hoping he'd have news on the headless woman and/or her head. He stopped in the road even with the barn bridge and turned the Duster's engine off. I hooked my thumbs in my front pockets and took a step closer.

"Good evening, Mr. Robison. Little late to be finishing the chores, isn't it?"

"Yeah," I said. "You coming from work, Mr. Birr?"

"Shop's always busy the first weeks after school's out. A certain element suddenly has more time and energy than they can manage in a law-abiding manner... Hey, I shouldn't be giving you a bad time about your chores. My hogs have probably climbed the fence and made their way over to Lucy MacRae's flower beds by now. Is your father around?"

"Nope. Session meeting. At church. Mom's around."

"Oh, no, I don't need to bother your Mother." He paused, his eyes moving around beyond me into the barn. "Well, I better let you get back to work. Probably see yer Pa on the road."

"I'll tell him you stopped—hey, Cambell saw Tim Gray today."

"'Zat right? Not every day a man gets to lay eyes on the King of the Jungle." He gave a commending nod of his head.

I laughed. "Never heard him called *that*. That's funny. Tarzan. Is there a Jane?"

"Ho-oh! That would be too much for the local gentry to take. The notion of Tim Gray procreating, that would call out the dogs and rope, wouldn't it? Well, I better—"

"Is there any new news on the head? I mean, the lady... her head?"

"No head yet. Not that I've heard. Just the body and Bobby Morgan's clothes. Just what you boys found. There in your cemetery." He said that slowly and his face seemed

73

to express sympathy but his voice put a barely perceptible edge on "your."

With that he headed out the lane. He was always saying things.

I walked on up the barn bridge passing my fingertips around the shape of the golden arrowhead in my pocket. At the doors, running footsteps turned me around to our drive leading to the house. Cambell was sprinting to the pickup, which was down at the chicken house. I put the empty sack flat on a pile of other empty ones, replacing the hunk of iron bar keeping them in place.

He raced out the lane, slowing down, marginally, for the stretch in front of the house. Dust. Mom didn't like it. I didn't know who his date was with but I thought it might be one of the McKee girls, the one closer to his age. She was a dandy specimen, all the bells and whistles. Her lips were kind of a little plump and looked really, really soft. Very, very soft. I stopped myself. Cambell had dibs on her, for one thing. For another, I wasn't ready for commitment.

Jacob called to me and I thought briefly of telling him about Sue McKee and me but I skipped it. He wasn't a big fan of girls yet. He joined me in the yard and presented his hands to me cupped and concealing something.

"Look," he said, "A peep frog." He cracked his thumbs apart slightly.

"Neat," I said. "He's really green, isn't he."

"Yeah. He's tiny, tiny."

"Where'd you find him?"

"In that little cigar tree by the crick."

"Was he hard to catch?" I asked, my mind flashing from this poor little caught creature to the bush in the cemetery—the cigar-ette bush—and a bigger poor creature named Boyd still eluding capture.

"Mmm... no."

"You're not going to kill him, are you?"

"Mmm... I don't think."

"Good. He's nice. Think he's thinking?"

Jake shrugged. "Maybe."

"What's he thinking?"

He shrugged again and then we just gave the frog a good long look. It was green as could be, like a new leaf. A perfect, pretty little being.

CHAPTER X

In case I forget to get this point across later I should say that this particular summer turned out to be hot and dry, beginning to end. So much so that people brought it up a lot and mentioned it at regular intervals, kind of like they did the Bad Ones, too, until they were shot. It seemed like the hottest summer I could remember in my relatively short life, which didn't seem short to me at all. I felt like I'd been around for a long time, had innumerable memories, and was kind of an important part of the history of Perth Hill, but, in actuality, I hadn't been, didn't and wasn't. Not compared to most people around here, old folks and parents and people like that. These were the people who really drove home what an exceptional year it was, hot and dry-wise.

Somehow, though, in our little neck of the woods we lucked into getting just enough rain at just the right times all summer long to keep it from being a disaster like it was I heard in other parts of the state. And it was the first of these lucky rains that led Burrhead to turn over his prize. The rain may have made digging easier. Or maybe Burrhead couldn't stand the thought of it getting wet. Or maybe the rain just put him in a good mood. Who knows. This was Burrhead we were talking about and he was tough to figure.

But the way it got brought to the public eye, the head, was that on the way to church Tom Orr looked in his mirror to check on the twins in the back seat and there it was, resting peaceably between them. Not completely out in the open—one of them was trying to keep it concealed under the flap of his little suit coat and as Tom put it, it was peeking out at him like a Halloween decoration. A pretty good one. He was biased of course. Since they were just about to the church they just kept on coming and once in the parking lot, Mrs. Orr, Beth Orr, went in and got the preacher.

Needless to say I do not know what all you are taught in a seminary but I would bet you many of the things Reverend Stone had to deal with that summer were not covered. Preaching was one of the occupations my Dad held in high regard but it seemed like there might not be any fun in it. Something you might guess from the Bible, which has a rather heavy bias towards wars and all manner of lepers. Don't get me wrong, there have been, I take it, in reality, lots of wars and lepers all over the place over the course of time and if you are a preacher you never get to pretend otherwise. You *never* get a break. That's all I mean. It just seems like it would be nice if there were a funny book in there somewhere.

Anyway, I was tense and weird and worked up, too, on this Sunday morning. Backtracking: Dad had come home three nights earlier from that Session meeting—the bad night of the you-know-what (liver and onions)—with the news from Ralph Alexander that someone other than Bobby Morgan had been grilled by the sheriff. It seems that they had found a cache of butts of cigarettes of a brand that not too many people smoked. A brand that, in fact, only one person in the whole list of congregants, living or dead, smoked. Only one, if you're not counting his son and his son's degenderate friends. These used-up butts were in close proximity to the body.

Luckily, Mr. MacRae had been square dancing with a barn full of taws over in Alexander's clean barn on the night in question. Mrs. MacRae thought it was amusing.

So he was off the hook and that should have been a great relief to me except for the way that Dad told us about it. He was very terse and abbreviated as if he were holding something back. All Mom said was: *See where smoking will get you.*

In the both of them there were signs of another shoe about to drop. Of that third bad thing about to happen. It's sad and pathetic but I must've actually, at that time, felt like a woman getting her head cut off, a man getting crushed by a tractor, and four 8th Grade derelicts getting nabbed for smoking—the third bad thing—were all roughly equally important and serious. Therefore, on the way to church that morning my hands were sweating and I was cursing the burning bush.

Mr. MacRae was greeting that Sunday. Just getting past him in the first place on the way in without fainting or blurting out something idiotic was a superhuman feat. Then we all saw Beth Orr as she came in fast and urgent, with a detectably victorious air, and said something to him, something with a little more oomph than "good morning, lovely day," then said something to Rev. Stone who was also loitering around out there. Then they all hustled out together in a fit.

A lifetime of sins suddenly swarmed into my memory. Tom Orr knew our evil habits. Beth Orr was his wife.

We could hear Rev. Stone plainly when he came back in to use the phone in the Cloak Room. "Hello," he said. "This is Rev. Stone at Perth Hill. I'm sorry to disturb you all at this hour but it's rather important. Is Mr. McDonough, John, there this morning, close by? I would like to speak to him please if it's not too much bother. Thank you... yes, thank you."

He was good. Very calm. An older lady had answered the phone, you could tell, because his voice had become extra pleasant and almost a little womanish. We waited anxiously, expecting anything. Gorty was on high alert. Jacob was coloring in the insides of all the a's and o's on the bulletin with a pen Mom had given him. Stan, from what I could tell from the back of his head, was cool as a big old cucumber.

The small cross on the wall behind the pulpit hummed and the clock on the wall to our left ticked. I fastened my eyes on the cross. I liked it. Some people didn't. It was fluorescent, internally lit by fluorescent bulbs. Bushy, Mr. Wilson, that is, made it. That seemed unlikely. Everything about it seemed unlikely. He *grew* things, didn't build them, and he was real down on flashy outward symbols. He was a seriously organic old codger. But there it was. Humming. No. No, I didn't like it.

"Yes, John. Sorry for the inconvenience. Something very interesting has turned up here at the church... the, uh, missing piece, shall we say... yes, Perth Hill, of course, Perth Hill... yes, the head."

He went on some more but the word was out and buzzing around the sanctuary like a gnat.

When Rev. Stone emerged from the Cloak Room into the sanctuary we all looked at him and he at us, hesitating for a tick, and then he walked purposefully to the front knowing we knew. But of course manners dictated that he announce it publicly just so we could all pretend we hadn't been eavesdropping. He prayed, too, something along the lines of "Gracious Father in heaven we thank you and praise you for your mercy and wisdom. We would ask, dear Lord, that you bestow a measure of this mercy and wisdom upon us and upon the family of the woman who was recently killed. Lord, we do not know who she is but we would just ask, Lord, that you comfort her loved ones when the time comes as you see fit. Heavenly Father, we would ask that you place your guiding hand on our law enforcement individuals..." and plenty more sort of basically like that

It seems like an unreal coincidence, I know it does, that head showing up like it did after that period of time, right on the door step of where its body had been. But it did. It was almost as if it had latched onto the scent of the rest of itself and tracked it down. For a brief spell we thought it had popped up somewhere in the cemetery, that it had gone undetected by the detectives. That's not what happened though. Bobby and Tommy, the twins, had hatched a scheme to make money from their prize by charging a fee to see it, a museum sort of thing for their little Sunday School friends. These two, they always even then had their eyes on the bottom line. The Orr twins *will* be rich someday.

The Rev cut things way short because he was learning that no matter how well prepared he was he couldn't compete with the surprises and ungodly miracles happening lately outside. I'm not sure why but everyone's guard went down, the parents', most particularly, and *everyone* got a look at it who wanted one. There were gnaw marks all over it. It had been worked over by skunks and coons and mice and who knows what all. *Burrhead.*

"Yeah, looks like some'n gnawed on it," I agreed. Charlie and I were staring at it through the back window of the Orr's Ford. "You heard about Mr. MacRae?"

"Yep. Close one. What'd Stan say?"

"I don't know. Where is—come on let's—wait, he's... Stan, look at that."

"That's a head all right. I wasn't allowed to play with severed heads when I was little," he said.

"Oh, sure," Charlie said as we moved away from the car across the parking lot to the grass bank of the newest part of the cemetery, "And I guess the next thing you'll tell us is that you had to walk five miles to school in the snow?"

"Ten."

"Jiminy... ten miles to school and no severed heads in your stocking? No wonder y're so screwed up," said Charlie sympathetically.

"Stan..." I interrupted, "What about your Dad?"

Stan shrugged. "He didn't do it."

"That explains your sorry-ass Christmases," said Charlie.

"Charlie—what'd he say?"

"Who?" asked Stan.

"Your DAD."

"Nothing. He doesn't keep tabs on that kind of deal. He never said anything about it."

"He just assumed they were his?" I couldn't believe it.

"Guess so."

"Geez... what if he hadn't been square dancing? He could've been in big trouble."

"Neaaah."

I looked at Charlie. He was watching the sheriff pull in and smiling.

"You two are killing me," I said.

The sheriff beat McDonut *again* even though no one at Perth Hill had called him. He put on little white gloves and retrieved the head with the utmost care, placing it in a special bag with an odd amount of ceremony. I mean by this time it had been a *dog's* possession, not to mention a child's toy.

For the record, Burrhead is sort of a collie or a German shepherd or a Great Dane kind of a thing, sort of a pure bred, a mixture of fine things with probably a little setter and cocker spaniel in there somewhere, kind of the standard breed for the area. It's basically derived from whatever breed of dog some New Sterling twerp or Point Fiver got tired of having around and dumped out here since the beginning of time, all ignorant and worthless. Tom Orr castrated his particular version, Burrhead, early on so he wasn't exactly known for footing across the whole of the countryside spreading his goodwill like some do. In fact, in spite of the diminishment to his manliness, he wasn't known to have any goodwill at all except towards the twins. They were the only ones who could stand to be around him and vice versa. He probably was blood somehow to the Bad Ones but had never got up a violent taste for sheep, perhaps due to Tom's intervention.

Old Burrhead. He sure did the twins proud, bringing that thing to them to play with. How unfortunate to be deprived the God-given right to use it for unburdening your little Sunday School classmates of their collection money.

Well, as things go around here, that is, never too smoothly, the head turned out to have no physical connection to the body, past or present. That is, it was *not* the head we were looking for.

CHAPTER XI

In all honesty? I had had bad feelings about that head from the start. It just didn't seem quite right, if you know what I mean. There was something very unhorrifying about it, almost like it had been cleaned up and sterilized for use as a nice visual aid in science class. It seemed to've been rinsed of any connection to a living person. Truthfully, and I am not just saying this, it was hard to get all emotional about that particular head.

Nobody had been. Probably because nobody had admitted yet that the lady in our cemetery could've actually been killed in *our* neck of the woods.

It took over a week for the truth about the head to come out. Tommy and Bobby got to wallow in their celebrity for one more Sunday. Tuesday is when we found out at home;

I remember because that's the day the auction over in New Cornwall had their feeder pig sale and Cambell came back with the news after taking a load of pigs there. He got it from an Amishman. An *Amishman*. An Amishman had the word before we did.

It wasn't even a female's, for the love of Pete. And it'd been separated from its original owner some considerable time before our corpse once thought to be Bobby Morgan (our *other* Bobby some referred to it) met its untimely end. The sheriff and his posse of state lab guys and investigators and what not had determined this about immediately but kept quiet as they scurried around trying to scare up whose head it could've possibly been. They didn't. Still haven't. Dad knew all this a day before we did and hadn't let on. He has a little bit of Amish in him, too, in that, sometimes, he can be just as hard to figure out.

That night at supper, Jacob tried to lift us out of our disappointment by giving a brief tutorial on how to properly *shrink* a head as per according to some brand of Indian in Ecuador. He got a book from somewhere. Dad, Mom let him go on as long as they did because it seemed to have some genuine scientific merit. Well, I don't know about scientific. But he wasn't just dishing it out to make us feel creepy.

"When somebody gets killed it hurts everybody's soul and somebody drinks a special magic drink and goes to this river where the dream ranch is and they dream down there to see if they should get the head of who did it and if he should he goes and gets his other Indians and they go kill him and cut his head off clear off and then you're the Lord of the Trophy.

That's the head the Trophy but it has to be specially prepared or you might spoil it and the spirit will get you. The head is not the whole head. Do you know what it is? It's the skin. That's it! They only skin the head and shrink the skin!"

Mom told him to keep eating and he took a couple of bites, bite of pork chop, bite of corn mush, chasing them through his puddle of syrup.

Bites duly chewed and swallowed, Jake continued on with extra vigor, "You have to boil the skin then roll hot rocks around in it then hot sand when it gets small enough you keep doing it forever for days and weeks until it's the right size then you *cleverly mold it with the fingers so the features are retained and it becomes the head of a small dwarf,*' the right size is an orange, that's how big it is an orange it's orange-sized not bigger like an orange, an orange dwarf—"

"Jake!" I was laughing, we were. "It doesn't turn into an orange dwarf."

"I know," he went on barely with a breath. "It has magic powers and you wear it around your neck and pet its hair and the chief blows tobacco juice mixed with spit up your nose and everything and gradually if you do everything and you only eat small birds so the spirit can't find you the head's spirit and you 'abstain from sex' and you gradually wash the head with a magic 'slution and the spirit becomes a 'will-less instrument and your obedient slave'... Neat, huh?"

He put his elbows on the table with his hands palms up. He had a motor going sometimes. Mom's face was stuck somewhere between horror and amusement. Her eyes widened momentarily and her calmer senses returned.

"Jacob? Your elbows?"

His eyes went to hers; he processed the information, his brain scrambling to be in our world. Mom reached over and lightly tap-tapped his elbow. He took them down, only a half-comprehending look on his face, and started to play with his napkin. He redirected his eyes down the other end of the table.

"Have you ever seen a shrunken head, Dad?"

"I have not," he answered.

"There are pictures in my book. I'll get it. Mom, may I please be excused, please?"

"You certainly may not. Finish your mush, and your salad, please."

A week passed, then the next one, with no new head. The saga of the twins' fame took a slight turn to the sad when the official word got around that "their" head was not "the" head. But don't feel bad. Burrhead produced *another* head. An *additional* head. Not the same one. *Another* one. *TWO*. Burrhead had a running total going. No kidding. And this was the one.

CHAPTER XII

This really sounds made up now. There's not much I can do about that. And believe me I get zero joy out of singing Burrhead's praises. Nobody would except the twins. Yeah, and suddenly, their shameless father. He, almost instantaneously, grew an affection for the scruffy animal.

Suddenly he was explaining to everybody, including the *newspaper*, how exactly he had castrated that dog. With a sheep band. You know, the same ones you use for castrating lambs. No one ever told him you could do it that way with a dog; he never heard it anywhere. It just came to him: *And now would you just LOOK at old Burrhead!*

I wish it was made up. But it was in the papers. If you're a reader you know.

For a little while, some people, like, for instance, Mr. Graham, started to wonder, the way the woods had lately seemed to be bristling with noggins, if there wasn't a mass burial out there somewhere, Indian, of course, and over the course of all the years enough layers of soil had eroded away to allow an enterprising, if despicable, animal such as the Burrhead to stumble into. So far this has proved to actually not be the case but you'd think that all these arrowheads that people find around here had to've been up to *something* once upon a time.

Mrs. Orr called their woods the "jack-in-the-box." She had been very watchful of her boys and their "ball" games and discovered head numero two-oh as soon as it was delivered. Because of all this, in spite of it, whatever, I never completely figured, the sheriff and all really focused their looking and prying for a time on the Orr place. And the Orrs. It was impossible to imagine why they would've killed this person.

Any of the Orrs, excepting, obviously, Burrhead, had to be the very, very remotest of suspects and their place wasn't even near the cemetery but there they were poking and prying, through the woods, in the barn, the sheds, everywhere, tramping everywhere, tramping into the house with their muddy boots on. Oh, man. This really got to Beth Orr.

Well, the paper gave the head and heads plenty of coverage. The *New Sterling Intelligencer* is the one I mean. It was probably in the Youngstown paper, too, and Pittsburgh's, but we didn't get those. We got the *Intelligencer*, in the mail, day late. (I have never seen a paperboy in Perth Hill. To tell you the truth, I have never seen a paperboy.)

Anyway, before they found out whose head this was exactly and became all grave and serious the *Intelligencer's* headlines were things like *FOX TOWNSHIP: HEADS UP!* and *TWO HEADS BETTER THAN ONE FOR RURAL PERTH HILL* and stuff like that.

They made fun of our constable, too. As far as they were concerned we were all Amish out here, just quietly a-till-till-tilling the soil, weaving our own clothes, going to little prayer meetins', having quilting bees, 'warshing' on Saturdays down in the crick, eating potatoes with the skins on, yodeling... dim and dirty and delirious, the kind of folk who just whistle all the livelong day.

We did have our share of whistlers (Iz) but we also had our share of ne'er-do-wells. That share was, admittedly, pretty small, probably because, compared to a place like New Sterling, this wasn't a very friendly place for out and out ne'er-do-wells. They would actually stick out out here. Yes, there were bad kids. Mostly from Mt. Air and Quarry and Lost Acres. But they were primarily nothing more than pumpkin hooligans being stupid.

Well, almost overnight, things had changed. For the better, according to Jimmy Alexander.

To his credit, McDonut seemed to keep a pretty level head about everything, not puffing up to a point bigger than he was already puffed up to, you know, in order to fit the new level of crimes and everything. Yes, he wore cowboy boots but they were a present.

"She's pretty," said Izzy looking over Mom's shoulder at

the newspaper resting on the kitchen table.

"Yes," Mom said. "She was."

She was. And she was taking up about a quarter of the front page and half of my brain and smiling.

"She's not wearing one of those things," I pointed out.

"Habits. I think most nuns are 'plain-clothes' now," said Iz.

"More comfortable that's for sure," said Mom. "The poor girl. Twenty-six. What a waste."

"D'joo know there was a monastery in New Sterling, Mom?" asked Iz.

"A convent. No. I'm afraid I did not."

"So she was Italian," I said. "Mr. Birr guessed that."

"Anna Caravengelo. I'd say so." Izzy knew everything all of the sudden, of course.

"Dad was right, too. About where she was from."

"Mmm-hmm. But your father also said she was some down and out street bum. She was on her way to El Salvador. To a mission."

"Through Perth Hill?"

They ignored my observation. I was standing on the rug between the door and the table. Cambell and I had come in to make a phone call. He was over out of sight on the cellar steps at the other end of the room, the phone cord trailing around the wall. He'd gotten over there on another rug, cater-pillaring it so he never actually touched the clean floor with his boots. We were checking around for links for the manure spreader's web which had broken again. He was checking around. I had followed him in because it was hot outside and I was thirsty. Following him in seemed... sensible.

No one had commented yet on the most obvious fact about Anna Caravengelo that Dad had guessed right. So I did. "She was Catholic just like Dad said."

Without turning from the paper Iz said, "A nun? Catholic? *Reaaaaally*?"

Cambell emerged off the steps onto his rug and hung up saying, "We won't hold that against her!"

"Oh, Cambell," Mom said heavily.

"Just for your information, you're the one who said it was just jewelry, Iz, the crucifix." I rattled the ice cubes in my ice tea, which I had had to beg her to get for me.

She lived in a convent. Not Izzy. Wouldn't that've been lovely? The *sister*. The sister sister. In St. Joachim's in New Sterling.

Cambell rode his magic carpet back across the kitchen and we went back out.

"How about that, a nun," he said. "Of all the things I heard guessed... nun wasn't in there. Russian spy, yes, could be. Elvis, quite possibly, wouldn't be surprised. But a nun?"

"Weird."

"And what's a nun doing looking like that? Nuns aren't supposed to be drop dead gorgeous, are they? Anna Caravengelo. Sister Anna Caravengelo. Come on, Boyd, humor me. I need some answers."

"I don't really have any."

We walked slowly across the front lawn toward the road and the barn. Different thoughts were jumping around. The body in the cemetery, the head, the picture of Sister Anna Caravengelo and... *Burrhead*. Burrhead. He had her head in his mouth, that pretty hair, face, smile, and he was trotting around through the woods. I must've looked ill or something because Cambell poked me in the arm.

"Boydo? You swallow a bug?"

"I was thinking about Burrhead."

"Tom Orr's pride and joy. Did you know that the Celts thought your soul was in your head?"

"Oh yes. Of course I knew that. Where do you get this stuff? College?"

"Yep. It can't be right though."

"Why not?"

"Too many screwy things up there already. They wouldn't get along. Except, possibly, in Sister Anna Caravengelo's case. She looks pretty righteous to me." He thought for a second. "Which reminds me, you should be nice to your own sister. If you know what's good for you."

"Why?" I asked.

He hesitated, then burst out, "Oh, you stumped me again!" We laughed. "No. You should. She's about the only one we have, you know. She can't help it if she acts like a girl. She's pretty good 'z far 'z sisters go."

"This is really sweet. Are you trying to make me cry?"

"Yes. And—here's the important part—that girl doesn't need any Burrhead to cart her around, she's got tentacles, Boyd, eyes in the back of her head, stooges and stools and pigeons all over the place. She's like Santa Claus. She knows if you've been bad or good. She's incredible. The things she can know about a person... she's scary."

He was joking. Half joking. I picked up a rock to calm myself and looked at him. He nodded and laughed once, as if to say, 'you better believe it, pal.' That spiky black hair of his, very short and foreign and completely confident of its position, could make you think he was adopted or something but to me it made him seem exceedingly wise, the holder of many facts. I wound up and tried to launch the rock into the old, roofless, brick silo. Didn't come close. The rock sailed off into the pasture.

"She can be scary, I know that... but what do you have to worry about? You're in college."

"Me? I'm not worried. I wasn't talking about me."

"Oh..." I searched his now unsmiling face. "Riiiight, you're the driving snow, I forgot that." I forced out a laugh. "You're scary, too. You are both scary."

"Oh, yeah, go ahead and kid. Mark my words, friend. Watch that back. I kid you not."

He broke into a bigger, rounder, joshing laugh. I relaxed a little.

But he wasn't joshing, I didn't think.

Nobody wanted to hear information like that. It could ruin your whole sordid life, some omnipotent presence like that. But... come on, nobody was superhuman, not even Isabelle. God willing.

Well, as for the *Sister* Sister, her Sisters, or fellow Sisters, or however they want you to say that, were, according to the newspaper, all beside themselves at the convent and upset. They had followed the Perth Hill Murder Case as they called it (although technically they should have been calling it the Perth Hill Murder *Victim* Case because no one knew *where* she had been killed, I mean another crime scene *was* possible) from the very beginning because they had a special interest in Perth Hill. Their accountant was from Perth Hill. He worked for the firm of Loggi and Pristnello. They called him "Bobby Morgan."

That took some getting used to.

It really did.

The Mother Superior had the warmest feelings for Bobby Morgan, thank heavens, and thought only the very best about him and his work.

CHAPTER XIII

Mrs. Morgan wouldn't lie about anything. If you knew Mrs. Morgan you'd know that. Poor woman. It sure was hard not to stare at them, though, and just wonder about things. The odd, tiny clan. The oddly tiny clan.

Yes, I had been batting that around in front of the usual eminences, Charlie, Stanley, and other older experts such as our leprechaun sawyer, Mr. Bell, and was able to coax out a twitch or two, and perhaps a squeak. There were no big secrets here, only long-gone things that weren't happy or useful (like Murray Glenn's missing finger), and, therefore, not worth dwelling on.

First, little Bobby's father was dead. I *was* aware of this. But I didn't know how *long* he'd been dead. He'd been dead for a long time, so long that I basically knew him about as good as Bobby did. Died of a heart attack broad-casting rye grass in a pasture at the age of 33. Bobby was about nothing at the time, not even hardly born yet, or not *even* born yet. Second, Bobby's grandma, his father's mother, went cuckoo. And third, his great-grandpa was born without a throat.

Charlie: *Oh, I have a hard time swallowing that one!* But it wasn't a joke. It was true. Adam's apple completely not around. Simple shape of the matter was that, for the Morgans, there truly was a long, wide acre of pathetic biological mayhem stretching back to the mist.

And now we had a decapitated nun wearing little Bobby's clothes. When it came to biological mayhem, this seemed to be kind of a corker. You've heard of the luck of the Irish? The Morgans hadn't.

You wouldn't guess this dismal history by knowing Mrs. Morgan. She was tough. *Raised those kids by her lonesome and worked like the dickens besides.* Mr. Birr said that. They had sheep and some Herefords. Still had some sheep. Merinos, I think. *Bobby isn't normal but he's about half-normal, which is half-again 'z normal 'z he mighteh been.* Mr. Bell said that.

Bobby's sister, now she was a bright spot. Ellen. She lived near Pittsburgh, had a nice husband and three cute, clever children (so they said, Mom, the ladies, etc.). They appeared dressed all the way up, to the nines and twinkly on Mother's Day and other notable days. We, in fact, had seen them not too, too long ago. A gaggle of Ellen's old cronies such as Beth Orr always glommed onto them between church and Opening Exercises laughing and coo'ing and all that garbage.

But for the love of Pete, they had to be operating, ever and always, under this slowly circling turkey vulture that was the Morgan past. One eye up, nervous, ever and always. You would think anyways.

There was, to tell you the truth, before any of this, something about the Morgans that was kind of sad, vaguely sad. You couldn't put your finger on what it might be, or why you yourself felt that way about them. Maybe it was simply their limited ranks and modest physical sizes situated there at the end of the extra long Glenn pew—the Morgans didn't even warrant their own pew—and the Glenns, plentiful and large as they come, horrendously robust, bearded and flushed, wide, dense silo-people.

Every Sunday now, like the one I'm talking about right here, these kinds of unsettled thoughts would crowd to the front of my brain as Cambell raced us to church like it was going to be interesting or something. And the weird thing, it usually was.

To the right of the Glenns, Mrs. McKee got up from their own short end pew. The McKees had pretty daughters. Unfortunately, Cambell would never tell me much more than that obvious fact.

"Uh, Patrick, my uncle... in-law, I guess you'd call him, Ronald Lewis, a lot of you know him, he's fixed the plaster in probably everybody's house down around us by now at least once, is in the hospital again with his knee and I wondered if we might could say a prayer for a fast recovery."

Mrs. McKee sat back down while Rev. Stone jotted a note. He looked back up at us from the pulpit. "Anything else, prayers or concerns, we should remember?"

Gorty had one. He always did. Usually for Stump, his boss at Stump's Dairy. Today he had a concern for Stump's foot, which hurt.

As the Rev. dutifully jotted this down, I heard a bulletin crinkle behind us, not right behind, about three pews back, then Jimmy's Mom's voice. It was the nice friendly one with a little quaver in it. "Reverend, I think we should all be praying for Anna Caravengelo and her family... and all the people at the convent where she worked and lived."

"Thank you, Gwen. We certainly should. Everyone." The Rev. paused, a bewildered and sad expression on his face. When he started again his voice was softer. "We certainly do need the Almighty to guide us through, especially, of course, the people who were closest to her...."

I turned away for just a second to see what Jacob was coloring on his bulletin that day (I can't remember). Then I looked over at Cambell. He was engrossed in picking hay splinters out of his hands... the field that I'd raked on Friday haunted me briefly. I had been half-daydreaming, half-sleeping, thinking about the sister while I was raking, about her picture. Her hair was loose and curly. You'd call it a pageboy if it were straight hair. It was black—*black*. Blacker than Cambell's, way blacker, blacker by a dozen crows. You couldn't tell what color her eyes were but I'd have to say they were caramel, about halfway between the color of my arrowhead and the earth that held it, some very particular, perfect shade that I was afraid no longer existed. She was pretty but looked kind, like she would go ahead and try to be your friend even if you were stupid.

Every round or two, on the straight part of the field, I'd pull that picture out of my front pocket for an inspection. I had gotten it that morning. I had volunteered to burn the trash because there was an empty milk jug in the can. I lit the fire, then stuck the jug onto a stick and proceeded to melt it. The orange, flaming globs of melting plastic whistled softly and sizzled as they cascaded back into the fire like drops of volcano. So beautiful. Working the stick back and forth over the fire and twirling the stick, raveling the plastic to make it last as long as possible I was suddenly struck by a face staring out at me from the flames. Anna Caravengelo.

I grabbed the edge of the paper and yanked it out, stomping the flames. I had saved her. So I did save her, carefully ripping the blackened, sooty borders from the photo. Maybe other people did, too. She had that kind of face, the kind you wanted to hang onto and look at.

I was driving along, her picture in my shirt pocket, thinking, and came to the end of the field and just kept right on agoing right into the woods bashing and crashing through wild red raspberry bushes and saplings and low branches and whatnot, just that whole thicket there at the shared edge of field and woods. I got stopped before I ran into anything too deadly but that particular windrow trailed away to nowhere looking as if someone was in there pulling the whole field into the woods by a string. If anybody pinned me down about that windrow I was going to say I had to go to the bathroom really bad. There's a cucumber tree in there. Big leaves. If you couldn't find nice, furry grape leaves, cucumber leaves were the best. That's what I'd say. Always the convincing detail. Learned that from Mr. Ken Orr.

Later, I stuck that picture in my Bible. I did, however, hesitate for a moment because, well, you know, I didn't know if you should really put a nun in a Presbyterian Bible. But I did. But... I'm not some kind of weird freak—don't worry about that.

Between church and Opening Exercises for Sunday School we stood along the wall of the sanctuary, as was our new custom, not feeling very welcome in the cemetery anymore, and shot the breeze.

Stan told us who did it. "The family did it," he said looking straight ahead over the rows of pews and talking out of the side of his mouth, shady-like.

"Whose family?" Charles asked.

"THE family, capital f. The Family. The mob. Mob hit."

Charlie stepped away from the wall to face it and us. "Let me guess, Mac. You're Marlon Brando. Right?"

Glen, facing the wall, too, said, "Marlin *Perkins*."

We laughed. Stan didn't. "I'm serious. This has all the signs. Lookee here: brutal murder, vanished weapon, no witnesses and... *Catholic*. And not just Catholic, a nun. The Pope is mobbed up big time. Everybody knows that."

Charlie busted up, pressing a hand to his round stomach. "Mobbed up? What have you been watching?"

"Not Mr. Rogers like you."

"Isn't a mob what they call a bunch of penguins or sea otters or something, Marlin?" Glen grabbed my arm and continued, "Jim here will attempt to sneak in and infiltrate the dangerous mob of penguins and capture one in this bag to take back to Mutual, Omaha. It's risky business. Penguins are by nature not—" He stopped, a smile creeping in across his orange, glowing face. "I mean they are calm. They are not flighty at all, but they do not take very kindly to captivity, particularly in this bag that Jim's about to use."

Stan laughed, a bit reluctantly at first.

Jimmy hit Glen. "Penguins *can* fly, you know. But they have to buy a ticket like everybody else."

"Rule change. No more penguin jokes. For future reference, it's Mutual OF Omaha. And a mob is sheep."

"You like sheep, don't you, Lane?"

Janie and Jody walked past between Glen and Charlie and the pews, working their way to a back pew for Opening Exercises.

"Are you being nice, Benjie?" Janie asked. She pointed at him. "You guys look like y're up to something."

"I'm always nice," he replied as they moved on. "Not that it's any of your business."

"That's an inbred trait," I said, suddenly feeling keen and perceptive. "Sisters think it's their job to monitor your behavior."

"Your sister's nice," Ben said. "You're lucky."

I chuckled bitterly.

"No. I've noticed that, too," Glen nodded. "It's inbred but I've found that you can beat it out of them."

"Right, Wallace," Stan said, "I've seen with my own two eyes Mary beat the living crap out of you."

"Actually, Stanley, it's never been proven that Mary is a girl. Mom and Dad only gave her that name because she looked like she belonged in a manger."

Through various independent sources, standing around here and there and eavesdropping, it became clear that Stanley's theory was not *too* widely held, openly anyway. But I did find out that the Pope "irritated" at least one person: Glen's Grandpa Dungan. Of course, who *didn't* irritate Grandpa Dungan?

The Deacons, all ladies, organized a plan to take food to the convent and also to get a group volunteered to attend the funeral. Mom wasn't a current Deacon but she was going to do both. Taking food to the family of some regular person who just died is pretty easy to figure because you know how many mouths are going to be around eating up your casseroles and meat loafs, sweet rolls, baloney cups, etc., but this convent caused some head scratching. A lot of hypothetically speaking and calculating and worrying went into the plan.

How many nuns? What did nuns eat? What day should they take it? Not Friday! What *type* of nuns were these? Were these St. Joachim nuns some kind of 'special' nun that ate only certain food? Mrs. Orr (Ken's Mom, not Beth) had read about a certain type of nun that ate primarily nuts. Nuts. Imagine that. Primarily nuts.

I liked nuts.

This was not a simple problem. You didn't want to offend the nuns, mercy no, also, you didn't want perfectly good food to go to waste, *mercy* no.

The delegation charged with funeral duties grew to a size that I believe was considered to be safe. It included the sincere and fearful, and the curious and fearful. Fear bound them all together, sincerely and curiously. Who knew what to expect? Somebody or other knew somebody or other who had a cousin who had been to Europe and gone inside some of those big, famous churches in some country, *Italy*, and they had seen... *relics*. Bones. Human bones. All manner of bits and pieces, all stored in little bottles and in jewelry. Yes, jewelry.

But that wasn't the worst thing they had seen. The worst thing was... a bishop. No, no, not just any bishop. A very old bishop. How old was he? 90? A 100? Hah! 300! He was *300!* In a glass trophy case. Not a statue or a painting or a wax replica. The actual bishop. The *whole* contiguous bishop. He was pretty wrinkled but they had found a way to pickle an entire bishop.

And there were candles, heaps of candles, and incense and clanking chains and little old women, beads clutched in their gnarled digits, rocking back and forth and muttering to these bonelets and pickled bishops. Praying. To bones and pickled bishops.

Nobody believed a single word of it... all the same, safety in numbers.

After Sunday School we made our way out to the car, Mom was last—finalizing that whole expedition. We were anxious to get home but the delay allowed us to witness a remarkable thing, particularly remarkable what with the pickled bishop so fresh in our minds.

They came around from the west side of the church: nuns. As if they had heard us talking about them. Reverend Stone was leading them, talking to one. There were four.

"Well, I'll be," Dad said quietly from behind the wheel.

"Why would they want to come out here?" Izzy asked.

"Blest'f I know," Dad said.

Jacob, then, his voice faraway and unusual, said, "They come to mourn."

Izzy and Cambell and I laughed briefly. The way it had come out was kind of weird and funny.

"They always wear black," Izzy said.

"Anna Caravengelo didn't," I said. "Not in the newspaper, I mean."

"Not for that picture anyhow."

We watched them go, moving down among the gray stones and the Ben Franklin trees, floating.

CHAPTER XIV

During the next couple of those early July days I wondered why would we do all that—Perth Hill, I mean—take all that food and go to the funeral and everything when we didn't even know Anna Caravengelo? Mom said to be nice. Isabelle said because we felt bad and sort of... responsible for it. That was the stupidest thing I ever heard.

They went anyway, of course. It was in the morning, during the week. They reported back over lunch.

We had left-over fried chicken from Sunday, left-over ham from Monday, left-over potato pancakes made from Sunday's left-over mashed potatoes, a waffle from sometime (cut up into fourths so each of us whiny kids could get a piece) and apple sauce. And two brand new peanut butter and honey sandwiches (in quarters as well, a very nice polite size).

And one very small shape of orange Jell-O with strawberries in it from some other time and another of sweet and sour pickles. Bread and butter and strawberry jam, too, naturally.

"It felt a little like calisthenics class, didn't it, Izzy?" Mom said.

Z-belle agreed. "Up, down, kneel, up, down," she chortled. "Catholics should be the most physically fit people on earth."

Dad laughed. "You just described your mother at meals," he said, referring to her jumping around, in and out of the kitchen, getting this and that, refilling serving dishes from the stove. It seemed like it would be easier to just plop the frying pan on the table and the whole bottle of catsup but she never did that. Everything had its own nice little serving dish.

"Well, a body has to do these things," she said. She paused waiting maybe for some additional smart remark, then continued. "I have been to a mass before. As a mere child I went with a friend to her oldest sister's wedding. Tenny Murchik. She sends a Christmas card. They have two boys."

"Don't you want to know if we kneeled?" Izzy asked.

"D'joo kneel, Zeezie?" Jacob asked.

"Mrs. Keegan did right away, huh, Mom?"

"Went to her knees like lightning struck her! Heavens. And Mrs. Morgan, poor woman. There was quite a debate amongst the rest of us. We decided there was no harm in it."

"Kneeling always seemed like mock piety to me somehow," Dad said matter-of-factly.

"Oh, I don't think that, Timothy. The Episcopalians kneel."

"God knows if you're humble or not," Iz stated. "Kneeling or sitting."

"Well, He better. Righto?" With that Mom got up and took the plate the potato pancakes and waffles had been on and disappeared. She came back with three warm potato pancakes and cut them in half. "Eat up you'ns guys," she said, handing the plate to me. "Supper time's a long time... well, for good or bad, we knelt but we didn't have communion, which was okay by me. They used to use real wine. I suppose they still do."

"Mommm, we almost had communion."

"Ah-hah! The truth comes out!" kidded Dad.

"Speak for yourself, Isabelle. I didn't know that's what they were going to do. I thought we were all going to do a little dance or something."

Dad laughed. "*Rrrose.*"

We laughed, too, but Mom kept a straight, innocent face. "Well, how was a bod to know? I thought we might. A little dance would be okay, right?"

"Around the golden calf?" Dad asked, raising his eyebrows.

"Be nice, Timothy."

"How did you almost have communion, Mom?"

Z answered. "Everybody got up, so we did, too. Like robots, huh, Mom?"

"We didn't know," Mom said. "But Mrs. McKee pointed out a little paragraph in the back of the hymnal that said they didn't want us to. It didn't seem, shall we say, overly polite, did it, Zeezie?"

"No, it didn't," stated Z firmly. Then she got slightly dreamy and said, "The priest was handsome, though. What a cutey."

"Oh and such a nice voice. It sounded kind of foreign, didn't it, Zeez? A young fellow. Heavens, he was young."

"Did they say anything about her?" I asked. "You know, Anna Caravengelo."

"Well, yes. He did. A little. She did a lot of work at a community center on New Sterling's South Side—there was a goodly number of, well, black people in attendance... but the poor girl had no immediate family apparently. Her parents were over and out long ago. We had to fill in the blanks here and there but she grew up in a special school or home or convent in Titusville. Did you get that, Zeez?"

"Mmmm-hmmm. A convent, I think. A saint something. Wow, just think about that. She was a nun in diapers."

"But a free-spirit. Didn't you get that impression? From the way he said it, it made me think her mission trip to down there—"

"El Salvador."

"Mmmm. It wasn't officially approved or condoned by everyone. Or someone. Or however they do it."

"Do you think she could've been wearing those clothes, Mom, to sneak away?" Z asked. "Carla heard that."

"I never thought of that."

"Paper said they knew she was going," I said.

"It's a cover-up," said Cambell plainly. "She tried to escape and they killed her." He was sounding like he really knew.

"Cambell. These women did not look capable of that."

"Not them," I offered. "The Pope. He sent a hit squad."

"A hit bishop," corrected Cambell.

"Did Mrs. Graham go?" I asked, cleverly switching gears, I thought. "Ben said she was."

"And Janie. They rode with Ruth. It was a bit much for poor Janie, I think," Mom said.

"Really?"

"She was crying, poor thing. She's unusual."

"She's a handsome kid," Dad said.

"She's working for Duff Taylor this summer. Did you know that?"

"Doing what?"

"Well, I don't know exactly. What does a person do in an orchard before things get ripe?"

What would be great, I started to think would be to get in a situation like that where Janie was crying and I could be there and offer her my hanky, a nice clean one, and I could comfort her and everything. That would be pretty good. She'd probably be appreciative and think I was kind and nice. And the possibility might arise that she might want to kiss me, which would be really good. She's unusual so it was possible. This is when I made the decision to start carrying a spare hanky. A clean one. For occasions.

"Aaron Birr was also there, which I thought was nice of him," Mom said.

"He goes all the way in there to church?" asked Jake.

"No, no. Unless he's switched. They go to Cyril and Methodius in Quarry."

"Oh."

I dropped the clean hanky in Janie's lap. "Why did *he* go?"

"Well, I'm just not too sure. I really didn't feel it my place to ask him that."

"He came late," said Z, "right from a hearing. McDonut caught some baddies taking apart the Township grater—"

"Wha—"

"To sell for scrap," answered Z, creepily apprehending my question.

"Who were the rascals?" Dad asked.

"Mmmm, I don't know," said Z. "Two boys from 'Cuttown."

"Starlings."

"Boyd, that's not nice." Mom frowned at me. "'Cuttown considers itself to be separate from New Sterling anyway. Aaron Birr pointed one of their mothers out."

"'Zat right? Leave it to good old Aaron Birr. No doubt gave her a ride from the hearing. Hard to rattle that bird."

"There was quite a variety there," said Mom with a tilted, slightly amazed nod. "Mostly of the Italian flavor."

"How about that nun who talked to us and Mrs. McKee?"

"Did you see any bones?" Jake interrupted. "Saint bones?"

"Are you interrupting, Jacob? We didn't see any saint bones. She was lovely, wasn't she, Izzy? An older woman with such a lovely soft brogue. Oh, I could've listened to her all day. She could've been speaking gibberish and it wouldn't've mattered. She said very nice things about Perth Hill's cemetery and church. They reminded her of her home church in Ireland. It was stone but still."

"I thought Catholic churches had to be gigantic," I said.

"I guess not. Cyril and Methodius isn't overly huge-huge."

"Where was yer friend from, Rose," Dad asked.

"The south... of course. Near Galway, she said."

"Can I ask a question?" Jake said. He was being more careful.

"Yes, you may."

He snuck in two questions all in one quick breath. "Were there any bishop pickles or mobsters?" He looked through his glasses blinking expectantly at Mom... then Iz... then Mom.

Mom shot a reproachful glance at Cambell and me as if our innocent comments about hit bishops and so forth had brought this on. Mrs. *Glenn* was the one who'd heard of the pickled bishop in Italy. "Why would you think there were mobsters, Jake?" Mom asked.

"Stanley said there were."

"MacRae? Honey, I hardly think Stan MacRae is any expert on the Catholic church but...."

"Of course there were, Jake! In other words." Isabelle laughed. She was kidding, sort of. New Sterling probably did have some littler-type mobsters. Jake got my attention, though. Even though he had remained hidden from us or invisible, he had been listening in to our conversation in church on Sunday. Little bugger. Between him and Izzy, if Cambell's warning could be believed, a person could never let their guard down.

CHAPTER XV

We had one field that didn't make any sense. It was down towards the Francis Forge Road end of our place but over far enough towards Stearns Road that you would naturally think it was one of Gil Moore's fields. You could get to it through a narrow strip of woods at the edge of our sheep pasture, which was the shortest way, but bumpy and through a creek, or you could go on the roads. Bill Wendt told Dad that it was Moore's field 150 years ago but the man who would've been Gil's great-great-grandfather had given it to the people who homesteaded our place, the Kyce's, as payment for something. This was the kind of stuff Bill Wendt somehow knew.

Well, we were on our way back from that field, Z, me, a load of hay, a big load, 110 bales, the whole field, tightly built and rock steady. Or, not as tight as some, actually, and I was riding nervously on the shelf at the front yelling at her to take it easy as she yanked us out onto the road, the tractor and the baler and the groaning, creaking wagon and me, when we saw the car, Z stretching her scrawny arm out towards it.

A big black Cadillac, clean and shining, parked about half way down Frank Stearns' lane. There was zero normal about that. Mitchell Brothers, the undertakers who had their office or whatever you call it—parlor—in Quarry, were the only ones from around here who had a Cadillac and this wasn't it.

Occasionally, people with really clean cars would find their way out here from somewhere for a Sunday drive and they stuck out like sore thumbs. Perth Hill isn't exactly Lancaster, you know. They might slow down or even stop very briefly to get a better look at a pig or a cow, some exotic creature like that, but they never out and out parked and left their car. Z kept her hand on the accelerator but didn't twist it down; we rolled past the end of Frank's lane, slowly and quietly, staring at the black car. Who knows why but seeing it was eerie, kind of spooky and ominous, as if it were a spaceship come down from some vastly superior civilization with no warning and no hint of intent.

Old Frank... more and more stuff started to go on in his life now that he was almost dead. Couple days later Mom came home from Agway with some teeth for the rake and some links for the manure spreader web—we'd depleted Van Spoets' entire supply (we must've replaced the entire web by this time on the jinxed machine)—and Cambell and I were standing in it pitching the same manure for the second time, this time *out* of the spreader, into the field along the road below the chicken house.

"I would've been back sooner, boys, but I got stuck on Forge behind a truck hauling the largest piece of equipment I have ever seen. Moving on a road, I mean. It turned onto Stearns Road."

She put the brown paper sack of links on the seat of the tractor. "I'm sorry this keeps breaking. You poor fellows. Maybe we can get a new one?"

"That's what Boyd wants for his birthday, Mom. He was just saying. What was it?"

"I don't know. A crane or something. Maybe the railroad's putting up another tower. What time do you goofballs think you'll be in for lunch?"

"What're we having, Mom?" I inquired.

"I made bread this morning so we're having fried dough. Along with a few odds and ends. Does that meet everyone's approval?"

"I love fried dough. Did you make enough for all of Cambell's stomachs?"

"We'll see," said Mom widening her eyes.

"What time do you want us?" Soon I hoped.

"Well, it won't be ready for 15 minutes or so. What're your father and Jake doing?"

"Clipping needle teeth, giving shots," said Cambell as he eased a little fork load of manure onto my boot. "They can come whenever, I'm sure. How 'bout... half hour? 'Zat okay?"

"That'll be lovely. Toodles."

We finished cleaning out the spreader then went to get Jake and Dad with about ten minutes to spare. We told them about the crane.

Dad said, "Well, we don't want to rush your Momma—maybe we'll take a little jaunt in that direction before lunch."

We headed for the pickup but before we got there Myron Rantle drove by and knew all about it already.

If there'd been enough warning, if we hadn't gotten picked off out there in the open lane like sitting ducks, we, including Dad, would've tried to run and hide. Mr. Rantle liked to visit. I mean *VISIT*. And stay. Stay and stay and visit and visit even when you'd used up all the useful topics and there was not one more word to say. His trouble was that he got laid-off periodically and had time to kill and he was at this time, laid-off. Being laid-off was hard on his family but it wasn't any picnic for anyone else either. Honestly, he could waste more of a person's time while providing the least information or benefit than anybody. Except for today.

"Gentlemen," he said, very seriously as always. One arm hung limply out his window along his pickup door. His head was sweating. He had a very nice round head, that was not quite officially bald, I will say that.

"Hello, Mr. Rantle," Dad said, rather flatly. "What has you out and about?"

"A few chores. I seen yer neighbor's gunna strip," he said.

My eyes flashed to Dad. He had very definite feelings about stripping.

"Not that I know of," Dad said, but his expression had, in a heartbeat, become confused and sad with dissolving disbelief—it was the same expression Jake got when he realized he was about to actually get paddled.

Mr. Rantle raised his listless arm slightly in the general direction of the Stearns place. "Stearns. Just come by there. They was riggin' up the dragline even as we confabricate, if yeh get my drift."

"I wish you were joking, Myron. Y'r not, though, are you?"

"I am not, sir. Blackstone Mining. I stopped in and had a yack with the crew. Blackstone's one of them Bavarro fellows."

"Blackie Bavarro, I believe. They've been out snooping around before."

"'Zat so? They're gon'neh take that field next to the woods. Frank had beans in there last year. They drilled test holes over there a couple years ago. crew says."

"I don't know anything about that." Again, Jake's about-to-get-paddled look clouded Dad's face. "News to me if they did... Frank, that rascal..."

Just then Mom's voice came singing down the draw from the back porch. "LUHHH-UHHHNCH!" It wasn't irate yet. "DO ANYBODIES HEEEEEAR ME?!"

Dad hollered back, "We HEAR yuh, Ma! Be there directly!"

Miraculously, Mr. Rantle didn't invite himself in for a free meal but buzzed away of his own accord, more or less, feeling pretty good about himself for dispensing some useful, non-worthless information.

CHAPTER XVI

Severed heads and dead bodies were upsetting enough to our leafy little neck of the woods but strip-mining equipment was actually horrifying. A place or two had been stripped 50, 60 years before, before the idea of reclamation had been discovered. These places were barren and shaley and peculiar. They had hills that were the wrong shape for around here with big jagged washes. They were pricked here and there with scrawny pine trees and, thanks to birds, wild cherries. Things hadn't gotten desperate enough yet to try that again. As Mom said, it just wasn't nice.

My parents moved here from 30 miles away 20 years prior to this and they were still considered rootless vagabonds. Shoot, according to Charlie Lane *I* wasn't even from here—and I was *born* here for the love of Pete. But even we crazy immigrants knew it wasn't *nice*. Not in Perth Hill. I mean, the road going through your place had your neighbor's name on it; Fergus Woods weren't owned by any Fergus, their house and barn just happened to be much closer to them than the Wallace's who did own them; the creek that ran through your place and had your name on it also ran through five other places. And so on. These creek names and road names were still people names. The families who came here 200 or whatever years ago and put their names on things were *still* here. And none of them thought stripping your place was a very good idea. Except, apparently, for one.

Well, they kept bringing in equipment, Blackstone Mining did. The name didn't inspire too much confidence in their expertise. *Blackstone?* Couldn't they think of the actual name for it? After a couple of days, though, everything stopped. None of the crew was even around. Seemed like the calm before the storm.

Things weren't all doom and gloom, though. The black raspberries were starting to ripen. The tame red ones had started a bit earlier and they were good but the black ones, with their dense and perfect shape and color and a flavor your mouth was always set for, were oh so good. That's true.

Mom had picked the very first few of them after supper from one of her 'secret' early bushes and we had them on vanilla ice cream during the late news. The phone rang and she went, unenthusiastically, to get it. Usually at that hour it was some strange person wanting to complain about the school board or the 4H or something.

She answered it. "Oh. Hello, Aaron Birr... quite fine, thank you. Are you looking for TR?... one second please, Mr. Birr. We'll have to dig him out of his chair—*Timothy. It's Aaron Birr.* Oh, you are most welcome, Mr. Birr. Good night."

They were on the phone for a while but I didn't get much of what they were saying. Those raspberries... everything around me seemed sweet and silent and good. That passed. Jake was on the couch next to me reading a book on guillotines.

Dad came back in the living room saying, "Aaron Birr should worry about his own place 'z much 'z he does about Frank Stearns'. Bless his heart."

"I put your bowl in the freezer," Mom said. The house was still very warm.

CHAPTER XVII

Mr. Birr got the stripmine stopped, temporarily at least. Not him actually because, firstly, he was a Justice of the Peace, and, secondly, he wasn't a lawyer. Little quirk there in my particular branch of judgedom, he said. Legal training not absolutely required. So he got Mr. Zahnhiser to do it. Poor Mr. Zahnhiser. By this time, he was trying as hard as he could to be otherwise tied-up, cutting silage, making wills, taking Carla's little sisters to their eye specialist in Pittsburgh (those little girls were born about blind but they could see a little bit), but old Aaron Birr, he got him to tangle up Blackie Bavarro's lease somehow. Which only seemed right. Seemed fishy, or at least uncouth, that they would wait till a man was almost dead and couldn't talk to roll in and start ripping his place up.

In spite of that little sparkle of good news folks had really clammed up at church, and all during church, during the "prayers or concerns." I mean, when Rev. Stone asked us if we had any. Nobody had any. Pretty hard to believe. *That* summer?

Well, listen, nobody ever really went running off at the mouth during "prayers or concerns." That book, something about why bad things were always happening to good people? Easy. I'll tell you why. It was because some people flopped down to their knees at the drop of a hat and tried to pawn off their petty little problems on an already very busy, not to mention, tremendously inscrutable God, when what they should really've been doing was rooting around down there for a four-leaf clover.

But you could usually count on one or two "prayers or concerns" just to be nice. A grandpa's bum kidney or something. Nothing. Not even from Gorty. Rev. Stone was left carrying the ball. He prayed for justice and tranquility. And also for our nun.

"Our" nun. He was the first one I heard say it out loud and right up from the pulpit, loud and clear. Well, kind of mumbled, actually. But he said it. And it wasn't a slip, or else he wouldn't've had time to think to mumble it. There was never any comment about it. In fact, spontaneously, this was how almost everyone from then on referred to Anna Caravengelo.

Our nun. Very strange. For a bunch of Presbyterians, stranger than manna. *Stranger than manna, plagues and Picasso all balled up into one.* Mr. Zahnhiser there. He liked to say goofy things. No other Zahnhiser did but he did.

I think he thought them up on those long drives to Pittsburgh. He spoke in parables, or tried to I should say, which made him, according to Charlie, a Parabola.

How *did* we get to "our"? Glen, kind of a Parabola himself, was slightly more helpful than Charles in interpreting Mr. Zahnhiser. The "our" business was two things, he said. First, for a bunch of Presbyterians with what were turning out to be rather limited affections for anything having to do with the Catholic faith, it was warped. Second, it was inevitable.

Second first. She had lit on our good ground, out of the thin air, from the heavens as it were, Glen pointed out. Our good ground, Perth Hill's, had claimed her and that in itself had to count for something. She might not've picked Perth Hill, but God evidently had picked it for her—things didn't just happen; there were reasons, clouded and tortured though they might be. Her blood was soaked into our soil, and this, as they will be only *too* happy to inform you, was exactly how Charlie's and Stan's and Glen's old ancestors had come into it, the soil, these fields and woods, in the first place. Their old blood was soaked in there, too, along with Anna Caravengelo's, mingling. My lucky arrowhead might even contain a trace of it. I pointed that out.

She had stirred up quite a mess, though, moving on to the warped part now, and nobody felt happy about that. Really was not appreciated. And she wasn't done stirring either, prophesied Glen, that was the thing. And we even *knew* she wasn't done stirring when she became ours, officially, from the pulpit. She wasn't quite done shocking us, the dead nun, *our* dead nun. She had been violently unhinged and rearranged and in the process was kind of rearranging us, too. More trouble was on the way, more discombobulation, and still there we were claiming her.

And the discombobulation? She was little Bobby's girlfriend. There.

I said it. It was true. Some of us never quite got over that one. Little Bobby's girlfriend. Our nun.

Little Bobby finally remembered this small fact and mentioned it to the Sheriff at a luncheon they gave for him over at the jail.

This got talked about, sure it did, but not very much to tell you the truth. No one had ever tried this before: dating a nun. We weren't sure if there was something perverted about it. Particularly with this *particular* nun, who, to refresh the memory, had been beheaded. It was very difficult to overlook that part and very difficult to talk about any of it out in the open air without seeming kind of perverted your own self.

But she was ours. Bobby Morgan had managed to merge the warped and the inevitable. She was more ours than we could ever've guessed. And the thing was, this *could've* had a happy ending—admittedly hard to imagine—if she had escaped from the convent and become a nice Presbyterian and all, Bobby's little wife and all. But that's not what happened. But you know that part.

CHAPTER XVIII

That same day she became our nun, all of ours, we were out on the bank of the newer part of the cemetery during Sunday School under the row of beech and white pine trees Bushy had planted umpteen thousand years ago. Since Bobby Morgan kind of abdicated as our teacher we somehow convinced the powers that be (Murray Glenn) that we would finish out this term through, get this, self-study. Stanley negotiated this little gem and we all loved him for it. The idea was to take turns being the teacher. Each Sunday somebody else. Quite an idea.

This Sunday Jimmy was the teacher and he had actually read the lesson and studied it and thought up a thing or two to talk about—he could be like that. He gave it a good try, too. Thirty seconds in, though, the focus had shifted, pretty decisively, to jokes; nice ones, mean ones. Practical ones. Glen had kind of secretly slipped up into one tree before the lesson even started. Every minute or so, a little piece of gravel came down through the boughs and branches and konked a head.

Ben thought it was a squirrel (throwing *gravel*). He said he *saw* it.

"We're darn lucky Burrhead found that head," our teacher mused. "What if our nun's besainted someday? That head'll be worth some serious jack."

This took a moment to sink in and we stared at Jimmy.

"Hey!" Ben whined. The "squirrel."

Jimmy shook his head impatiently at us. "For *relics*. Some Catholic church will pay cold hard pesos for that head. Think of all the teeth! Maybe even wisdom teeth! The twins might turn a buck after all."

"Does Cyril and Methodius have any relics?" I asked.

Charlie laughed. "A *baby* tooth."

"Cyril's gallstone," Glen chirped from up in the branches. Ben still didn't get it, didn't even look up!

"Who was that anyway?" Ben inquired. "Cereal and that other one."

"Commodious," said Jimmie.

"Saint Breakfast. Sister Restroom," Charlie said, chuckling proudly.

Scratching his own empty head, Ben asked, "Where *is* our nun's head anyways?"

"The sheriff's using it for a door stop." The big worm of regret burrowed into me the instant my stupid mouth let that out.

The girls couldn't take it any longer. They had been ignoring us for the most part.

Jody Dyson, Janie's best friend, said, "For *crying* out loud, you morons, she was a *person*. A real live person." She took a breath. "She had a family. She had friends. You'ns... are... *sick*. How would it be, Stan, if someone brutally murdered Linda? How would *you* feel?"

"Good?" Stan replied.

We didn't get to laugh at that as much as we would've liked to because of how serious and mad they were, Jody and Janie, both of them. They always got mad together—they *were* close. "The Strips." Charlie called them that, after raw bacon strips that you couldn't get apart. They stomped off.

That was about the end of that class. Glen quit dropping little pieces of gravel down and started hurling them instead. Poor Ben's head, speaking of relics.

That night in more reflective moments I thought about how ignorant and stupid we probably looked to The Strips. They had been disgusted. Jody, her high voice gone into its growling flute, perched there on her perfectly shaped legs, tanned lightly to a ripe peachy color, and Janie, there, in her longish blue tea dress, which was about the color of Johnny-jump-ups, the high, before-lunch sun turning her blond hair into a halo. And us, there, all ignorant and stupid.

Whoever married either one of those two was in for a steady supply of morality and goodness. And that is notwithstanding the fact that sometime later one of them, sort of, turned up pregnant. A nice couple from Wisconsin adopted the baby. Happy ending. More or less.

In the meantime, we were pathetic. That was sad because the Sunday School hour had started out so promising with me showing Janie my lucky arrowhead. She said it looked like the sunset and I said that was *exactly* what I had thought the second I found it! I prayed she would factor that into her overall assessment of me for that Sunday.

CHAPTER XIX

That afternoon Stan said something that maybe some of us had thought about but had never come right out and said. We were sitting around eating some raisin pie his Mom wasn't too proud of—thick crust, "just mortified," unfit for church picnic, her son/his friends uncouth: eat anything—and a watermelon after trying to get the car to jump over a log and he said, "My father would kill me if I married a Catholic. Skin me alive. And he would use something dull and rusty."

He stood up and spit seeds out to the grass. His head looked more triangular than usual. It was that melon, the wedge; it brought the natural shape of his head out more.

"What're you gawking at, Red?" he asked.

"Your head," I said. "It, uh... D'joo know you could skin a head? Headhunters do. That's what they shrink. Just the skin."

"Not that yours could get any smaller," Jimmy said, stepping off the porch giving himself a little head start if he needed it.

I'm not sure why Stanley brought this up because when it came right down to it none of us were ever actually going to get married. It was kind of a nutty idea.

Other people did though, like for instance Tom Orr, and suddenly it became obvious that you couldn't tolerate a Catholic, or a lousy pie maker, for a wife. Cooking was fairly important, I knew that part from my own personal life. Mom spent endless, and I might add futile, attempts to help Izzy learn this. Cooking was a little bit competitive around Perth Hill. Berylie McHenry and Eleanor Morgan, in particular, had a running, "good-natured" battle going over pie, beans, whatever. Old Berylie could be a little vicious when it came to Mrs. Morgan's pie crust. I've heard some of that myself.

The Catholic angle, though, was still pretty fresh as it pertained to wives. It should've been obvious, I guess. How many Catholic wives did I know? One, Mrs. Birr. And she was neatly married to Mr. Birr, a Catholic. Stanley was apparently way ahead of the rest of us on the Catholic angle. Aside from having just the sort of head for working out new angles, there was one other reason the thing was ricocheting around in there. We'd find out about that soon enough.

Sunday's evening then came and we were eating popcorn in the living room ("party") and Jake asked a simple question.

"Does 'bestow' mean give?"

"Yes."

He then informed us: Ireland first bestowed on mankind the art of mechanized head chopping, the guillotine.

Smiling proudly, he added, "We're Irish."

In a mock insulted, mock, I think, tone, Dad said, "Not of my account."

"Your father's jealous, Jacob," Mom said. She didn't look up from the paper. "We invented many useful items."

"Name one," Dad said.

"Chocolate."

That wasn't what we learned in school but she sounded definite. Later, when we'd gone to bed, I moved our nun to Judges. I was reading it, actually I was. It was violent and except for a virgin who got burnt-up all the women in there were always beating up on the men, pounding stakes through their heads and dropping millstones on their heads and cutting the magic hair off their heads, etc. Whatever was in II Kings couldn't top that. Our nun could use some revenge. I looked at her there tucked in among the sacred scriptures.

Jacob was reading under his covers with his little pen-light he got from Grandma and Grandpa, and I, by my bed lamp, which was bright enough to attract the bugs outside. They thumped and rasped against the window screen. Maybe it wasn't the light. Maybe they were attracted to *her*. My gosh, she was pretty.

So Stanley's Dad would kill him would he? Mr. MacRae's opinion on the matter, I was coming to understand, was probably not a rare one. I wondered about my own Dad and my mind started wandering.... How can I say this? If it ever came out we'd both be ruined. But it wouldn't matter. We'd be martyrs for love so deep it was in China. She'd swear off her vows, be cast out from her church. And I from mine. We'd move to Texas and ranch. Or Chicago. I'd apprentice under Frank Lloyd Wright. He built Falling Water. We'd build new lives, from the ground up, by our own rules. Architecture would be nice, a nice clean line of work with regular hours, away from strip mines and manure spreaders. On the weekends I'd write letters, longhand on Big Chief tablets with this fabulous Italian fountain pen we found—*no one missed it?!*—between the cushions of an old sofa we fished out of a dumpster, while she worked on her impressionistic watercolors across the room by the window taking advantage of the natural light. I drifted off wondering if she, as a spirit, had seen us out there wandering towards her, smoking.

The next morning feeding the pigs, I thought to myself: it is such a great feeling knowing that you had all those thoughts and... *kept them to yourself.* The lucky arrowhead was working and I prayed that it would continue working.

After breakfast, moving tools and boxes of nails and staples and bolts out of a granary that we would need later for storing oats, I could hear Dad and Jacob jockeying ladders around at the back side of the barn. Dad was getting set to replace missing slate. Jake was giving a seminar on packrat middens and then—*suddenly*—Komodo Dragons. The Dragons were interesting but I wished he wouldn't've left us hanging right at the point where we were about to find out what the oldest thing ever found in a packrat midden was.

In a bit, Aaron Birr came along: down the lane, tires munching up the limestone and its crinoids. I peeked out the door at the end of the granary row to make sure it was him. It was. He was bringing the slate he'd scavenged somewhere.

I opened the gate to the pasture, shoo-ing away King Festus, the boar (Duroc, red, hairy), so Mr. Birr could pull around to the back of the barn. As he got out of the cab, Dad said, "Heh-*LOW*, Aaron Birr!" but he couldn't turn around as he was at the eave of the roof tying the roof ladder to the top rails of the ground ladder he was standing on.

Aaron Birr answered, "Good morning, gentlemen. You are going to fry up there on a day like today, Timothy."

"Afeard you are right about that. Beats the dickens out of waiting till December though—Jacob, you can go down and help your brother and Mr. Birr unload. I'll be all right. Thank you."

We unloaded the rock planks, stacking them vertically against the stone of the barn foundation in the foot or so of shade that was there.

The tin roof on the nearby open air shed tinged and popped, expanding in the elevating sun, as we worked.

Dad finally made his way down the ladder and eyed the slate. "That looks in good shape."

"Some of it's questionable. The greater most'll shed water, I believe. Not yer usual gray is it?"

"Not at all. Might've been something fancy. Was it on a barn?"

"Spring house."

"My gracious... you must've cabbaged the whole roof."

"Not a slate less. The old fellow was tickled it was going back onto a farm building. He showed me the foundation. It was substantial."

"Spring active?"

"Not that I could see. Will this hold you for a while? I've still got this much again at my place."

"This'll fix us in splendid shape. Thank you, Aaron ."

The judge moved toward his truck then stopped and looked up as if to check the condition of the barn's roof. It seemed to jog his memory.

"The sheriff's people were out in your cemetery again this morning," he said, slanting his eyes back to earth.

"'Zat a fact," said Dad his voice lifting.

Mr. Birr nodded, "More evidence out there than they first supposed..."

He didn't know more than that but he didn't have to. I knew what it had to be. The bush. I heard Mr. Birr say, "Be careful up there. You felluhs keep an eye on him," and I stumbled over to get the gate for him. He smiled at me as he pulled out, a weird smile that could have meant something.

Theoretically, that threat had passed but the bush still bedeviled me badly. My guilty head rang with the choir of little children singing: *Hide your light under a bushel? No! I'm going to let it shine, let it shine, let it shine...*

Unfortunately, our degenderate charade of being upright youngsters, relatively speaking, depended on *not* letting it shine. We needed that bush to keep our dirty secrets. But little Bobby our old Sunday School teacher had recently been teaching us a brand new lesson: while the Almighty might go ahead and allow you to keep your light, your talents and all, hidden safely away under a bushel, He'd take great pains to eventually expose your seamy underbelly for the whole wide world to behold. Sister Anna Caravengelo had proven, unintentionally, of course, to be His able assistant in the job. Little Bobby had learned this first hand.

Closing the gate, I heard the tractor approaching the chicken house and Cambell singing. I went down there. He backed the spreader in between the rows of farrowing crates in the half of the chicken house not occupied by chickens, shut the tractor off and hopped down.

I said, "Hey, Olivia, they can hear you clear out to the main road, yeh know."

"Really? Over the tractor?"

"You can't even hear the tractor."

"Hmmm, lucky I have such a super voice."

"For a hyena."

"Be nice."

We started to pitch. I wanted to ask him how mad Mom and Dad would be if they ever caught one of us smoking or drinking. I decided not to.

"Cammm—," I grunted, struggling with a piece of stray binder twine buried in the manure, simultaneously releasing the rest of my brother's name—"—BELL!"—and a manure missile against the outside wall of the spreader.

"You should try getting some in the spreader once in a while."

"Sorry. It's a small target. Are there many Catholics at Penn State?"

"Mmmm," Cambell stopped pitching, straightening up. He looked at me. A droplet of sweat hung from the end of his nose. Jutting his jaw, he blew it away in a spray into the air. "Yeah, I suppose so." He tucked back into the pile and heaved a fork load into the spreader. "Why?"

"Just curious. What do you think Aaron Birr, the Birrs, what do you think, I mean, what the heck are they doing living out here?"

"Beats me. But they've been in Perth Hill a long time. As long as Wendts or the Kendalls probably. IN—in the spreader. "

"Speaking of them, how was your big date last night, Josy-wosie-breath." This was a pure guess. But delightful Miss Jo Wendt was as good a guess as any.

Cambell laughed at me. "Nice try."

"Becky-wecky?"

"Groping at straws, Bubba."

"Speaking of groping... come on, tell old Bubba."

"Why would I?" he laughed.

"Because y're my older brother. And I look up to you and respect you and I need guidance on the type of girl to go out with."

"You? Why not start with any girl?"

"Even a Catholic one?"

"Anything human and breathing would be a good start."

"Funny. Do you think this has anything to do with the mob?"

"You not having a date? We can't blame everything on the Mafia, Boyd."

"Okay, here's another question. Komodo Dragons can consume 80 percent of their own body weight in one sitting. True or False?"

CHAPTER XX

Cambell got the right answer. He guessed. I can't actually remember the right answer. Let's say, true.

Also true was that our own starvation for some fresh bad news was ended that Sunday. Very galling how we got it—on the little cork bulletin board right there in the vestibule when you first come into church. It was right there next to the greeters, Mr. Wallace (Glen's Dad) and, get this, Tom Orr. Make that, the perpetually shameless Tom Orr.

The *Intelligencer* had done an entire article on Burrhead. *Burrhead*. Tom didn't even bother to pretend that he hadn't put it up there himself. In fact, he bragged about it. He bragged about how it wasn't even his turn to greet that day, how he'd had to get rough with Grandpa Dungan to get the spot. It was Friday's paper so most of us wouldn't be getting it till Monday but old Tom had it. He tacked it

up there right over the Christmas letter from our missionary in Chad. How perpetually shameless was that?

There was a picture of Burrhead and behind "him," a little out of focus, Tom looking very serious and businesslike.
It was all there. The castrating epiphany, the loyalty to the
home place, the humble lineage, the whole pitiful ball of
wax. And there was Tom basking in the flea-bit glow. Pretty
revolting and bad enough even if that's all there was to it
but it wasn't. Embedded down there in all the fascinating
tidbits about Burrhead, slipped in there like an after-
thought, was the conclusion the sheriff and McDonut had
come to that Perth Hill's cemetery was the crime scene. *The*
crime scene. Our nun had met her maker, or unmaker, however you want to look at it, right here in our cemetery.

The *Intelligencer* had the Bad Ones stealing away with
her head and it, the head, destined probably never to be
seen again, until, until, they came across the indomitable
Burrhead and his domain, at which point Burrhead single-
handedly faced those Bad Ones down and forced them to
turn over the grisly booty. This was all per Tom, of course,
not Burrhead, pure shameless conjecture that he somehow
made seem like indisputable Biblical fact. Sadly, it fit in
with whatever actual evidence the sheriff had.

There was a feeble ring of truth in it all because a human
head is exactly the kind of toll you would expect Burrhead
to extract from travelers daring to cross his wretched plot.
You couldn't deny either that if any dog could communicate
with the Bad Ones it'd be Burrhead, as he no doubt had
some relatives in there. The Bad Ones (which the paper

called the Hounds of Perth Hill as if they were something great, as if they were from *here*, as if they were more than just demented mutts abandoned by nitwits from New Sterling), in case you're wondering, were put out of business soon after by some deer hunters given an early and flexible permit. Burrhead, meanwhile, lives on.

My zeester got a phone call at supper the next day. She knew it was for her. She and the phone knew each other pretty good. It was Tammy Hill.

Who cared? We were having sweet corn and fried eggplant—*deep*-fried, with batter—and Ned and a little dish of cooked plums.

We were getting a few old ears by now, deep into the middle of summer as it was, but that didn't matter. And Ned was a little tough, partly because we had of course not come in when we said we would and he got a little too cooked but mostly because it was Ned and that was how he was. Mean and wiry and tough. He was the kind of little steer you didn't mind eating one bit, assuming your teeth were sharp and mostly all there.

Tammy Hill had called to find out what time something was and she also had sad news, which she thought we'd probably heard but we hadn't. When they were done Izzy turned from the phone, her eyes shiny.

"Mr. Wilson died this afternoon," she said, softly.

Dad stared at her for a moment. Then he made a quiet sound: *Huh...* a mixed-up sigh, part surprise, part resignation. He moved his head up and down once, then, slightly, side to side, some words coming. They didn't. He didn't say anything, he just stared at his eggplant with a long, long blink of his eyes as if he were trying to remember a name and then took his knife and cut a piece of Ned away from the bone very slowly and deliberately.

Mom snicked and said, "Poor Bushy. Did Tammy say when the service will be?"

"No. She didn't."

The rest of us didn't say anything. I was just learning to tune my general behavior in situations like this to the tone of Z's voice. I can't say Jake's reasons but he made no comments on the burial customs of the Mound Builders or something like that. I tried to think about Tammy but I didn't honestly like that name, "Tammy," and on the spur of the moment like this I couldn't even conjure up more than a sweater and mild acne.

Well. Seconds on blackberry cobbler would've lifted Dad's spirits, I thought, but he had a school board meeting to go to.

Seconds were great. Then I piddled around up on the barn floor braiding binder twine together to make a rope while waiting for Charlie to rumble down in the car. We were going to Alexander's to play basketball and box on that barn floor of theirs. Ralph, Jimmy's Dad, worked in a plant so their barn floor wasn't overly used, clean and tidy and square danceable at all times. The Alexanders were like that as a rule. It has something to do with working in a plant because I'd noticed it about McKee's barn floor, too. Clean, tidy. The plant guys themselves were a little different as a rule. Almost, I want to say, *happy-go-lucky*, a little more that way, more than real serious and perturbed like anybody else.

Anyway, it was nice their barn floor was that way and that our planned activities didn't sound like a lame cover-up for a drinking party. When I heard the muffler, *lack* of one rather (it was in the trunk with some of the car's other parts, had come off at Stan's when we were teaching Charlie to fly over the log, and saw dust rise at the end of the lane, I trotted up to the back porch, put my face right up to the screen door and told Mom we were going. She said: *Have fun. Be careful. Be good.*

Three-thirty-three was about my average concerning those. Nothing to sneeze at if you were an Indian or a Pirate but I was only a son. More and more I was wishing I would behave myself. But I didn't.

CHAPTER XXI

We picked up Mark Gorton and I told them Mr. Wilson was dead.

"Bushy?... dang it," Charlie said.

"I know," I concurred.

Then Charlie's eyes widened, suddenly. "Natural causes, right?"

"For once. At least my sister didn't say anything un-natural."

"That's nice. Good."

Mark asked, "Bushy who?" He was related to Gorty but lived out on the main road across from part of our land and didn't go to Perth Hill. They were something unheard of, Episcopalian, I think. His father worked in a mill; they didn't farm even a little bit. They just lived on a bite out of what would've been Fergus land or Reed land or Wolfe land or I'm not sure. Mark was a good guy; he didn't try to be cool, which would've been tough, as skinny as he was and with that consistently overgrown flattop mopping his head. He said he was even going to take a Vo Ag class the next year, forestry.

The Alexanders lived down a long lane that was all theirs; it wasn't a road going somewhere else, to some other road, I mean. Their house with the red trim sat up and across the lane from the barn on a slight knoll but the barn bridge was even with the lane, which made the barn seem like it was in a hole kind of but it wasn't. Besides being tidy the barn was extraordinary in two other ways. One, it had a fresh coat of paint on it. Two, the color of the paint was green. Like grass. In spite of that Ralph and Ruth always got high marks for never splitting the place up and for raising a few animals every once in a while, Holstein steers, pig or two, etc.

The barn doors were pushed all the way to the ends of the barn so that the floor and the bridge came together in one level, playing surface, though, technically, the bridge was outside and out of bounds. Jimmy and Paper Cut and Glen were shooting around.

"Hello, knuckleheads," Charlie hollered, running onto the floor stealing the ball from Jimmy and then dribbling it off his own foot on the way to the basket.

Ben laughed. "Oh, yeah! I want him on my team!"

Charlie, retrieving the ball from the empty mow, said, "Hey! I *am* good. But I'm modest. Right, Red?"

"Nothing but the truth," I said.

It was totally false. Charlie, Jimmy, Mark and B. C. Robison, in terms of ability? We didn't have any. And we didn't make up for it with heart, either. And our shortcomings were more pronounced than in football because of a sadistic wrinkle: *dribbling*. And shooting, we didn't exactly have the knack for shooting either. We didn't care. That was our secret weapon.

The court was the basic layout, hoops at either end, attached to the end walls of the granaries, a piece of plywood for one backboard and for the other an old oval aluminum snow saucer pounded almost flat. That, the *almost*, was, to a degree, a talent equalizer, as was the low hay loft at the other end which hung half-way over the basket at about eleven and a half feet. *Nobody* was very good at banking shots in off a convex backboard *or* shooting from the outside with the zero degree arc of Gwen Stott's pancake behind. When you add in the numerous dead spots in the floor and two ten-inch square posts in the center of the court supporting a crossbeam ten feet overhead you had a game way more interesting than what they made you play in gym class. A good bit bloodier, too. Those posts were upholstered with nose skin.

Stan and Greg pulled up in Greg Pulaski's parents' brand new car, a Thunderbird-type thing. This was a tense moment. Did they have the goods? Breathing stopped. Then Greg hopped out shouting.

"The beverage cart is here!"

He didn't know it but Ken's Mom had pulled up right behind him to drop Ken off.

Glen, hemorrhaging, shouted back, "Hi, Mrs. Orr!"

Greg spun around. Mrs. Orr probably hadn't even heard what he'd said but he patted Charlie's car and said, "The old... deatherrrridge Dart... they don't make 'em like this anymore! Hahahahaha...."

Believe me, it was just that lame. Greg was a buddy of Stan's, Greg Pulaski. He was from Lost Acres. Couldn't say what his Dad did. Let's say he was a... oh, I have no idea. An engineer maybe, or a bank loan guy. Greg was okay. Cocky, though, and he'd been on an airplane so he had this impression that he was kind of fantastic and vital to everybody.

Which he was, tonight. He had been held back a year or two in grade school and was older than us and looked older and everything.

After Mrs. Orr had backed around, waved nicely, as we did in return, and headed back out the lane, Jimmy issued a general warning, "We should probably keep it down. You know, as far as that goes."

Greg said he was sorry, but Stan, not too quietly, said, "Yeah, Ralph and Ruth don't know their son is a huge drunkard!"

We could all tell right there, by the over-boisterousness of that comment, that our two stewardesses had been wetting their beaks on the way over. They weren't overly out of control, just overly *them*. More them than usual, I mean.

After a fair amount of haggling we decided on teams. Glen was the problem because he was good. Played on the junior high team and all. So it was four on five: Glen, Ben, Charlie, me vs. Greg, Stan, Ken, Jimmy, Mark.

Greg was fairly good, too, and Ben and Stan weren't *completely* spastic. Ken was half-spastic and the rest were as noted, spastic to the core, controlled by whatever higher power that governs the comings and goings of headless chickens. In other words, this was a game between Glen and Greg.

Things went along fine. Then they deteriorated as they did, which was why boxing was always given equal billing on a night like this. It was recourse, regulated, sort of. And safe. Sort of. That's a lie, or at least not true—we boxed because it was fun to fight. Fun to fight, that is, and get away with it.

The start of deterioration was easily traced. Jimmy made an easy lay-up. Jimmy never made easy lay-ups. Glen called a time out.

"Charlie, stay out with me. Ben, Boyd stay underneath. Charlie, set a pick on Jimmy. When he does, Boyd, don't just stand there and thank him, slip over the middle and I'll hit you and you'll have an easy left-handed hook. Nobody will expect you to shoot—it'll be perfect. You are left-handed, right?"

"No, not really."

"Well, you're definitely not right-handed. So you must be."

"Okay."

"Oh, boy... don't worry. It'll work. No big deal if you miss. Ben and Charlie will be there to pound the boards."

So we tried this and it worked like a charm. Charlie picked and Glen, who was double-teamed by Stan and Greg, threaded a pass in to me perfectly in the middle only I didn't get to shoot because he hit me with it right in the hands, which are actually a vulnerable area for me, not my best feature physically, and the ball zipped into the mow beyond the granary—at least I saved Charlie the embarrassment of trying to "pound the boards." I apologized. We got the ball back and we tried it again. Then again. Each time it got less and less likely that Glen would pass it to me but he did and we really had them fooled. Each time, I apologized: I'm sorry, Glen... Glen, I'm sorry... I'm sorry. I was really sorry. Well, the last time I was sorry they got the ball and Jimmy made another easy lay-up. Glen couldn't take it anymore. He quit trying to include us, his teammates, in the game, which I might say was only sensible. He kept the ball the whole time and ran circles around Greg and Stan. It was beautiful and funny. Meanwhile, of course, he was also giving Stan a big dose.

"Stan, you're breathing kind of hard? Are you tired, Stan? Stan, are you tired? Why are you tired? I'm the one who dehorned 20 calves today and Burdizzio'd 15—I should be tired, you shouldn't be tired, Tired-Boy—then I put up a half-mile of woven wire fence, by myself, and that was all before lunch. What's your excuse? Huh, Tired—, TB?!, TB! Huh? Huh-huh-huh?!"

That was good for a couple baskets and the lead. Stan retaliated with his usual Holstein-superiority-complex thing.

"Hey," he gasped, "I wish we had miniature cows, too. I'd have the whole herd dehorned and castrated before breakfast—"

"And bred!"

"Hey! Any day you get tired of those little windup toys and want to handle some real cows come on over. I'll show you how it's done."

They were, at this point still, mostly joking around and laughing but then Ben had to put in his two worthless cents worth and things went southern.

"Real cows?" Ben said. "What kind of real cow makes blue milk? Why not just turn the faucet on?! What's the difference?"

Stan ignored this at first saying something about anyone who raised beef cattle had an IQ of 50. One hoop later, Ben said, "Yeah, why are you so tired? I'm the one who put up 1000 bales of hay today! A thousand bales and I'm not sweating! I'm not sweating! Look!"

"Hah! With a BALE-THROWER? What kind of a 50 IQ child uses a BALE-THROWER? I'll tell you what kind. A wimpy baby kind of child, that's what kind, with a 50 IQ. I could fill this whole barn in one hour with a bale-thrower."

Stan knew Ben's soft underbelly that was for sure. The old Paper Cut was sensitive about the bale-thrower, which only points out how stupid he was bringing it up in the first place.

They started wrestling around and that was the first time I saw it, or thought I saw it. Well, we broke it up and brought the gloves out to let them settle it in a civil manner. One pair was old. They were Ken's. He found them in his attic. The other pair was Stan's and they were brand new. His sister gave them to him for his birthday, with only the best intentions, I am sure. So they boxed.

About the time they started Mrs. Alexander walked across their yard and hollered down to us. "You boys be careful! I'm done fixing broken noses!"

She was actually pretty good at that—Ralph said it was because she worked in a hardware store.

Any rate, there was nothing to worry about. We circled them and they circled around inside us circling each other like roosters for all of one circle before it degenerated back into a wrestling match or regenerated or whatever and that was the next time I saw it and now this time I was positive: Stan was wearing a crucifix.

We broke them up. Actually Greg did, which surprised me. Until I realized something. He wasn't used to this breed of internecine warfare like the rest of us were. He was like the *Intelligencer*, like New Sterling in general probably, and thought bumpkin land was basically a bunch of dunderheads out shucking peas and do-si-do-ing till the cows came home, just old tobacco chewing cherubim and seraphim. The first generation of Lost Acre-ites knew otherwise I guessed but not the second or third. Oh well, be that and everything else as it may, this made Greg propose that we indulge in some pre-flight refreshments. And not a second too soon.

CHAPTER XXII

Fighting led to drinking, which I gathered was the opposite of the way it went in other places. We were an advanced civilization. Jimmy made for the house to get a sack of weeners and an old Farm and Dairy newspaper to start the fire.

We got ourselves up into the bed of Ben's pickup, not his, his family's and into Greg's car because it had a cassette deck and you-know-what in the trunk and went out the lane to a field road that split two pastures and ended in a set-aside field full of weeds. I gave Pulaski credit for one thing. He would take his parents' car *anywhere* for a good cause. We went along the pasture fence to where the woods started. The spot was behind the barn about 400 yards, concealed from the house, in the vicinity of a 50 year old pile of slash left from some old logging project. No hot dog in the world would be safe out here.

There were no apologies or anything between Ben and Stan because there never were. A spell of muttered sputtering and then they stopped and just didn't talk to each other or look at each other for a while.

Our stewardesses it turned out had actually already disgorged the loot at the edge of the woods under a fallen tree. And this was when we first detected a problem, standing there ogling the riches.

Lifting a bottle or two out from under the tree, Stan said, "Greg, did we leave anything in the car?"

"No."

"There's a bottle missing. I think."

"Should be three."

"One's gone. Which one of you yahoos has it?"

None of us yahoos had it, of course.

Glen said, "Chaps, this could negatively impact our operations." Supposedly, his Uncle Jon, a business-type man, actually talked like this even though he was from Squirrel Bench right up the road a mile.

Mark, more sensibly, asked, "Could a groundhog drag off something like that?"

"Fiend!" Jimmy hissed.

I said, "A packrat might. For its midden."

"Right. A rat," Stan said.

"A thirsty rat?" I posed, hopefully.

"A rat big enough to drag away a bottle of Boone's Farm would be thirsty, that's no lie."

There were no better theories except maybe that Greg and Stan had sampled an entire bottle to death on their way over instead of the *one* can of Old Milwaukee they swore to. Their veracity *could* be "impregnated," after all.

The question was this: Was their level of bright and snappy jolly ho-ho-ho-edness upon arriving equal to one-half can each of Old Milwaukee?

Glen brought this to our attention but we let it slide. There'd been enough fighting, and besides, any of us would've done the same thing. We, not the most righteous chaps in all the land, in case you hadn't noticed, knew enough to cast not the first stone. So we didn't.

Anyway, Jimmy got the fire going in one strike. He didn't even need the old newspaper. The wood was drier than paper. The sun was down and the last light was spread out in a hazy pink rim over the ends of the fields and the tops of the woods to the west. He had come out that afternoon and sickled down a patch of weeds to keep the fire in its place and to make room for a couple benches of straw bales and 2x12's.

The first cans had been popped, the Kool-Aid was rotating, and Greg gave a learned talk on beer brands.

"IC Light's better, no doubt," he said, choking down a gulp of Old Milk. "IC Light is so smooth. But we're not made of money, right?"

"Keep the eye on the bottom line. Prioritize and make that capital work." Uncle Jon, again.

"Glen?" Ken asked. "Is there anyone in the world who's more full of shit than you?"

"Oh my, m'boy, I wouldn't want to guess about something like that but just let me say... I'm... very... proactive when it comes to shit levels."

"Inventory, you mean," Stan said. "Shit inventory."

"Well spoken, old chap."

"Stroh's is almost as cheap," informed Professor Greg. "But Old Milk is actually smoother. Even though it isn't fire brewed."

Actually, I thought Greg had Glen beat, inventory-wise.

The cassette was going, Jimmy's Bruce Springsteen tape. We could really relate to him. On a fairly preposterous level, that is. We didn't like country music or blue grass though. It wasn't *smooth* enough for a bunch of operators like us.

Jimmy had also provided empty milk and pop jugs. We had a mysteriously, indescribably fun time for a while battling back and forth with flaming wads of melting plastic, catching each other on fire and acting like idiots and everything. It was pretty rowdy there for a while but then Mark asked if he could put in his brother's Blue Oyster Cult tape and things got a *little* moodier. We didn't *fear* the reaper but we were willing to give him a brief think when all the conditions were right.

I mean by the time everyone had showed up to play basketball the news about Mr. Wilson was well spread out there on the vine. Hadn't made it to Ben, though, maybe because of where they lived, a hole. Where *he* lived; Janie lived in a valley. He was truly shocked. As if Mr. Wilson hadn't been 180 years old for the last 30, 40 years or so.

"My grandpa had him in school. Dad, too," he said and took a contemplative swig of Boone's Farm Strawberry Hill. It was like he was attempting to discern the consequences of Bushy being gone, to his grandpa, his Dad, who knows.

Bushy'd taught three generations of future farmers so you'd think most of what he knew must've sunk in by now. Perth Hill, Fox Township would probably just plow ahead like ever. But this particular summer being what it had been to that point you were inclined to imagine something more weird about it.

Ken asked, "Did he... go from natural causes?"

"Is cancer natural?" Stan said. "He was in his nineties anyways. When y're that old y're a ticking bomb." He stared into the fire, poking it. His profile didn't have that triangular impression to it but it still made a heck of a big shadow.

Glen was beyond Stan on the bench and his eyes, you could see, had popped out. The white spot over his brow stood out in the fire's glow like a small headlamp. "Ninety? Holy cow... he was born in the *1800's*!"

"Back when dirt was a rock," said Charlie.

"Wow..." Bushy was giving Glen a slow, cool shock from the grave. Wonderment once again had control of him. "He went from horses to tractors to combines to man on the moon.... Flying around in spaceships for the love of—how did he not go insane? If I see things change that much, I promise you, gentlemen, I'm going berserk."

Stan said, "Come on. He was ancient. He was ready."

"Doubt it," said Ken. "He skinned the cat on his eightieth birthday."

"So?"

"You probbly can't even skin the cat right now, Stan," stated Ken, more or less matter-of-factly. I watched Ben, hoping he'd leave it alone. Stan was calm at the moment but it wouldn't take much from the likes of Ben to get him going again.

Stan snorted with amusement. "I can skin the cat."

"I bet. Let's see you sixty years from now."

"Hah. I'll skin the dog, too."

"Yer on."

"That's impressive," Glen said. "I never heard that. Maybe he's up there in Heaven right now skinning the cat."

"And planning bushes," said Charlie, not trying to be funny.

"How do you plan a bush?" asked Stan with only mild sarcasm looking over and giving us a taste of his isosceles-ness.

Charlie answered. "Oh, sure, *now* you ask. Wait till a guy's dead and then suddenly get all interested. Had a hundred years to ask and you wait till *now*."

Stan smiled and looked back into the fire. I couldn't see it now but I knew it was there, under his t-shirt. What did his Dad think of *that*? Stanley MacRae was not usually so perplexing.

The image of our nun's crucifix in my Dad's hand flickered briefly in the flames.

"She was only twenty-six years—"

I heard my voice and stopped it. Charlie had been bringing up the necrophiliac business again and calling me obsessed and everything. I was not a necrophiliac. And I wasn't obsessed. I just couldn't stop thinking about her, that's all.

Jimmy tilted the bottle of Boone's Farm towards me without removing his gaze from the fire. Held up to the firelight it was pretty—rusty pink, "old barn"—and felt almost cool, too bad it didn't taste as pretty as that. But... it was good.

"Wonder if she ever saw Drake's oil well?" Jimmy's voice sounded like a spoken thought, too, barely there, gone off.

"Why?" asked Ken.

"She was from Titusville. She might'eh. I saw it once."

"We all saw it," said Glen, equally gone off. I looked at him. Was he referring to our field trip? Or, strangely... to Stanley's crucifix? But he was lost in the fire, too, and ended, "Shoot, Bushy might'eh drilled it."

As for Jimmy, he was gibbering and I understood him perfectly even if Charles failed to, or pretended to fail to. Cooking up some connection with her, that was it. You couldn't avoid it. She was pretty, and rare, the rarest thing in the world to us at the time—a nun—but it was more than simple infatuation. It was *mostly* simple infatuation, of course, but there had to be a reason she landed in Perth Hill. There had to be. And we found her. Jimmy hadn't been with us but he'd earned an honorary spot.

"Stan," asked Charlie, easing the bottle out of my hand and now holding it out to him. "More communion?"

Charlie had seen it. I watched. Stan hesitated, peering at him, then the bottle. I waited for something to happen to his face, something like denial, shame, something, anything, anything more than a smile. That's what he did, though, smiled and reached for the bottle.

"That would be great," he said, eyeing up the level in the bottle. "Go to church. Drink. Go home. They ain't so screwed up."

Charlie's subtle accusation was lost on him—I thought—
and no one confronted him on it directly. Why, I'm not
exactly certain. Stan was big but not dangerously insane. So
that wasn't it. Something made us fearful, me anyway.
There was already a lot of screwed up, bad summer behind
us, right behind, trying to mill us up before we had too
much of any normal natural kind of fun summer. If Stanley
wanted to get all carried away and weird, let him.

Charlie chuckled and that was that.

So we stood up, sat back down, poked the fire, put
another plank or two on, and stared at it and thought or
didn't and listened to the reaper's never ending adventures.

This went on until Mark, anxious, said, "What's that?"
His bony, gnawed-to-the-nubbin-pear-core frame straightened on the bench next to Charlie. He was focused on the
woods, not the fire.

"A ghost," Ken said flatly, not even glancing over.

Glen said, "Coon maybe. A skunk."

Pulaski laughed. "It's that rat. Coming back for a beer."

He knew *zero* about packrats I can assure you. But I
didn't hear anything either so I didn't say anything.

We went back to nothing for a moment or two. Night
was in good by now and a slip of low clouds had eased over
on no breeze at all to cover up the stars before they had gotten much beyond pale. The only light there was for us was
the fire's and we were glued to it like June bugs.

I fell into one ember's spell, unblinking, watching it, its
orange and black colors shifting and trading places in waves,
saturating this part of the coal then another, back and forth,

back and forth, over and over. No one was making a peep but after a time, I don't know how long, maybe seconds only, someone asked, Glen asked, rhetorically you'd say, this question: Which way would you pick to die? Like our nun? Or... Mr. Wilson?

Charlie said, "Don't leave Frank Stearns out."

"He's not dead yet."

"Not technically."

"Too bad," said Ken. "Is Bavarro digging over there yet, Boyd?"

"Nope."

"Okay," Glen said, steering us back to his poll, "A—cancer; B—beheaded; C—crushed... hmmm... boy, they all sound pretty good. This is hard."

"Can we pick more than one?" asked Stan.

"Yeah," Charlie answered, "You deserve more than just one."

And I said, my hand sliding into my pocket and feeling the edges of my arrowhead and the tip, sharp, hundreds, maybe thousands, of years old and sharp, I said... nothing. I was going to say *something* but Mark again whispered, really loudly this time, "*Ssshhhh. Listen.* What *is* that?"

Charlie hit him on the arm. "Go look!"

"I heard it, too," Pulaski said.

"Somebody's spying!" I kidded, elbowing Jimmy. "Yer sister."

"Hey," Jimmy responded calmly. "It's just a ghost. Don't fear the reaper, man."

Ben started to laugh but then shot up on the plank and said, pointing, "There *IS* something. By the beer. I saw it."

"Wait... the beer?" said Jimmy. "Time to fear the reaper! This isn't funny anymore!"

Greg got up. "I'm taking that stupid tape out."

Stan stood up, voice hushed. "Flash your lights on for a minute while you're at it."

Greg opened the door quietly and eased into the seat, ejected the tape. There was a split second of blaring radio commercial and then nothing. The fire crackled. We, sitting, straight up broomsticks, waited. He hit the lights. And we saw it. A *packrat*—the size of a small man!

Jimmy was up moving and yelling, "*Tim?*"

At this we all flew off the boards like giant click beetles—*Tim Gray.*

The legend, the immortal... *sprite* had come close and we saw him sure as we had eyes and he was here with us, with *us*, mere humans and he had come to us to, to, to... to steal our refreshments? Apparently, yes.

Well, that fact didn't sink in right away and we were actually just scared and thrilled. Jimmy had gone to the edge of the woods and called into the pitch dark where Tim had retreated. In truth, I wouldn't've—most of us wouldn't've—known right off it was him, but Jimmy did.

"Tiiim!" he yelled, not screaming, kind of with a twang, kind of like his hillbilly switch had been flicked on, imagining, I guess, how Tarzan, if he were native to our woods, might wind up sounding. "Tim, Tim cuh'moan by the far... we're justa hangin' out. Cuh'moan 'n have ya a... bee-yerrr."

He whispered that last word. We waited, braced for something weird or unexpected. In a moment twigs were snapping and rustling, and before you could tell if they were coming closer or going away, he was gone.

CHAPTER XXIII

So Mom performed a miracle for Hugh Wilson. She managed to goad us into getting to his memorial service early, early enough even to get our usual pew, i.e. our pew. In from work, clean, shiny, in the middle of the day. She had gone over the critical nature of the timing with, and had extracted a promise from, Cambell at breakfast but it was still a miracle. We were appreciative in the end.

The church got packed up to folding chairs in the aisles and along the back and walls and then past that to standing room and then past that to sitting in the choir's loft to the right of the pulpit. The 'loft' is really a 'bump'—you didn't float high above the congregation up there, you basically stared it right in the eyes, so we felt for the Wallaces.

They were late and ended, up there staring back at us, sheepish and trying desperately instead to stare into the middle distance. I avoided looking at Glen—too painful—but I caught a glance at Mr. Wallace. Pitiful. Mr. and Mrs. were not choir types. There *was* something supernaturally off-putting and insulting about not getting your own pew. And to be thrust up there in the front, in front of everybody, and turned around... had *dunce* written all over it.

Worse, the people around them, their loftmates for the day, weren't from Perth Hill. Those Wallaces, every last one of them, were stranded and there was not one thing we could do for them.

Behind us, two pews back, in their God-given spot were the Lanes. Lots of others were mixed up and in and generally rearranged. All this smack in the broad middle of the day. Even from the relative safety of our own pew, it was discombobulating.

And our little heads were still reeling from "Tarzan," as Mr. Birr had called him. *Tarzan...* what a joke. But something bad had happened. Tim Gray had been picked up by the constable. Two things were bad about this. One, he was on a bicycle that belonged to St. Joachim's Convent. Two, he was drunk.

The opening hymn was *O Come Emmanuel*, the Christmas song. Mr. Glenn had to like that. Rev. Stone said it was Mr. Wilson's favorite. He had been humming it *just the week before* in the hospital. Well, if you live long enough your chances of being a prophet go up. His family had decorated the church, something he used to do every Sunday. His vases were all around. Day lilies and other fancy lilies, roses, different kinds, bleeding hearts, daisies, who knew what all.

And in his way, they were all arranged with wild things and weeds and stuff. Wheat, green wheat, pale yellow wheat, cattails, ferns, chicory, black-locust fronds, mint, etc. He had been doing that since "dirt was a rock" and it was nice because sometimes it was able to give your eyes something to do besides sleep. You could squint and twitch your head and there'd be kind of a flowery kaleidoscope on the vase.

Singing and twitching, though, couldn't quite keep my mind from going back over a disturbing visit of a couple days before from Mr. Birr and Sheriff Donrett. I had been crimping hay, yanking a clog out when they came driving out through it all like Greg Pulaski. I came close to seizing up like a sow bug, rolled up and paralyzed.

Just passing by, they said. Heard some young fellows had run into Tim Gray recently. Not sure, I said. *Something* was making noise in the woods. Could'eh been him. Had we ever seen him before around Alexander's? Nope. Wonder why he was out there this time? Don't know.

Well, that seemed to hold them and they made a chitchat comment or two about hay, which the sheriff referred to as clover, probably to sound knowledgeable, even though he was up to his ankles in, primarily, mowed alfalfa and I started to breath outward again. But when we were saying our fond goodbyes and nice-to-meet-you's Aaron Birr slipped in a weird comment: "Remember Tam O'Shanter's mare."

It wasn't a question. He had tipped his large, crewcutted head down and slid his eyes over the top of his glasses to peer at me. I managed a vaguely affirmative-type, frizzly chuckle.

My worrying could've gone on and on, except that the Grahams came into the church.

Janie was wearing a maroon dress the color of—and I gave this some thought—sweet gum leaves in the fall. *True.* I inhaled deeply. My senses were suddenly sharp.

It was then that I noticed a distinct aberration. We had been there a good five minutes already and only then did I notice it. Even as she, they, I mean, as the Grahams were wedging themselves into space that didn't seem to exist in Zahnhiser's pew next to some complete strangers I discovered that the church didn't smell like silage. We'd been through a lot lately but nothing compared to this.

Had I been blind and not seen the seating arrangement that afternoon, folks, refugees, turned out from their own pews and all jumbled up, from pulpit to narthex, Mizpah to cloak room, I still could have smelled that: the diluting power of aliens. I could've been totally blind. Berylie even had to notice.

It was hot. Zahnhiser's pew was by a window and I carved out a little block of time to envy them and look at the stained glass and the small transom-like window at the base of it, which was chained open and probably admitting a gentle, refreshing breeze. I looked at Janie, too, although I pretended like I wasn't.

Rev. Stone began the eulogy, saying, "There won't be a eulogy here today. There will be a, more or less, standard worship service. To the Almighty. Hugh was adamant about this. Ten years ago when I was first welcomed by

Perth Hill—he had instructed Rev. Marshall before me, too, without a doubt—was when he first gave me his reasons for this. There were two. First, anyone who comes to my funeral, he said, will know the truth about me, saint or woebegone rascal, so there will be no point to blowing smoke. We'll keep folks from rolling their eyeballs out of their heads, shall we. And, second, for some folks this will be a rare sashay inside the walls of a church and I'd hate for them to miss out on the benefit of a regular worship service."

That got a nice laugh. And talk about eyeballs. They were going back and forth, back and forth, trying, politely, to locate the rare sashayers. That was almost enough right there to kick up a little wind, those swirling eyeballs.

Well, after that, I didn't put much effort into listening because we got inside these walls on a regular basis and listening wasn't going to get us out of coming again that next Sunday. Ben messed me up, too. Minding my own business, staring at Janie, I kept running into *his* beady eyes roaming around on every pleasant breeze they were probably enjoying over there.

So I gave up on that and went and got Anna Caravengelo. We bicycled down to Miller's Pond (it was actually a snip left of a canal that hooked into the Erie Canal and therefore should've been famous but wasn't). She didn't have on Bobby Morgan's clothes. She had cut-offs on and a loose t-shirt that just barely revealed that she had, you know, a chest that wasn't too, too on the... ample side. It was alluring and all, just not, you know, overly... breastigious.

This was perfect. She wasn't hounded by every star athlete and we got along great. We pedaled to the water's edge and I told her about how this was actually a portion of an old canal that once, long ago, was connected to the great Erie Canal and provided goods and services to the people of Perth Hill and then at the end I said, *that's what they say anyway,* so as not to sound immodest and like I had done a bunch of original research on it or anything. It was late evening. The frogs were going and the crickets, too. The moon was up. I thought of even more actual things to say. We took our sneakers off and tested the water and then my voice started to sound completely like Rev. Stone's and there he was up in the pulpit pretending not to be giving a eulogy. There he was. Right under Mr. Wilson's humming cross.

"The righteous flourish like the palm tree and grow like a cedar in Lebanon. They are planted in the house of the Lord, they flourish in the courts of our God. They still bring forth fruit in old age, they are ever full of sap and green to show that the Lord is upright; he is my rock, and there is no unrighteousness in Him."

The Hugh Wilson Psalm, Dad called it. His family was up there in the first rows of the middle section. You could tell he was old when his *children* looked like grandparents. A couple of them were so old that they weren't even alive anymore; they'd keeled over before *him.* Edgar and Kyle were still kicking, though, and farming. One man I'd *never* laid eyes on, even at the Christmas Eve Candlelight service when relatives came flying, creeping, strutting out of the woodwork. It was never exactly like this day, of course, but there was a dilution on Christmas Eve, too.

The final hymn was "This Is My Father's World". Jacob had half the hymnal, nothing strange there, and we sang but we didn't need to really because everybody else was and it was loud. And sad, I guess. I didn't cry, though. I just don't.

CHAPTER XXIV

The reception in the basement was festive. Hadn't bargained on that. Had I walked in cold I would have thought: WEDDING. The food was even wedding: cake, punch, nuts, cubical mints. Weddings were themselves no laughing matter but in this case the atmosphere was a relief.

Wilson relatives greeting each other all over the place and Mom and Dad introducing us to people we "should know" but didn't because, as far as *my* memory went, years zero through four appeared to've been a total waste. Strangely, the furthest back memory I did have was of a family reunion, which this reception reminded me of. When they were over I always wondered who *were* those people. Complete strangers who were not a bit like us but who *looked* a little bit like us. There was something disturbing about that. Mystery-filled, too. Like a second cousin who lived hundreds of miles away and was pretty and you wondered about writing to her and what might happen, like moving to England because nobody would know we were cousins there.

Funerals, death, began right there, at Hugh Wilson's, to be like that, like second cousins, confusing and familiar and from the other side of the planet. And like dessert that was both salty and minty at the same time.

Eventually, Mom and Dad got caught in a conversation and their lines of gravitational force shriveled up and I spun away about the same time as Charlie and Stanley got free from their folks, too, free, free to grab a goodly supply of cubical mints and bust outside where there was air.

Charles McChain Lane yanked his tie off and wrestled out of his very tight coat. "I hope I die first. In my family," he said, at his usual intemperate yell. His shirt came half-untucked making his plumpness dapper and cantilevered.

Stan and I copied him, yanking our ties off, too. "Yeah! I hope you do, too," said Stan, at his even more intemperate yell. They laughed. Stan didn't have it on today, the crucifix.

Preoccupied, I said, "Where were they hiding him? I couldn't find him," and waited for them to quit ho-ho-ho-ing.

"Who?" asked Charlie.

"Mr. Wilson."

"He was cremated." Charlie stuffed his mints into his mouth then wiggled the fingers of both hands upwards through the air.

"Like burned?" I asked

"Exactly like that, I think."

"We tried to burn a dead cow once," Stanley reported. "It didn't work too good. Then we got some tires. That cow burned."

"Cool," said Charlie.

"Yeah."

We stepped through the Kyce twins who died when they were 2 ds. and 5 ds. of age in 1846.

"D'joo see Mr. Birr's here, Boyd? Yer buddy," said Charlie, balling up his suit coat.

"No..."

"Yep. Behind us. Did him and the sheriff ask about how Stanley was drinking like a fish and running around the woods naked on a pony stick? Did they ask about that?"

"No. But I mentioned it anyways."

"Funny. I'll laugh tomorrow. Remind me."

"I will, too, Boyd. I'll call Mrs. MacRae and tell her to remind Stanley to laugh about the time he was running around naked on a pony stick." Charlie stepped quickly between two markers to the next row.

"You better run, moron," Stan said, spitting between his front teeth.

We turned at the end of a row and walked towards the orchard instead of going down another one.

"Did you guys ever hear of Tam O'Shanter's mare?" I asked. "Speaking of ponies."

"Who's he?" asked Charlie.

"That's my question."

Ahead of us and off to the right 100 yards were The Strips down at the little pond. It wasn't the church's but you'd never know it. Mr. Taylor didn't care. Mostly it was covered with algae but today all the green was piled up at one end. Janie and Jody were at the other end, walking, then stopping and pointing. At minnows maybe, or their own reflections. A tiny breeze had come up and it pushed Janie's dress against the backside of her body. Aaron Birr gave Mom an article on the Book of Kells one time and that's what Janie reminded me of right then, one of the scrolled capital letters in it. The color of sweet gum leaves in the fall.

Charlie had brought up the Farm Show. "Man, summer's almost over," Stan said, spitting again. "That's right depressing."

"Right depressing all right. Are you going to sleep over this year, Boyd?" Charlie hit me on the arm, remembering that I hadn't been allowed the year before.

Before I could respond, Stan, pointing to the pond, said, "If she does, I am definitely staying." Then he lowered his voice one lecherous notch, tilted his head towards us and said, "I'd give her a blue ribbon in fitting. And in conformation, too."

"Who?" Charlie asked. "Janie?"

"Jody. Janie's too bacon-y. Too twiggy."

I kept my mouth shut. But my thumb knew ten times more about conformation, and fitting for that matter, than MacRae.

"You're too picky," said Charlie. "Ain't he, Red? Bacon's good. What are you showing anyway? I need to know what class to get into so I can be kicking butt and taking names. Taking names and kicking butt this year, you hear me, boy?"

"You're showing a Holstein again?" Stan was surprised.

"No. Just kidding," Charlie chuckled. "Don't worry. I have the Grand Champion Brown Swiss this year."

"Takes a man to show a Holstein. I'm not afraid of a little competition."

"Y're a brave, steaming pile of hybrid vigor, Mac. My idol," said Charlie.

"I know.... I have never won one ribbon and I'm proud of it. Competition does not frighten the likes of a man like me. I thrive on it. I eat it for—I eat breakfast."

"I've seen you eat breakfast."

"It's important."

I turned and walked backwards for a couple steps pretending to see an interesting insect fly by but I actually looked back down to the pond: *Might they really stay overnight at the Farm Show?*

Our aimless circuit was bringing us back to the Old Cemetery. Folks were starting to trickle from the back entrance of the church. Mrs. McHenry and Mrs. Morgan walked arm in arm the way old ladies do, particularly nearly blind ones... but to tell you the truth not *these* two nearly blind ones, not usually, on account of the blood between them, which, if we have to bring up pie again, was really not the best. Stan stopped and nodded across the array of granite and sandstone.

"They're going to dog her right along with Tim just like they dogged Mrs. Morgan," he said, moving on now. Tim Gray had "found" the convent's bicycle but couldn't remember exactly where. The sheriff was extremely suspicious of what 'found' might entail. He didn't tell me this in the hay field, he told Aaron Birr who told Stan's Dad who told my Dad. Then my Dad heard it again when Aaron Birr told him in person. Tim Gray had transformed himself from a 'worthless ninny' to a dangerous worthless ninny.

"Old Berylie?" I asked. "She's a Wells."

"So's Tim Gray. His Mom was a Wells. Mom said."

"Really?" I asked, mildly befuddled. "I thought he was more of a Fergus." The Ferguses were the only ones who ever had anything to do with him as far as I could tell.

"They're just cousins or something," said Stan.

"Whatever happened to Tim's Mom? Where the heck'ehz she?"

"Beats me. Timbuktu?"

"Is that supposed to be dirty, Stanley?" asked Charlie.

"It's a place."

"I know that, Stanley."

"Right. Anyway, she married a McHenry, too. After Mr. Gray flew the coop, I mean. They moved somewhere."

"Timbuktu," stated Charlie.

"Probbly."

"The Ferguses, the McHenrys, the Grays, they're all related? Why do people make fun of the Amish?" I said. "We're all as inbred as they are."

"Hah. You Robisons're safe, yer people're all from somewhere out east," said Stan. Right, wayyy out east: Grove City.

"Yeah, Red, leave the inbreeding to the experts, okay?" concurred Charlie wisely.

"Good idea," I said. Stan and I pushed him against Wm. Mawson and we stopped and curled around his grave to his side, or maybe right on him, which we were trying to avoid, of course, but you couldn't tell exactly because that stone was kind of catywampus towards the woods. We were strangely caught off guard, finding ourselves here, face to face with Cress Wells and we milled around for a minute under the tree by his headstone without knowing why.

"What do you think the other evidence was?" I asked.

All of us glanced over at the bush then back to the stone without speaking. Another moment or two of silence passed and then Stan said, quietly, very quietly for him, kind of a thought that just sneaked out with his breath, "I hope he's not able to look down and see us."

Charlie and I shifted our eyes from the stone to him taking a moment for his meaning to sink in. He was looking over at his ancestor's grave, Wm. Mawson's.

"No middle name for old Mawson," offered Charlie.

"He didn't jack around, old Mawson. Not even a whole first name. Waste of time. All business." Still quiet, Stan's voice.

Then Charlie spoke in a quizzical tone, "If he's looking down he's in Heaven and in Heaven you are *not* forced to watch the likes of us, Stanley, I guarantee you. That would be abdominal having to do that."

"Completely abdominal."

"Nobody should have to look out from Heaven and see his

degenderate great-great-great-great-great granddegenderate. They're all up there with Bushy just skinning cats. I hope."

Staring at the ground wondering if our nun's blood was down in there, I said, "That would actually be God, wouldn't it? Being forced to look down?"

"Uh-oh," Charlie said turning toward the church.

Jacob was running down a row tapping each stone on the top with a stick as he came. We said hello to the little pest but he ignored any kind of small talk like that and said, "Whuh'duh'yeh doin'? Everybody's in the car waitin'... hey, this is the spot...."

He looked up at us. His little bowtie was still clipped into his short-sleeved shirt perfectly. One pants pocket was bursting with cubical mints. Before we could respond he continued. "A head can stay alive if you pump in dog's blood. If you shout it'll blink and look right at you."

Charlie laughed. Stan said, "Why *dog's* blood?"

Jake shrugged. "That's just what they use."

"Come on, Jake," I said, taking his arm. "Let's go."

"Hey, maybe that's why the Grahams keep all those mutts down there," Stan said. "Just in case."

"I heard they're keeping a bunch of heads alive right now!" Charlie yelled, slapping a knee.

"You'ns're sick," I said. "See yuh later."

We left them there laughing at themselves. Jake asked, "Do they know what they're talking about?"

"That would be a first."

"That's what I thought."

Berylie and Mrs. Morgan were still out wandering blindly, chatting, up in the newer cemetery. Looked like they were actually *friends*. Maybe Berylie was getting tips on what kind of cookies got rid of McDonut and the sheriff the quickest. Maybe something slightly better than bad had come out of little Bobby's entanglements after all.

Describing a funeral as 'nice' never occurred to me until Mom said it on the way home and Iz agreed. She wished we'd had communion, though, Iz did. She'd been on a communion binge since our nun's funeral. She was getting to be a real professional at funerals.

"Hugh would've rolled over in his grave," Dad said.

"Why?" Z asked, a bit combatively.

"He wasn't overly enthused about communion even once a month. He thought it was too showy." Dad chuckled.

In the back, Jake clued me in. "Mr. Wilson couldn't roll over." He frowned and continued with the sad fact, "Cremated." A perfect opportunity wasted. There would be no keeping *his* head alive.

"Jake," I whispered, "I don't think even a dog could've saved poor Mr. Wilson."

Aaron Birr and his wife, nice and pregnant, were getting out of their car as we went by. His big straight-armed wave made me remember Tam O'Shanter's mare.

CHAPTER XXV

The Farm Show, as you might know, was like church and a lot of things. Once you were there it wasn't too bad. It was Wednesday, the first day. Cambell and Jake had brought the animals the day before.

Going down midway towards the barns brought on a pungent, confusing déjà vu. On every little breeze wafted the jumbled, cosmopolitan scent of Polish sausages and manure, cotton candy and horseflesh, roasting peanuts and rabbits. It was intoxicating. Folks were bringing in the last of the animals; others were throwing together booths and displays in a final-minute panic. Up behind us and the produce barns, wedged in next to the road, the carnies, with their teeth and whiskers, were bolting together their thrilling junk.

Half-way down the rows of cattle barns, Jacob waved me in the direction of Maple Leaf and proceeded on to the hog barns and Mr. Mud Pie. When I got to my heifer I was overcome with joy. We had an end spot, a coveted end spot! Joy to the world! Neither Jake nor Cambell had let on. And just as glorious—the spot next to us was still vacant, ultimately a no show! We had a *ton* of space— Maple Leaf and I were flying First Class! Hosannas! How decadent it all was.

Each cattle barn was really just a long, double-pitched roof, 40 yards about, protecting a narrow 30-foot wide strip of bare earth. Running longitudinally down the middle was a three quarters wall, like a changing curtain that divided the barn into two long sides. The animals were lined down each side, tied to eyebolts in the dividing wall. There were no stalls separating your own precious animal from those next to you down the row so you can see just *how* decadent and extravagant my situation was. The arrowhead had come through again like the priceless object it was.

One ominous note: Holsteins. They lined the rest of the barn. I eyed their big black and white frames unkindly. They all, on this side of the barn, were from one place, a place that called itself Far Mile Farms. *Far Mile Farms*. I divined this because they had hung from the rafters a gargantuan, varnished sign heralding their presence: Far Mile Farms. Nothing brings out the arrogance in a person like a Holstein. In the years gone by, the Milking Shorthorns were situated with the other more modest and likeable breeds like the Brown Swiss or Ayreshire. Alas, they were over the wall from us. Maple Leaf and I were overflow, cast out alone into this kingdom of Goliaths.

But I didn't let it get to me. Quickly, I set to my first order of business, posting the vacant spot next to Maple Leaf as native ground. I took the hay bale and the straw bale and the half bag of feed and bucket and pan and my box of grooming tools and stationed them around the area in a way that would be construed as haphazard and unintentional.

As I was completing the task I noted a girl far down the row. She was a Far Mile girl and she was wearing very tight pants. Perhaps I had judged her family too hastily.... She bent down to pick up a halter. The eternal optimist, I decided to hope for harmonious relations with them after all. When she disappeared beyond the end of the barn I gave Maple Leaf a rub behind the ears and an encouraging word, then headed for the hogs.

The dirt track linking all the barns together was actually the continuation of and the extreme northern end of the midway, but it was all animals, no booths or commercial activity. If you were down here, you were either a farmer or you were lost or you had come to amuse your little city-bred offspring. It was bustling already. Some of the beef classes were being held that day and kids were yanking their critters to and from the washing racks. It was, *always*, comical and embarrassing by turns to watch. The yelling, cajoling, hitting, purring, running, stomping people and the standing, running, frozen, compliant, crazed animals.

The sheep and hogs shared a barn, a substantial open-air pavilion-like place covering a large square chunk of land criss-crossed with pens and walkways. I located Jacob's watering bucket, an old metal 40W gear oil container. He wasn't there of course. He and his friends would have to be reminded repeatedly about their bare minimum duties in this operation. Mr. Mud Pie appeared to be content, however, nestled in for a mid-morning siesta.

I gazed around for a minute at the big demented tartan of swine and sheep, black and white Hamps alternating with red Durocs alternating with white Yorks and Landrace alternating with black Poland China and odd Mulefoots, all napped together with Suffolk and Merino and Rambouillet and Cheviot. Give me a cow any day.

Beyond the rippling surface I spotted Glen out on the track with his cousins leading in a load of heifers. I ran out and grabbed one of the three ropes he had in his hands. The back of his t-shirt was soaked and untucked.

"How many are you showing, Glennard?" I asked. A lot, obviously, but they were surprisingly well mannered.

He said nothing, then laughed, "I don't know for sure. Too many. Whah'duh'yuh hear from yer neighbor?"

"Mr. Birr? Nothin'."

"I wish they'd figure out who did it."

"Me, too. I hope they don't find out too too much from Tarzan... yeh know?"

"Yep."

We walked back to the end of the barn.

"Where are you?" he asked.

"Up a couple barns. With the Holsteins. We have a choice spot, though. On the end and everything."

"D'joo you see Stan yet?"

"Nope. He should be up around there though."

We said adios to his cousins and started in the direction of the Holsteins. Glen tucked his shirt in and pushed his thick, copper hair around.

"Man, it's hot."

CHAPTER XXVI

It took some impassioned finagling but I convinced my folks that I really should stay overnight at the Farm Show grounds on Thursday even though I didn't really want to the way it was so hot and everything and with all the bugs. Maple Leaf's class was the very first of Friday morning. By being there the whole night through sleeping with one eye open I could intervene during any impromptu manure incidents—before she lay down and things really soured. And, in addition, I could, up to and including, hit the ground running Friday morning applying the finishing touches: polishing her hooves, wiping the sleepies out of her eyes, powdering her small white markings, getting my own good show clothes on, etc. It was all so very, very plausible.

That night, Wednesday's, Jacob's stomach was growling up a storm just after we'd gone to bed. I tried to ignore it.

But then out of the blue it growled two bars of what I swear was Jingle Bells. That's how he heard it, too—Murray Glenn would be duly informed. We chuckled a good long while before dozing off. When I did I had a dream. It was all about Anna Caravengelo's fingerprint. It was pretty nice.

"What is that?" asked a girl's voice (not a dream voice, a real voice).

I turned away from Maple Leaf's ears, which I had been wiping out with a cloth wetted with alcohol to see the Far Mile girl. Tight pants. Cowboy boots. *Cowboy* boots! Where'd she think she *was*?

"Maple Leaf," I replied without thinking.

"I mean, what is she?"

There was a Grange Speaking Contest brightness in her tone and the tilt of her head was synchronized perfectly with the lift of her eyebrows. She *practiced* conversations, you could tell. But I put off hating her.

"A heifer—Milking Shorthorn, I mean," I answered.

"I see. A Milking Shorthorn. How old is she?"

"Year and a half."

Her round eyes widened and she cocked her head briefly towards Far Miles' cows—her nose was smallish, of the upturned puggish variety—then she cocked back to Maple Leaf, quickly. The whole procedure was supposed to look like a reflex.

"A year and a half? My gosh! They don't get very big—I mean... she must be very economical to feed."

I ran my hand down Maple Leaf's back and quoted something Dad had said. "She's very 'typie'."

"Oh," said the girl. Then she turned on her cowboy boots and left, giving me a sharp little finger wave.

And there I was, about to offer her the use of the vacant spot next to Maple Leaf. She hadn't improved my opinion of big time Holstein farmers that was for sure. But those pants... there was a certain diplomatic quality to them. She had stiff beige hair that looked as if it required a good deal of attention and her face, overall-wise, was about cute enough to be a Dairy Princess' on a so-so year. Those pants, though—they were really top-notch.

A little later I went down a barn to have a meeting with Stanley about all of this but it was hopeless. They, and all the other Holstein people, were full steam ahead in showing mode. It wasn't really mayhem in Far Mile's case. They'd been doing this all summer, moving around to different shows taking all the prize money. They had *five* people getting the cows ready, hired guns probably. Miss Pants didn't have to do *one* thing except get her own hair ready.

Black and white swirled up and down their long vast reach of the barn, their domain, like gigantic hornets, buzzing out to the washing rack, then back, in squadrons of threes and fours. There was a flurry of teasing tails and shaving udders, buffing and preening, primping and polishing. To the casual observer it was a frantic rush but they knew what they were doing. If you've ever seen one of those belt-driven threshing machines they get up and going for a demonstration about how great the good old days were you know how it was. Noisy, bashing and billowing and threatening and nerve jangling and then, at the end, a surprising, beautiful, refined product.

They were beautiful, too, no question. Gleaming in the afternoon sun. These were not cows. They were Bovines. So black and so white, the contrast so intense, so hugely displayed, splashed across acres, stories, of hoof and hide, from horn to dew claw, you might want to just punch yourself in the stomach and shout something for no good reason at all. Were those kingly, proud-headed beasts with names like Far Mile Parlor Sphinx and Milkinator and Maids' Revenge, were they, I mean were they *actually* related to Maple Leaf?

The Holsteins went on all day. Class after class after class. Every class had at least ten cows, sometimes, twenty. For most breeds there was one judge. For the Holsteins it took two, tag teaming for lunch and bathroom breaks and to relieve the mind as well. As the classes piled up a punishing numbness started to grow, no doubt, from the brain out. Ben and Charlie and I went over to the show tent late in the afternoon for a small dose of the torture after gorging ourselves with vinegar fries and candy apples.

The tent, a wedding tent sort of, was a modernization. A really good one. Showing a cow is basically like being in a beauty contest and the Farm Show Board finally conceded that a little shelter from the elements might be a beautiful idea. The show 'ring' was a big patch of beaten, dusty grass flanked on one side by a small set of bleachers, fifteen rows high or so. More folks were there than I expected and there were also a few familiar faces. Some Glenns and McHenrys and MacRaes bunched up in the lower rows to one side forming a Perth Hill rooting section.

We traipsed through them saying our howdies. I felt kind of bad and nervous going by Berylie because of Tim Gray and all but she greeted us as if there was nothing new under the sun. Actually, she greeted Ben and Charlie and my *father*. I wouldn't have said anything, of course, but Mrs. Glenn kindly did.

"That's Boyd, Berylie. Timothy's middle boy," she offered loudly, patting Mrs. McHenry's leg.

Berylie raised her hand in apology. "Oh my, of course it is," she said, her wattle quaking. "Pardon an old coot, Boyd."

As was my custom I turned dangerously red and laughed weirdly. "No problem, Mrs. McHenry. We all look alike."

I was trying to make her feel better but it sounded stupid.

We went to the top bleacher.

Charles was having trouble controlling himself. In a loud whisper, a *booming* whisper, he said, "*Note to file: Boyd gets the liquor from now on!*"

Ben, louder (of course), added, "Yeah, you won't even get carded!"

I craned my neck at them like an irate goose. "Would you idjits like a bullhorn?"

They laughed. Having a lovely time. "Calm down, Red," Charlie said, softer. "Yer Dad's the one who should be mad. Berylie thinks he's in 8th Grade and looks like... *you*."

"Very funny. She's going to hear you, you know."

He slapped the bleacher. "Hah! Hardly. Blind as a bat, too. And everybody's worried about *us* getting behind the wheel."

"Yeahhh."

This was actually a good point.

One class was wrapping up and the judge droned on about withers and carriage and teat placement, trying to justify his capriciously random order of placement.

"Best thing I ever did was not show Holsteins."

Ben and I grunted sympathetically. "How come y're not even showing any brown cows this year?" Ben asked.

"Ah, Ben," Charlie said, "I felt bad hogging all the ribbons all the time. It wasn't fair."

I leaned forward looking past Charlie to Ben. "He has an interesting memory, huh?"

"Good question."

"Wait... you thought I was talking about this Farm Show?" He pointed into the air in front of himself.

"And you were actually talking about the alternate-universe Farm Show where you win ribbons and go out on dates?"

Charlie stood up, saying, "Well, no. But... where is that? It sounds like a good place." He reached his fingertips to the canvas roof briefly liberating a stout ring of white stomach from his shirt. "This is one hot tent."

Ben stood up and touched it, too. As he did, Charlie said, "I heard on the news it's supposed to snow tonight."

"Yeah, I heard that," I added.

Ben's eyes lit up. "*Tonight*?"

How could his sister've been so perfect?

In due time the next bunch lumbered in and now there was something to watch. I mean not only Miss Far Pants but also the competition itself. The class featured one of ours, Mark McHenry! He was a nephew of old Berylie, grand, grandnephew possibly, and I hoped he would provide a bright spot in her life. Right off the bat you could tell he'd come to play ball.

At that time Mark was in sixth grade but was not much bigger than Jacob. The difference in size between him and his three-year old cow was comically enormous. Mark's Mom had turned him out in brand new jeans, board stiff, razor creased, and a supremely white, snap-buttoned square dance shirt. His hair was well combed and spit upon. The perfect little mantle figurine, he was. The cow as well had been fitted within an inch of her life. Nearly all black, her finish was opal-like, a shimmering pool of oil. They were, in fact, an earnest, wee tugboat and mountainous tanker calmly plying the treacherous shallows of the Farm Show ring. They were indeed.

Two times around and the judge stopped them for the first time in a straight line facing the bleachers. Their order of entry had put Mark near the right end of the line, our right, the end where the bottom of the class would eventually wind up. It was unfortunate happenstance that could affect the subconscious of a judge. But this was a careful one who had just gotten back from a bathroom break. He walked deliberately down the line pausing frequently to run his hand along a neck or ask a question. When he got to Mark, he seemed to give the cow an extra measure of attention and inspection. And so our excitement started to slowly build.

Charles had already made a decision. "I'd give the blue ribbon to that one."

"The hair girl, right?" Ben guessed.

"Ohhh yeah."

Only I knew the truth. "That's my neighbor. *Farrr* Mile Farms."

"There's a lot to her that meets the eye," Charlie said.

Ben summarized, "She's very completely all there."

"She hurt Maple Leaf's feelings."

"So?"

"Right." Another good point. These degenderates were on a streak.

But I had been diverted. Janie Graham came walking down the tracks along the ends of the barns towards the ring. I tell you, honestly, with my arrowhead, I had to only think about her for a passing second and she would appear. Her strides were strong, they meant something, her slender form stretched out, angled into her direction. Her dusty blond hair swayed. At the base of the bleachers she fixed us with a look then moved her attention downward to share a brief nicety with the old women and the others. Then she trooped up and my stomach tightened. She wore gray-green cotton janitor pants and a Slippery Rock State t-shirt, all loose fitting but not without a tracing of bodily charm. She was really gorgeous.

At the top, the end of our row, she considered each of us in turn briefly. Then—"Mom wants you, Ben," she said, friendly enough.

"Me? Why?" The idea was absurd to us as well.

"I don't know. She's in the Grange Tent."

"Now?" he challenged.

"Yes, Ben. She wants you now."

Suddenly he turned fearful. His mouth dropped. "Am I in trouble?"

"You will be if you don't go." Her tone was becoming less friendly.

Ben looked at us. It was pathetic. We were powerless, too. He became frantic. "What did I do?"

"Benjamin... go."

He rose stiffly. "You can't call me Benjamin," he said weakly.

"See yuh, Ben," we said, not entirely at ease with the situation.

He shuffled out, his sister backing against the top railing to open the way. Down he went muttering.

What *did* he do? *Something*, that was a fairly safe bet. And not something right either. Mrs. Graham was a raw, strapping woman who was very fond of discipline. If Benjamin was in trouble there was a middling to astronomically high chance that we were, too. His departure was a mixed blessing, a rarity in that respect. Janie took his spot on the bleacher.

"What did he do?" said Charlie trying to not sound guilty of whatever it was.

"Nothing." She laughed, slapped her knee.

Charlie beamed at me, relieved, saying, "Your Mom didn't want him?"

She pursed her perfect lips with uncertainty. "Not really. Well, kind'uh. Mr. Gorton is supposed to show up with some firewood. He could use a hand to unload it, right?" Her smile was motherly. "He'll get to do a good deed. He'll like that."

We laughed, a bit sadistically. "He's going to kill you!" said Charlie.

"Hah! He's tried." She watched the ring for a moment. "And round and round they go.... Little Mark is adorable. And brave, holy...." She leaned forward, elbows on her knees, and looked over at us. "So, d'they start stripping yer neighbor's place, yet, Boyd?" She turned back to the ring still bent forward.

I made a quick study of her hair and her neck and her shirt and her back and her... everything and then looked some more at her face and then her shirt. Charlie elbowed me.

"Nope. Not yet."

"That's good."

"Yep," I agreed.

"You guys saw Tim Gray, I heard?"

"Sort of," said Charlie.

Janie's creamy eyebrows crinkled. "So, what were you boys doing out there at Alexander's?"

"Nothin' much," said Charlie. I shrugged noncommittally.

"Riiight. So..." she hesitated one, two seconds, looking away, down over the bleacher rows then back again at us. "What's this I hear about Stanley MacRae getting himself a little girlfriend?"

Our big heads aligned, mirror image-like, found nothing useful, only bugged eyeballs, four of them, then swivelled back towards Janie.

"News to us," offered Charlie. All we knew for sure were Stanley's opinions on Jody Dyson's developments.

"Really? Jen Lydczny? News to you boys?"

"Pulaski's neighbor? Yep, news to me. You, Red?"

"News to me." Big news, I thought.

"That explains his purty necklace," said Charlie, a bit snidely. "MacRae... what a—"

"Jen's nice," said Janie. "I like her."

"Sure she is. Stu said his Dad would kill him if he ever dated a Catholic."

"Married a Catholic," I corrected.

"I'm sick of all this Catholic business. Jen's just Jen, okay?"

The discussion ended abruptly. Our people, especially the McHenrys, and Mrs. Glenn who was giving a play-by-play to Berylie though she could surely see something as big as a cow, were on the edge of their seats and giggling nervously. The final drama of the Holstein–Friesian Three- and Four-year Old Open Cow Class was being played out.

What happened was this. When the judge had guided the showmen and their cows back into line, he had moved little Mark McHenry clear up—up, up, up—to Third Place! This sent a spark down every Perth Hill spine. Who could remember when a local Holstein cow had finished that high up, in the *good* ribbon colors? It looked like this would be the final order.

The judge went down the line and came back. He eyed the first four animals for interminable seconds, chin in hand, elbow on crossed arm. Slowly, he swung clear around the entire row to regard the cows' backsides. Then, taking our physical breath away, he eased in next to Mark's cow.

He pulled his hand down across the animal's withers, his brow furrowed with intense concentration. There was something about the conformation of this cow that impressed him exceedingly. He asked Mark a question. He smiled at the answer. He placed his right hand on the cow's hipbone and hesitated. He would move her up. One place? *Two* places? Then suddenly, with absolutely no warning whatsoever his *left* hand went up as in slow motion and came down on the back of the Fourth Place animal—Miss Far Pants. The left hand came up and went back down and came up and went back down on Maids' Revenge, he was tapping Maids' Revenge, and nodding his head, while his right hand slid unceremoniously away from Mark's animal down to his side. The worst of all possible horrors, he waved Miss Pants not just up a place but into *First* Place. Mark was demoted. Fourth Place. A green ribbon... weed-green.

A loud crack, like a belly smacker off a quarry cliff, split the air under the tent. It was Mrs. McHenry's hand slapping her own thigh. In a poisoned hiss, she spewed, "That man has the sense of a billy goat!"

Oh, she was fuming, the flab on her arms undulating, head wagging. If the judge heard her, he ignored it. And Mark was a stoic little trooper, showing only his perpetually eager expression while resetting the cow up, nudging her hooves back into perfect position with his own bitty foot. But old Berylie, she gassed on for some time, right through the judge's labored explanation of his ranking, before Mrs. Glenn got her feathers smoothed down somewhat. It was quite a show, in and out of the ring.

Miss Far Pants' shiny, round face was aglow with victory. It went right to her head. What a surprise.

"He is a goat," Janie stated forcefully. "That cow's hind legs are about as straight as the rows of corn in that field Boyd planted."

Charlie loved this. But she was just being playful.

I mused: *I can't ask but I wonder... is she staying overnight here at the Farm Show tonight with her fellow piece of Bacon, Jody Dyson?* That would be great.

CHAPTER XXVII

That night Glen, Charlie and I set up camp among the bales of Maple Leaf's sitting room. Stanley MacRae would not be joining us.

"He stayed last night," Glen offered.

"Right." I was quite suspicious.

"He did. Him and Jimmy and Ben."

"Why not tonight?"

"Maybe he has more important things to do. If Janie wasn't pulling yer leg, that is."

"More important than this?" Charlie snorted in disbelief, waving his arms over our swanky lair.

So we forgot about Stanley. He could go and make a shambles of his life without our expert assistance if he wanted. Good luck! We continued arranging the bales into sleeping platforms. The excitement of being on our own for an entire night with absolutely zero parental supervision electrified the process. We bustled around, talking loudly, joshing and carrying on. We had leapt into a pond of happiness so deliriously refreshing and awesome that we could hardly bear it. We were, in a word, *tetched*.

It sounds, probably, as if our emotions and our perspective on the world had retreated backwards in time to our gently imbecilic grade school years. I assure you, by this night we had lost even a *hint* of gentleness. The word on the street, out along the cow path, was that there would be several groups of female showmen also spending the night to tend their cattle and/or lesser animals. This was not firsthand knowledge, of course, but we had no doubt whatsoever that our wildest, fleshiest dreams would come to pass.

We tromped up one barn and down the next for an hour without locating even a *single* human female, girl, lady, witch. Nothing. What we did see occasionally were other ratty nests of blankets and bales wedged in between hot, reeking animals where lurked other shadowy figures with demented expressions on their faces that seemed painfully familiar. Back in camp, Maple Leaf even ignored our presence. I recounted my neighbor's post-victory activities hoping to stir up some kind of twinge in our dismal hearts. Lust, hatred, envy, *anything* would've been an improvement.

She had come by springy-toed and bubbly, and noticed my blankets. She stopped, put her hands on her hips. "You're sleeping out *here* tonight?" she asked with an imperial nod.

Deluded, I said, "You bet! Are you?"

"With all these bugs? Your family didn't bring a camper?"

"A camper?"

"To stay in." She cast her orbs about the trappings of Maple Leaf's and my life, the swanky lair. "This looks like kind of an adventure, though. My gosh, it sure does. What's your pet's name again?"

That did it. Her pants couldn't pull it off anymore. She was invincibly unlikable.

"Let's go see if we can find her," Charlie said, a flicker of life entering his voice again. Squatting on his bale of straw, his round face searched the darkness beyond the swath of barn light like an owl. He pulled one piece of straw after another out of the bale and threw them down. He was desperate for activity.

"What for?" I asked.

"I dunno," he answered.

This was plenty good enough for us and we took off. Every year two dozen or three families would lug in their pick-up campers or pop-ups and spend the week, as a vacation sort of. Their spot was a flat area where a few trees were scattered. It was out beyond the barns a ways towards the expanse of open field reserved for general day parking. One side of the area was bounded by the equipment dealer displays so if a family had little kids hours of amusement were right there.

We approached through all this new stuff, shiny tractors and combines and balers and plows and on and on. We had no real purpose for tracking her family down, obviously, and being in the middle of so much new equipment made it all seem even more unreal. The thought did, in fact, occur to me that Charlie might think it appropriate to throw some rocks at Miss Pants' camper or to let the air out of its tires but I didn't worry because there would be no way to single hers out from all the rest.

It was extremely easy to single hers out from all the rest. Even *without* the sign, a twin to the one with their cows. We stood in the shadows of tree trunks and gazed at it. It was unearthly, amidst the finest trees, away from the rabble in rusty pull-behinds and patched up Army tents. A small courtyard had been fashioned out of Chinese lanterns and there was a table there and folding lounge chairs. There may have been a fountain. And the whole beautiful enclave was anchored by their massive dwelling—a shimmering hulk at anchor in a harbor of oriental hues. And it was droning... droning, droning, droning a message: *I am air-conditioned. And bug-free.*

Miss Pants' family had themselves what I think was called an Airstream. It was no pop-up. It was sleek, silver and riveted. It was big and... big. It had all the subtlety you'd expect from a big time Holstein farmer.

"That's a camper?" Glen said, dumbfounded.

Around each curtain-drawn window glowed a misty fog of soft blue light. She was in there, she was, with her pants and her stiff, beige hair, watching a TV show, watching it in cool, cool comfort.

As the spell of general wonder was suspending us there under the rustling leaves, Glen saw the statue.

He broke the silence in a low whisper. "Maybe Stanley's in there."

"Hah!" I said, and waited for the punch line. Glen just kept staring though, so I said, "What do you mean? Why would Stan be in there?"

"Mary. They're Catholic."

"No joke... they are." It caught me off guard. "Farmers? Catholic? Like Mr. Birr?"

"Not quite."

We'd seen her before. In little concrete hutches in yards in Quarry and Lost Acres and New Sterling. We had never seen her at the Farm Show before. All the Catholic farmers we knew we could count on one finger. And he wasn't primarily a farmer.

"How do you know Stan's in there?" asked Charlie.

"I was kidding, Ben," answered Glen.

Charlie failed to respond to that compliment and we watched again, mute, the deep colors of their place and the trailer. And little Mary poised in the hazy dark. She beckoned us with outstretched arms from her position alongside the propane tanks. She wasn't smiling but had a contented look on her smooth plastic face. She was kind of pretty, actually. Finally, we had found a girl.

After a time, Charlie broke free from the spell. "Maybe Stanley *is* in there. Let's find out. Let's throw some rocks," he said, adding level-headedly, "then run back behind the combines."

Glen shrugged this off with a grunt and a, "I don't think so."

"Okay," Charlie negotiated, always a bit of a vandal from time to time. "I'll run to the poultry barn and get some eggs."

"Are you just an absolute Ben Dudley? We are not tossing eggs at that thing, Charles."

Charles was peeved now and his voice rose. "*What* then?"

"What what?" Glen asked.

"What're we going to throw? You pick."

"Nothing, Charlie," said Glen with a gentle snort, "we're not going to throw anything."

"Oh man... they made fun of Maple Leaf... right, Boyd?" He ached, truly, to throw something.

"Maple'll get over it," I said. "Do you think they'd mind if we came in and watched some TV with them?"

Glen's voice became very distant again, tinged now with longing to be inside that cool, cool camper. "Away from the heat and the skeeters...."

Well, we lingered there a while longer knocking rocks out of Charlie's hands until driven away by those very skeeters.

"One rock was all I needed. One... you woossies."

The night was about shot. The skimpiest directionless breeze stirred around the scents of dying sausage grills and cooling peanut roasters with those of cows and the checkerboard of snoring hogs. Then, powerfully, came the sweet, ripe smell of chew. I looked over to see Glen collecting a big wad of Red Man from its rumpled pouch.

"Hey, Glen," I said. "How about if I try some of that?"

This whole blessed night was slipping away and with it the opportunity to do something truly novel and stupid. Glen was only too happy to oblige me.

Soon I became astoundingly ill. My friends were delighted. After I had heaved for an extended period of time there at the end of the Angus barn, Glen said, "You shouldn't chew, Robison."

"Thanks, Glen," I said, straightening back up. "...Everything I do seems to come back to haunt me. Why is that?"

"Maybe you should try being a good person for a change," reasoned Charlie thoughtfully. "Instead of the evil, conniving, tobacco-addicted drunkard you are. How about that?"

"Mmm... no, that wouldn't work," I said.

CHAPTER XXVIII

Jimmy's Mom said nothing was spontaneous at a Catholic mass. This was soon after our nun's funeral and the deacons were sort of unofficially reporting back during Opening Exercises. Opening Exercises leader Murray Glenn didn't mind a bit; saved him from having to say something he thought up himself. They read everything, those Catholics. Even the prayers. All scripted. It sounded mechanical and clock-punched to me but she explained it differently. She got the feeling they were pulling God down into the church with this ceremony they performed instinctively so their hearts could concentrate on convincing God that they were serious. There was something very physical and real about it. She thought we were a bit more cosmic and trusting, as if God would most certainly be paying us mind if what we had to say was worth a penny. The Catholic Mass, she reported, reminded her of a Shakespeare play, one that she "quite liked."

And a "slavish pantomime" is what it reminded irritable Grandpa Dungan of. Arguments to Glen's Grandpa Dungan were like salt and butter, without them life would be similar to Ben's, pointless. He argued about 'hanger noise' one time—he had a problem with the hangers in the Cloak Room. He must've forgotten that, though, because one of his main arguments against Catholics was that their churches didn't have any place to hang your coat.

Every once in a blue moon or two something did spill out of him that sounded kind of accidentally sensible. Catholics *wear* the cross. *We* have it inside us. *We* are capable of greater sacrifice. *We* are capable of being more Godlike. *Put yer faith in a batch of hocus-pocus and omelets, if yeh like, but the Almighty wants results.* He presented it as a theory, naturally, making no personal claim at all, and said 'omelets' to keep it lighthearted.

A tempting theory, when it came to grownups anyway, (and ancient peoples like Wm. No Middle Name Mawson), hardworking and serious and perturbed as they were. But then you got to this choice piece of unavoidable evidence: their seedy little spawn. Evil, conniving, tobacco-addicted and all the rest. We had stuff inside us all right.

Mrs. Alexander, Grandpa Dungan, and others besides—our nun, in spite of herself, made them think out loud. She really did do that. But I didn't think on purpose. She had come out to say goodbye to little Bobby before heading south to that mission. That's all there was to it. That's what I thought, not that anyone ever asked me.

I lay there on my bales staring over at Maple Leaf, who had beshitted herself in a spectacular fashion while we were out, really spectacular, and wondered if Satan seemed like a real person to a Catholic. He was starting to, to me.

Sleeping conditions were not superior, as you might imagine. The lights were left on all the livelong night, every bare bulb on every third rafter. They were low watt bulbs, the exact intensity that all insects were programmed to enjoy. And they did. Though it was oppressively muggy, we had the blankets pulled up to our nostrils in defense. A certain amount of miserable time passed in a silence sprinkled with an occasional cuss and thrashing around and other various emissions. Then, with his head completely encased in blanket, Glen told what would eventually become, after a few warm-up tellings like this first one, his famous bathroom story.

It involves his Uncle Jon (o' course), and his Uncle Jon's boss' head, which is highly flammable. Glen takes about an hour just telling this part and the moment of ignition because you shouldn't rush through something like that and because it takes place inside a ladies bathroom. In the end, though, the major point is that Uncle Jon becomes a hero and gets promoted because he extinguishes the head before the flame rampages out of control over his boss' whole body. He does this by ramming his boss' head into a toilet. That's the more major point, I think, the swirlie. He gives his boss a swirlie. And gets a raise.

Glen told the whole uncut version and believe me we welcomed the diversion. He used many business terms, such as, 'In Box' and 'paper work' and other pertinent expressions, and since this was the first time Glen ever told it, it was still funny and we laughed pretty good, Glen so hard we thought he might inhale his blanket. He had one long, hideous conniption that was as funny as the story. He loved his Uncle Jon, that was plain. He was smitten with the whole idea of swirlies, that was also plain.

After a few repetitions of gathering himself back together and then spiraling back into spasms, he, and we, got settled down enough to discuss the story, each one of us retelling different portions and all that sort of thing. Physically worn out, he fell asleep first, lapsing into a snore, a half-cat purr and half-choking-on-a-chicken-bone kind of a thing. It was kind of scary sounding but Charlie and I decided after a few minutes that it wouldn't actually kill him.

He'd never admit it but Glen had a little Jimmy in him. There was something out there, in addition to the promotions and swirlies and all, in the cities and big places far away from Perth Hill that especially attracted him. I'd bet he himself couldn't put his finger on it, which is maybe why he'd never admit it. No point.

Sleep, not always the easiest thing for everybody, even in the best of places, didn't happen for Charlie and me until our tiny brains had time to get back to where they usually got back to that summer. We went rambling on from under our sheets like ghosts, unholy ones, for who knows how long.

Charlie brought it up and I started to think.

"What exactly is the point of nuns?" I asked.

"Beats me," he said.

"I mean, why are there nuns?"

"I give up. Why?"

"I'm serious. Why was our nun a nun?"

"She was born one. They all are."

"Do you think little Bobby and her ever... did stuff?"

"Yeah. He's not a complete fruitcake."

"Then she must not'eh just been born one."

"What's your point?"

"I dunno," I admitted, and mashed some straw down that was jagging my neck. Maybe Janie was right. Jen was just Jen. That depressed me almost, almost to the point of being sad.

"Charlie," I said, finally, bouncing my head against the bale to create a divot. "Do you think an accountant could kill a nun?"

"Yeah."

"Me, too... Charlie?"

"Yeah?"

"Why would he?"

"Dunno."

"Charlie?"

"Yeahhh?"

"Nothing."

Well... I showed Maple Leaf. I'll get to that and it'll be mercifully brief. But the mood of the day was well set when the eyelids fluttered open to the soft static of a light constant rain on the tin roof and a heifer whose only manure-free surface were her pupils. Her wretched condition was nicely complimented by the flavor medley in my mouth of Red Man and reworked stomach contents. I punched the heaps of fried bug carcasses and the ones that had exploded from a nightlong blood feast off my blanket and got to work.

Why, I do not know. Placing third out of two animals should've taken no effort whatsoever. I wish I were making this up.

When I got to the ring and saw only one other animal— there are not many Milking Shorthorns in the world, I think because their only sure trait is being super friendly, making them no more in demand amongst the farmer set than, say, hamsters—my spirits shot right up through the roof of the tent. This lasted approximately fifteen seconds. The judging was *quick*. Quick but intensely painful, like having a tooth snapped out of your head.

You would think capturing third out of two would be insulting enough to Maple Leaf's proud ancestry. Not so. Maple Leaf didn't even get to get Third Place all to herself. She *tied* for third. Out of two animals, *two. Tied.* Are you getting the picture here because this really was extraordinary, kind of unheard of, a kind of a record sort of.

The judge said we were both Third. The first two places in every class went to the State Fair in Harrisburg and "obviously" neither of these animals was "of that caliber."

So instead of claiming the fat Third Place purse—$6— all to myself, I had to share it with some other equally pistol-whipped loser. Three dollars. We didn't even look at each other or mumble. We just kind of shuffled away.

Mom was waiting at the edge of the ring. "That judge is not a nice man. What does he know?"

She patted Maple Leaf on the poll. Maple Leaf was tops in her eyes.

"It's okay, Mom. We didn't want to have to drag all the way out to state anyway."

I started for the barn. But it took a stout tug on the halter to get Maple Leaf moving again, away from the ring. What a cruel irony that she seemed to have a genuine taste for the limelight.

Mom followed along beside us in silence. The drizzle continued and she tiptoed her freshly laundered, oven-dried sneakers around the puddles. She and Izzy were meeting my aunts that morning for their annual "Farm Show Day." But her mind was still on the, uh, *competition.* After some seconds she said, "Who does that man think he is? *Oh*! I am so mad... I could spit!"

It wasn't like Mom to spit but he had hit a nerve, that judge.

"It's okay, Mom. Really. We don't care. We don't, do we Maple Leaf? See? Maple Leaf doesn't care either."

"Oh, honey... I know. I'm glad you're taking this so chipper. But... I have a mind to write a letter to that Farm Show Board—" She hesitated as if contemplating just what she would write, then said, firmly, "Yes, indeed, I will."

A vision seized me. Maple Leaf and I would be hauled before the tribunal and we would be ridiculed. They would laugh, really hard, I mean.

"Please, don't, Mom," I said weakly.

"Well... I just might. I'm going to talk to your father."

Back at the barn she got her mind off the mean Judge by shaking out and folding our sleeping blankets. "Did you boys have a nice time last night out here all by your lonesomes?"

I swallowed. The flavor of vomit was almost gone. "Yeah. It was okay. Kind of buggy."

"So did that work out good, keeping Maple Leaf clean and ready to show?"

"Oh yeah. Pretty good. She needed a little touch up this morning, that's all."

"Well, good. You don't look too, too tired. You look so nice in your white shirt."

Well, I felt stupid in my white shirt. Mom went to meet everybody. I gave my brave heifer a bucket of water and ditched the show clothes. The effect was immediate. The day improved.

CHAPTER XXIX

You know why the day improved? Let me inform you: my arrowhead. Trotting up the midway I discovered it again in my pocket and gave it a quick look. More perfect and translucent than ever in the rain. I had forgotten to transfer it to my nice show jeans. I would not tell Maple Leaf this.

Even the rain had become a blessing. Any kind of critical fieldwork at home would be put off; for the foreseeable hours my experiment as a life form independent of adult supervision would continue. A giddy tremor went down through me similar to the start of the night before. Perhaps I (the daytime, wise me) wouldn't squander this opportunity by doing stupid things?

So, the first order of business: beeline to the Commercial Displays Building to acquire some free samples.

I detoured through the poultry barn just to see if they had anything really weird in there. Anything with very long spurs or huge toppies. They did and they were neat. There were some eggs, too. I'd tell Charles.

Outside the food wagons weren't too cranked up yet. The rain held every kind of smell in place anyway. The rain made everything smell a little more like earth and a little more normal than you'd ever expect at the Farm Show. The rain was a blessing. Thank you, arrowhead.

The building, green corrugated sheet metal, housed two long aisles packed with booth after booth of business and government and election campaign displays. They all wanted to give you something. I chose one aisle and proceeded directly to a construction company's booth where they were handing out dandy six-inch rulers and big plastic *bags*. I was not a beginner. A bag was a coup. The pace accelerated. Fly swatter, peppermints, bumper sticker, *yardstick!*, campaign button, visor cap, electricity pamphlet, pencils, little thing that made a noise, small tablet, little other thing that made a little bit different noise.... Near the end, euphoric, my hand fell on something very unusual. Something I had never seen before in the Commercial Displays Building, a miniature deck of cards. The logo on the box was a very, very black Queen of Spades. What a find. Although I never played cards, I was thrilled. Who ever heard of getting a free deck of cards? Unique, shrunken cards? I couldn't believe my luck. But then, I turned my head upwards to see who the benefactor was and I saw the banner: *Blackstone Mining*.

"Howdy, Rusty," the lady behind the display desk said, as if she knew me. She had a cigarette-voice.

"Hi," I said back, very self-conscious all of a sudden.

She was old, 50's, with eyebrows so far north of her eyes they looked like they belonged to someone else. They were brownish, painted on; she looked *polled*. Her hair was red-dish-blackish-shortish but definitely fixed. She wasn't exactly ugly but it took a moment for the eyeballs to adjust to her. She had cowboy boots on and creased blue jeans with light cream stitching. I think she thought she was fitting in.

"Cute little cards, aren't they, hon? Help yourself to another deck for a friend."

I stared. "No. I mean, no thank you. One's good enough. Bye." I bolted.

"Have a nice day, hon," she rasped after me.

"'K, thanks—"

I peeled around under the narrow eave of the building. My heart was racing. Setting my bag of loot down I pawed through the odd little deck. Every card in it had the Queen of Spades logo on one side so that it would always look like you had them turned face up. There was something vaguely creepy about that. They stared at you, too, all of those tiny Queens—that was creepy, too. They made *me* feel creepy. Somehow they did that.

I put them back in their box. One thing was certain. I didn't want anything Blackie Bavarro was handing out. I moved away from the wall to find a garbage can and was startled that although I could still hear the rain I could not feel it. Senses sharpening, I looked up. Ah-hah... a *tent*. The Grange Apple Butter Tent to be specific, one side tethered to the side of the Displays building. Refuge.

I stuffed the deck in my pocket. Gorty, loyal Grange member/rabid volunteer, was there stirring the kettle ever so slowly with a long-handled wooden hoe. Something made me think he'd been watching me, something in the tilt of his head, the way he was so super-naturally focused on the bubbling sauce.

"Hiya, Gorty," I said.

"How's Mr. Boyd?" he replied in customary form.

"Just fine, Gorty, Mr. Gorty. How's Mr. Gorty?"

"Oh, well, fine. Stump brought me, you know. He's going to work on equipment today. I'm here. He said it was okay."

"I should say so. Looks like y're working pretty hard."

"Workin' hard 'r hardly workin'." He snort-snorted a laugh. It was easy to get him to say that and it seemed to make him happy.

Then he caught me off guard. He said, "Did you take a little deck of cards?"

"No—" I stopped. "I mean, yeah. I did, Gorty." I reached into my pocket. "One of these, yeh mean?"

His face was shaved, poorly, as per his system: let it grow for six days then shave it, poorly. Spooky tufts of gray-black hair sprang out on his neck and under his nose.

He squinted at me and answered, "Yep."

"Did Gorty get a deck?"

"I don't play cards," he frowned, eyes back in the cauldron. Back and forth, back and forth.

"These would be hard to shuffle," I ventured.

"I don't like strip mining, either." His tone wasn't agitated or accusing. It was quizzical, I'd say, as if one more sensible reason for not taking a deck had just risen from the swirls of apple butter.

I stared at the thick brown soup and his work. Back and forth. Was Gorty trying to give me a gentle lesson? Back and forth. He turned his head and we looked at one another.

"Our nun was his cousin."

My fingers squeezed around the little cards. "Whose cousin?"

"Blackie's. Stump said."

"No kid—that's weird. That's weird, Gorty."

"Blackie tried to kill Mr. Frank for his coal. Stump said. Stump said he killed our nun probbly."

"Why would he do that?"

"Stump said."

"Oh."

"Mr. Frank better not die."

"Yeah."

"I pray for him."

"Mr. Gorty... you're good, you are."

Expressionless, he went back to work.

"Gorty... see yuh later."

"Okay."

Back and forth. Back and forth.

I left. I wanted to show somebody. Janie. Show her these cards and tell her about the creepy Blackstone lady, tell her about Gorty, about Stump, about Blackie Bavarro, our nun.

CHAPTER XXX

My Dad was right. It didn't make sense that Frank Stearns would pick rocks from a field he intended to strip. Less sense even than the limited amount Mr. Stearns reportedly had. But... stupid and bad accidents did occur. People did stick their arms into running combines. People did saw their own legs off. People did fall asleep while raking hay and come a cat's breath away from demo-ing the family tractor against a cucumber tree.... People did get run over by their own tractors. It was a fact.

At the top of the midway I veered off to the dirt road that ran parallel to it, behind all the food buggies and trailers. I was avoiding Mom and my aunts. They were by the candy apple stand sharing an umbrella and one candy apple. All four of them had transparent, plastic scarves tied to their heads. The ones that open like an accordion. They were having a big time. Their bags were full of free stuff, too. I had forgotten mine at the apple butter tent. Didn't matter.

I hustled, not running but walking fast, kind of hopping probably, with my hands in my pockets, the left pressing my arrowhead to my thigh. Strange that I had found it the night I'd gone over to Mr. Stearns' place. Had it not been for his bad luck I wouldn't have found it. Was there a big equilibrium of luck in the world? All the bad and all the good perfectly balanced?—in one instant he was crushed into the good earth and in the next there I was plucking an exquisitely shaped and colored charm from the same earth. If he had married the Stewart girl it might've all been very, very different. But he hadn't.

The drizzle had become rain and I trotted. It felt good to trot. Trotting gave my kneecaps something to do besides pop up and down under the skin. I was nervous—Janie's fault. I also had to use the bathroom so beyond the midway, I accelerated and skirted wide of the barns and headed in the direction of the outhouse stench.

Two deep breaths and I went in. Alone, I thought, I stood at the urinal—a piece of rain gutter nailed to one wall at a slant—and hummed to keep my mind off the smell. The kneecaps were going again. I rehearsed what I would say to her. I didn't want to sound stupid or over-excited. Never in my life had I sought her out, by myself, to share a secret or a conversation or anything at all. Never... *any* girl.

The downspout at the gutter's end started delivering to the pit and I rehearsed aloud. Just as I began there was a noise to my right—feet shuffling! My heart leapt and my eyes shot down to the floor of the stall: *wingtips!*

I was *not* alone. Even in the dim light of the outhouse they shined. My kneecaps stopped. Everything stopped. They were awful things. Once they had been only the footwear of Bobby Morgan. I stared down at them momentarily paralyzed. Who wore *wingtips* to the Farm Show? Bobby wouldn't. Nobody would. The pants had a narrow cuff and a sharp crease. Dress pants... business pants. Who would dress so inappropriately?

Drained of all logic, my mind twirled.

Who would dress like this.... Someone with money, a money bags.... Someone from outside.... Someone from the city, someone who didn't belong, someone up to something, someone intent on blatantly walking around in expensive, outsider's wingtipped shoes dealing two-faced cards and taking things that didn't belong to them!

The feet shuffled again. Adrenaline rifled through me. I shook, tucked, zipped, and shot out the door like a pumpkin ball.

A 10-gauge pumpkin ball. The rain hit me and the fresh air and I staggered only for a step or two before regaining a measure of self-control. Of all the things to be frightened of....

I got to the barns and walked under an eave behind a long line of Herefords. An enormous bull there had drawn a small, appreciative audience, variously entranced and amused, pointing and giggling. As far as I could tell the object of their scrutiny was a stream of urine exiting the animal with typical fire hose-like force. *New Starlings.* My word—the Farm Show was crawling with inappropriate people! They seemed to be in the majority, in fact.

Now I felt even sillier, more infantile and stinky—any number of different kinds of people could've been wearing wingtips. Some insurance salesman or bank guy, no doubt, come to bid up the grand champion hog. In retrospect, mobsters didn't even wear wingtips. They wore girlish Italian loafers. I knew that for a fact. Stanley told us.

I went by Maple Leaf. She glanced at me over her delicate shoulder blade. I gave her another slice of second-cut, dark, dark green and prime, and informed her that soon I would no longer be talking to her like a pet. Her pampered life away from the cruel herd was winding down. I hustled on, ignoring the Parlor Sphinx and Maids' Revenge and the rest of the Far Mile empire.

Finally I got to the gated community of hogs and sheep and immediately slipped back into my original nervousness. Kneecaps on, throat dry, hopping. I saw a girl's back. But it wasn't Janie. It was old hamburger-y Jody Dyson talking to some guy wearing a Black Minquaas FFA jacket.

I was relieved actually. My desire to tell Janie what I'd heard had been squeezed out of me. I decided to check on Jake's hog. Halfway down the aisle, concentrating on not looking over to Jody and her friend, I felt a light tap on my shoulder—my heart jumped and I spun around.

"Kind of a jumpy old knucklehead, aren'tcheh, Red!" Charlie chortled.

I hit him in the stomach, harder that I meant to, and then showed him the little two-faced cards.

"Weird," he said, handing them back.

"They're from Blackstone Mining. Bavarro. He's here."

"Yeah. I can read. So?"

"I dunno. It's weird."

"Yeah. Well... weird's startin' to be normal."

Charlie hit me in the stomach then and congratulated me on getting a ribbon. He was impressed that Maple Leaf got a higher place than Mark McHenry and that fancy bovine of his.

CHAPTER XXXI

Church attendance that Sunday was sparse. End of Farm Show week: Folks were getting a jump on bringing their animals home. You had to leave them there until it closed down late on Saturday night—some kind of rule. They were giving as many city folks as possible an opportunity to see where meat came from and get their share of all the great bull urine giggles, I guess. There were a couple patches of Glenns and Wallaces in front of us and behind us the other fifteen or twenty who had shown up.

I don't know what the guest minister thought of this. Nothing probably. He was a prehistoric retired missionary who had spent something like a hundred years of his life in Central America—to Jacob's delight. He didn't preach on headhunting, though, and because he was ignorant, evidently, of our local tales of horror and woe, his prayers focused on the pretty day, the birds, butterflies, all creatures great and small and so on. It was pretty nice that way.

All the same I wound up not paying attention. I just sat there leaned forward with my elbows on my knees, head in hands, in the shape of someone paying attention, but I wasn't. I was looking around with my eyeballs, here and there, mostly at Mrs. Morgan. What possibly could've been going through that poor lady's head? Every Sunday, always there at the end of the Glenn pew, never not showing up, never hiding. She was brave. This day she had a brown, pill-boxy hat on, one of the ones with the wiry lace spooled around the sides like a bug trap. Her face was square and impenetrable as always, her posture fabulously erect, a bookend for the Glenns. People used her posture as a benchmark for their kids.

But to tell the truth, to me, she had been looking bigger. You might think it was because of the season. You might think it was an optical trick. They did fluctuate in size, the Glenns in fact did, with the seasons, and winter was their really big season. But by any measure, in any season, even a dryer one like this, the Glenns were not small people. It may've been an optical trick but there was some realness to it, too. Her son had somehow failed to compress Mrs. Morgan. Had the cross inside her, would be Grandpa Dungan's explanation. Anything's possible I suppose but I just thought she was tough.

After the sermon, Glen Wallace and I held up the back wall behind the pews and talked.

"She looks nice, doesn't she," he said, nodding towards Jody Dyson. She was talking to Mrs. McHenry.

"Yeah," I agreed. "So does Jody." I laughed at my joke.

Glen looked at me without expression. "You're perverted."

"Thank you."

"I saw her last night at the tractor pull. She's expanding her territory."

I nodded. "Guy from Black Minquaas? I saw 'em on Friday."

"Big moron, probably."

"Definitely. Complete loser."

"Black Minquaas of all places."

"Swamp. Set-aside. That's it."

"That is really about it, 'z far 'z anybody can tell."

We stared. She did look nice.

"She always goes after the older guys," I broke the silence. "Why does she always do that?"

"Because we're immature, probably."

"Immature? Us?"

"What we call youthful, or spry, they call immature."

I laughed. "*Spry*?"

Glen slapped the top of the pew. "That's right, by golly. For our age."

"Maybe we should date third graders."

"That is exactly my point."

"Third graders would understand us better."

"Yes."

Tom Orr went by then and we shook his hand.

"Mr. Orr."

"Mr. Robison. Mr. Wallace. A meeting of the minds back here, I take it," he said gravely.

We chuckled. "Indubitably, sir," Glen replied.

"Is that any kind of language to use in church?" Tom said, pressing himself against the pew to let the sole representative of the Graham clan sneak by.

The kindly, passing smile Mrs. Graham had been giving us developed an immediate hitch. Only Tom's silly comment must've registered. She narrowed her eyes and wagged a finger but kept going without a word. Tom's face got big and surprised and happy.

Glen let out a punctured breath.

"Sorry about that, Glennard!" Tom sounded dubitable.

We took turns hitting him on the arms and stomach and then he gave Glen a fatherly tap-a-tap on the shoulder and moved on, laughing.

"So where's Father MacRae this morning?" asked Glen. "Not like him to miss chur—mass."

"Maybe he went last night," I answered.

"If the Pope ever finds out he was ridin' around naked on a pony stick he'll be burning on a stick. He'll have to be a Presbyterian again."

"Yeah. Presbyterians are all for the pony stick business. Rev. Stone would ask him to preach on it. By the way, Glen, we made that pony stick thing up. Remember?"

"We did?"

"Yes!"

He looked at me and blinked. Then frowned and said, "Left out of the loop again."

"Tarzan's more in the loop than you."

"Don't even joke about that."

So, the wild and exhilarating days of Farm Show week were behind us then like a rather pleasant nightmare, leaving us only with the prospect of a summer's ending. Three hot and thick, but fleeting, weeks till school began again. The clock was ticking. The thumbscrews and whipping posts and Mr. Peckett, the infamous geometry teacher, were being lubed up and stropped for a fresh crop of bizarre morons called "us." All you could do was try to pretend it wouldn't happen.

CHAPTER XXXII

Which brings us to farrowing crates. Someday you might find yourself with a few hogs, through inheritance or whimsy, and in that case you'll want to know what we made our farrowing crate platforms out of. We made them out of tulip poplar. That was definitely the way to go. This was because tulip poplar had some magic rot resistant property, and the additional charm of being soft and easy to work with. The platforms still fell apart from time to time, the wood worn thin and punched through by the hooves of an endless shuffle of sows and their litters. When that happened we took the iron bar crate off, lifted the platform up, batted and shot at the rats who had been making a nice living under there from feed that sifted through the boards, and replaced it with a new one.

To that end Dad and Campbell drug in a poplar log from the back woods, which Dad had cut some time before, and we wrestled it onto a hay wagon to take to the sawmill (home of the ear wiggling leprechaun). About 18 feet long and 3 feet in diameter it taxed our native engineering skills and the muscle of the poor old Ford's front-end manure loader. It was a good thing we never had to build Stonehenge or anything big and complicated like that.

After we got it tied down Cambell and I took off for Mr. Bell's and Dad and Jake went and did some buckwheat thing. Cambell drove and I perched myself up on the fender next to the blaring radio. We went kind of a weird way, over on Forbes, down Stearns, then over on East Francis Forge and through Lost Acres. This was not the most direct route, but the flattest—according to Cambell. What he meant was that Trudy Schuster lived right along the main road through Lost Acres and she was the exact opposite of that, of the flattest, and she was excessively pretty to boot. You'd be pretty stupid to argue that point.

As noble as that reasoning was I still hated going through Lost Acres on a tractor. I would be sure to keep my eyes concentrated on the log as if that was an important job and pretend not to see them out there in their little garden gloves with their electric trimming wands and whips and tiny riding lawnmowers. Gloves. In August. Cambell would probably wave at everybody like the Grand Marshall.

Anyway, we were coasting down past Stearns', Cambell gearing down pretty good because of the hill there, and we saw some guy walking from the house. Cambell caught the littlest gear and we slowed to a crawl. The dragline was stacked out in the field, waiting, menacing. Then the guy hears us and looks out at the road and waves with his Pirates hat. It was Mr. Stearns.

We waved back, dumb, little half-waves. I swiveled around and kept staring. Cambell turned onto East Francis and he looked over, too, back through the road trees trying to confirm the sight. Then he cranked the accelerator and shouted over the engine and the radio, "So much for being dead!"

Well, how about that? That was good news, particularly for Mr. Stearns. Came to find out, he had posted one of those big time comebacks, the kind that has all the doctors and nurses scratching their toppies. This did seem like good news, indeed. Our neighbor would no doubt waste no time chasing Blackstone off his property. What were they trying to pull anyway? A man doesn't pick rocks from a field he means to strip. Of all the bad things happening that summer a sparkle of good had finally lit.

Then before you knew, Blackstone was back out there hitching up their dragline and getting ready to dig. When somebody asked Mr. Stearns the burning question—"Why were you picking rocks in a field you meant to strip?"—all he said was, "I needed some rocks."

All our theorizing and "hypontificating" about Blackie Bavarro ill-getting the rights to strip the Stearns' place were off the mark. Frank Stearns had inherited a showplace and he wanted to strip it, simple as that. Wanted to turn it

inside out, wanted to peel down through 200 years of crop-
land and umptold years of arrowheads as if it were mere
dirt, as if it were not happy hunting ground and soil and a
showplace. Well, it was only one 30 acre field, not the whole
farm, so that might be a slight bit of over drama but it was
the principle of the thing. It really was.

Still, what remained very, very, very high on my list of
the despicable and the distasteful was the purported fact that
Blackie Bavarro was our nun's cousin. Her I had no problem
with in Perth Hill affairs. Him, yes. Yes. For reasons which I
guess eluded reason, I continued, for a respectful while, to
hold him responsible for her death. My gut told me he was
offended that she would robe herself as a Presbyterian
accountant (as a man, a Protestant man—a Roman Catholic
nun?) and he quite basically flew into some type of righteous
Inquisitorial rage, like any good Mafia mobster would, and
sliced her head off. This is what my gut had to tell me.

My gut.

What seemed to make all these matters worse was that
Mr. Stearns started coming to church. Being almost dead, I
guess, had somehow revealed to him the importance of regular church attendance. So now we had to see him every
Sunday and be nice and everything to his face, real wel-
coming and all, even though he was about to create Perth
Hill's first strip mine.

"It's like He was trying to decide which one to keep, Mr.
Wilson or Mr. Stearns. And He picked Mr. Wilson. Mr. Wilson
would plant a bush in Heaven. Mr. Stearns would invite

Blackie Bavarro up and strip it. Who would you pick?" Some theology there from our Gentle Shepherd, Charlie Lane.

Mr. Stearns didn't go to Sunday School, too, that first Sunday he popped into church but I gather he was the lesson, more or less, in my Dad's class. Grandpa Dungan almost had to be physically restrained he got so riled up. He, obviously, and actually, most everyone, shared Gorty's opinion of strip mining. Most folks could control their emotions a little better than Grandpa Dungan, though. At least I thought they could.

CHAPTER XXXIII

So one Sunday evening, the chores done, I skulked along the edges of the woods. The corn was stunted in the outside rows owing to the shade. It was about the only place this time of year, when the fields were grown-up, that you could still easily look for arrowheads.

I carried along an old two-gallon ice cream bucket because it was also a likely place to find blackberries. And *blackberries*... blackberries in my mother's hands, a pie, blackberry pie... pie, pie, pie. Pie.

I hadn't been out long and hadn't found anything when lightning began to strike in the west and a breeze quickened. A storm! I felt almost instantaneously rejuvenated. The summer had been a strange hybrid of endlessness and blinding quickness but always—*always*—hot. We'd had rain enough to keep everything going but just enough. Real storms had been rare.

The flash of bolts was distant and their accompanying thunder was still a low grumbling when the ground opened up ahead of their coming and started exhaling. I walked head up, inhaling and watching. The new-old scent of earth and woods floor filled the air. White light sparked across the darkening sky at the horizon. In a matter of minutes, seconds really, the world around me had changed. It was thrilling.

Rain wasn't falling yet but the thunder and lightning were close and all around when I got back to the front yard. Z, who had been on the front porch steps sewing some needle-pointy thing, had come down in the grass and was pointing. Off to the northwest in the direction of Gil Moore's and the Stearns' place a gray-brown plume of smoke pushed into the roiling cloudbank. Then, as if she were conducting them, sirens went off.

Dad got up from the top cellar step holding the boot he'd just taken off and said, "*Uh-oh....*"

Z and I followed him around to the back yard for a less obstructed view out over the garden, field and back woods.

Dad periodically reminded us of the big fire the Glenn's had. He'd usually do this when we'd yank a bale out of the mow and find it was fermenting, creating its own heat. Part of a load made when the hay was a little tough, if it was buried in the mow deep enough to be insulated from cooling outside air it could, supposedly, get hot enough to, as they say, spontaneously combust.

That was the theory. And that was the theory for what burned the Glenn's barn down. I was little and remembered it as an incredible, roaring mountain of orange and black. In the background could be heard the indescribable tinkling sounds of hand-hewn mortis and tenons bending and creaking, resisting with all their might the heat of the flames. When they couldn't anymore, tree-wide beams crashed down and the shape of the building gradually dissolved. Then it was just a brick silo and big, hot fire.

I can't remember anyone even trying to fight it. I remember old Mrs. Glenn standing and watching and quietly crying. They hadn't got the calves out. That was only part of the reason she was crying, of course. By the next night a smouldering, black mound, still incredibly hot, had taken the place of a 150-year old barn. A 150-year old project, actually. Glenns had started it and Glenns had seen it end. We kids felt horrible for them. I was certain their lives were over, that they would have to move to a city and become beggars or mill workers or something. I mean, how could you go on without a barn? At the time, it was unfathomable. We asked Dad what on earth would they do now, and he said, simply, "Build another barn." Oh. Good idea.

Mom came up from the burn pile with the wastebasket and joined us there in the back yard. Something about the light made her hair appear extremely black and her face extremely pale.

After a second, she said, "Stearns' place?"

Dad answered, "Could be. Or Moore's." He hurried

back to the porch to put his boot back on, saying, "Reckon I better head over that way."

Out of the buckeye tree, between thunderclaps, a voice hollered down, "*Can I go?*" This was followed by a noisy cascade of snapping branches and grunts punctuated by the sudden emergence of Jacob on the ground in a rain of buckeyes. It was like the tree had spit him out.

Mom made sure he was okay, then got mad. "What were you doing in a *tree* in the middle of a lightning storm! You know better than that."

"Sorry, Mom," he said, jiggling his legs to expel leafy debris from his pants. "I fell asleep."

"In a tree?"

"There was a chipmunk. I was just trying to be still. Can I go, Dad?"

Before he could answer, Mom said, "I don't think they should." Her expression was worried and pleading.

Dad went to the truck. "Don't fret, Rose. They'll keep a distance."

Excited, Jake bounded towards the truck but Dad caught him by the shirt.

"Not in your bare feet, you don't."

"Can we ride in the back?" I asked, hopping onto the tailgate. Jacob was sprinting to the porch.

"Suits me," Dad said.

Mom stomped one foot and shook her head emphatically. "They are *not* riding in the back. You'll get hit by lightning!"

She drove the wastebasket to the ground with both hands and started towards the bed of the truck. I popped into the air and over the side before Dad was done saying: "You heard yer mum. Come on in front."

We collected Cambell from the barn floor and the four of us sped up the lane. On the main road the first huge raindrops plunked the cab's roof and marked the macadam with dark craters. They seemed the precursor to a torrential opening of the overhead. The back of a car a quarter mile in front of us, moving as rapidly as we, turned out to be Aaron Birr. We lost sight of him at the bend just before Stearns Road. Rounding it, we found him stopped and talking to a car going the other way. Dad pulled into the shallow ditch behind Mr. Birr and we spilled out.

"Stearns' place," the other guy said before we quite got to them.

It was Hank Paden. I didn't know him except to see him standing around with a shovel with the Township road crew. He was the one who looked like Elvis if Elvis had made it to middle age without turning into an engorged tick. He had slicked back hair and a tan, always a tan, and always smoking.

"We figured," said Dad. "Barn?"

"Yuhp," Hank said, blowing smoke out a corner pocket he had made in his lips. He transferred his cigarette from his right to his left hand and dangled his arm along the outside of his car door. He was very calm.

"They don't need any extra hands?" Aaron Birr asked impatiently.

"Nuhhh," Hank flicked an ash, "Larry and them got it licked pretty good. Myron Rantle's one who seen it. Driving by."

"What started it?" asked Cambell.

Hank shrugged, his cigarette hand rising, then falling back. "Not lightning. Wires, maybe. Larry smelled gas in the milking parlor. His big John Deere was on the barn floor. Could'uh been leaking. Some hay in the mow—last year's?—is what was mostly burning."

"Holy mackerel!" Dad said, his jaw dropping, as he imagined the big, old, dry barn. "Bless Myron's heart. Fancy old barn like that...."

Mr. Birr looked directly at Dad. "I'll second that."

"Frank's not around, I take it?" asked Mr. Birr.

"No. He's there. In the house when it started, I guess," he paused, then said, matter-of-factly, "When're they gon'neh start moving dirt?" He pulled on his cigarette, let the smoke billow part of the way out of his mouth, then in a quick, short breath sucked it back in.

"Too soon," Dad said. His face was stony.

Hank gave a squinting nod as he took another puff, then he coughed and said, "Yuhp.... So I heared Bobby Morgan's not in jail?"

"Nope."

"Tim Gray?"

"Nope."

"Anybody?"

"Nope."

"Here's an idear for you'ns. Let's stick Frank Stearns in jail and call her good."

The men looked from one to another with stiff chuckles, Mr. Paden blinking through a minor cloud of smoke.

"Wellp," he concluded. "See you gents down the line."
And he eased away, off towards his finagled acre-ette along
the edge of the Burns' hayfield.

There was nothing rising from beyond the hill on Stearns
Road. now, no smoke, only the half-black clouds, stalled,
but still keeping their rain. Mr. Birr had more to say.

"New Sterling's finest are not through with Mr. Bavarro,
however."

"'Zat so?" said Dad, his head canting, "Were he and his
cousin close at all?"

"Not particularly. I don't believe. They don't come much
more pious than Blackie Bavarro, naturally. And Anna C.,
in spite of herself, had been described by her friends and sisters in Christ, even before all this Bobby business, as a hoy-
den—so says our own able constable, who, T.R., is a man
not without his own theories."

"That's a comfort. Two and half months into the thing."

Mr. Birr made a grim, tumbling laugh and said nothing.

Dad's eyes stayed on him. "Are they worth repeating?"

Straightening, Mr. Birr said, "Forgive me, gentlemen, I
was being half-sarcastic. 'Fraid it's the same old business,
crime of passion and all that foolishness...." He stopped,
glancing quickly, a little shyly, at Jacob and me. He registered then my Dad's unchanged expression of interest and
continued. "But I will dare say that Mr. Morgan's whereabouts the night it happened have always seemed to possess
a certain *wishful* quality."

"With his mother at home? Is that wishful? Reckon yeh
can't prove that either way, Aaron Birr."

"Unless Mrs. Morgan's own whereabouts can be affixed otherwise, Mr. Robison."

The conversation stopped. The next moment, in which they traded cautious, searching stares, passed in a silent agreement not to continue. That's how I saw it. Whether they were simply afraid to go on or didn't on account of Mr. Birr's official duty to keep some things secret, particularly from the likes of Jake and me, I couldn't tell.

They switched then, awkwardly, to chewing over Blackstone Mining's other mining projects and then the weather.

Mr. Birr hooked around in the intersection with Stearns Rd. and eased alongside us saying so long to Dad and Cambell as he slid past the cab. "Hang on up there, young'ns," he said to Jake and me in the back. I was ready for some peculiar, suspicious, Tam O' Shanter business from him but it didn't come.

Dad turned up Stearns' Rd. under the soft booms of thunder receding eastward. Knowing they had the situation in hand and not wanting to simply pester them, we drove by without stopping, waving at the volunteer firemen and at Mr. Stearns like friends.

CHAPTER XXXIV

Popcorn that Sunday night, every Sunday night, was divine, and I mean that. Every kernel heavily baptized in butter and salt. I never controlled myself. It would've been improper. Napkin after napkin disintegrated into shreds while I struggled to keep my mouth fully stuffed but my digits clean enough to maneuver around a National Geographic all at the same time. There was some show on TV that Iz and Cambell were watching and our little brother was eating preserves.

Mom and Dad were in the kitchen having a minor argument. Mom had seen Jake and me in the back of the truck when we came back from the fire.

Dad without agitation: "Calm your feathers, now, Rose. The storm was well beyond us."

Mom sternly: "It wasn't raining when Cress Wells got struck, either."

Dad with agitation: "*Oh Rohhhse*... you're badgering me about a hundred year old wive's tale? For heaven's sake...."

Mom said something I couldn't make out, then they came into the living room, Mom carrying a tray with ice-filled glasses, and Dad carrying his popcorn and two plastic bottles of pop.

Normally, I would've kept my face in the bowl and magazine—theory: remain very still and perhaps you will be invisible (grouse and other animals with small feathery heads utilize this defense)—but the name jangled me. So I asked.

"What happened to Cress Wells?"

Z, not swaying her eyeballs from the TV, piped, "He was killed by lightning chasing cows. Right, Mom?"

"That is right, Isabelle. And it was not raining. And he still got planted right where he stood. Fried to a crisp. That's why you should listen to me when I say be careful when it looks bad out. You really should."

She had given up on convincing Dad. She bored her eyes into Jake and me between pouring each glass. "Do you hear me, Jacob?"

He didn't but he nodded anyway. Like a bug reacting to some vague, mild stimulus. I watched him for a second eating jam and drawing pictures of different styles of guillotines and rolling heads and decided to quit asking questions and to try to ignore everybody, too.

Later, I went out to make sure the truck and car windows were up. That's what I said but mainly I was going out to tinkle. I liked to tinkle outside at night. The storm had swirled over and around us dumping no rain to speak of but enough somewhere to clear the sky of muggy haze. If you were good at constellations this would've been your night. They were all up there twinkling away.

I shook and zipped, peering up. The stillness of this night was stunning. You could almost feel the earthworms out breathing, out basking in the thin light from all those twinkling specks. Sometimes, when I was out like this with the worms, I'd think up some ludicrous romantic thing about Janie or our nun; sometimes it, the thought, might drift and become a smidgeon rascally; something Jimmy might've been proud of. But not this night. My head had gotten too full.

To keep a full bucket from sloshing when you were carting it around to the garden or the hog troughs, Dad showed us, put a stick in there, floating on the surface of the water. The stick somehow kept the water quieter and in the bucket better. Perth Hill used to have a stick like that. But it seemed to have been stolen. Things were riled up; things from deep down there in the bucket were getting riled up to the top. All sorts of weird stuff. Actually, more than stolen, the stick seemed to have been grabbed and was being used as a stirring stick, plunged in there real deep and disturbing. And it wasn't just Perth Hill stuff either. There was New Sterling stuff in there, too. That shouldn't've been in there but it was.

We couldn't help knowing Perth Hill had a long history, Charlie, me, Stan, everybody else, but we had thought most of the important stuff had started coincidentally when we were born. It was a jolt to realize there was more to it. It was a jolt to feel yourself getting stirred up into a bunch of stuff you knew nothing about.

I think, truly, though, that my friends knew about most of the old stuff, more than they ever let on. Had been born knowing; it had been sledged in there with their genes and pulse and all. They didn't not talk about it on purpose. It did perturb me when they would say I wasn't from around here; I mean, I *was* born here, but when it came to old stuff that was out there idling along with the birds and the bugs across the fields and the woods and back again, quietly, invisibly, I guess it was true.

Gradually, however, slowly, without any real premeditated plan, bit by bit, I believe I was overcoming this curious birth defect. Like it or not, I was.

I strolled to the front yard. Lightning hitting and burning down a barn was unheard of around here. Our barn's dark silhouette was crowned with the reason for this. The spires of lightning rods, four of them spaced evenly along the ridgeline of the roof, poked blacker than the night up into the stars. They were pretty in the daytime. Milk glass balls ornamented the spears. They were grounded by copper-sheathed iron that went down each end of the barn as a smooth twisted cable, and because they had aged a delicate olive green, they made a nice contrast to the soft, weathered red of the barn siding. They were prettier than they had to be.

Old, well-cured hay didn't start fires, either.

But... if Perth Hill was still, in someone's mind, like a happy hunting ground, kind of a communal-type area not lightly messed with in some big drastic new way and that somebody wanted to send a message to Frank Stearns? A little smoke signal would be the fitting thing. Wouldn't it?

I pressed my arrowhead against my leg and went around past the millstone that old Mr. Wendt said the Kyce women used as a step to mount their horses and buggies and stood for a moment by the split rail fence that was the boundary between the yard and the hay field. It wasn't quiet anymore. Something had wound up the bullfrogs at the pond. They chugged along in their rubber bandy conversation talking about who knew what, mating probably, sounding old and young, without any age, all at once.

CHAPTER XXXV

So here's another good one, besides the Birr family, which had been around forever, there was once upon a time another family of Catholic farmers in Perth Hill. There had to have been because the cows that Cress Wells was chasing out of his field in the middle of a lightning storm that struck him dead a hundred years ago were Catholic. Their people were, I mean. That's the tradition anyhow among Berylie's people, the Wellses.

Blackstone Mining was Catholic, too. Or at least, Blackie Bavarro was. But Bobby Morgan was the one who was put in jail the day after the Stearns' fire. Not for the fire, for the murder of Sister Anna Caravengelo.

There was no murder weapon, no evidence at all that Bobby had killed our nun but there he was. Just because she had died in his clothes. And, I suppose, because Tim Gray, pillar of society, had placed Mrs. Morgan's whereabouts some other where than about her own homestead the night it happened. Little Bobby's alibi? Whatever was worse and more airy than *wishful* is what it had now become.

Tim Gray had found the Morgan's very old, unused summer kitchen to be a cozy nighttime spot for a brief spell the previous spring and remembered being rudely awakened in the late night by Mrs. Morgan returning home. She had been away since he had nestled in that evening. Bobby's vehicle was likewise not around. That Tim Gray could scrounge up from the grungy hallways of his fun house mind such a fine detail like the precise night this occurred was something to scratch over. McDonut and the sheriff maybe hypnotized him and made him remember the shape of the moon or if the stars were here or there or somewhere but I never heard they did.

Over the course of an evening and the next day, this development worked its way from a rumor, courtesy of Izzy's friend Carla Zahnhiser (still listed as a probable in the webbed foot department), up to a sorry fact, courtesy of the feed mill where Dad and Jacob were getting some barbed wire. The feed mill is in Mt. Air and they get the *Intelligencer* on the same day it comes out.

Regardless of little Bobby's predicament, if Tim Gray could be believed this development was a very sad one. It would mean Mrs. Morgan had been fibbing. *This* could not be believed. She was a wholesome grandma. One who had already had more than her share of heartache.

"Why can't they leave that poor woman be?" said Mom. She burrowed for something near the bottom of the freezer in the cellar alternately handing things to Izzy and taking them back. "Timmy Gray's memory is surely as addled as he is."

Outside, just beyond the cellar's screen door, I was petting the gray cat and waiting for Dad and Cambell to come back out with the fencing stuff.

"I'm not sure what to make of it," answered Dad. "Tim Gray's a ninnyhammer but so is little Bobby. I don't like the sound of any of it."

Neither did I. Tim Gray's name, particularly his, had lost all mystery and charm. I could only imagine what the whirring pulley sounded like when the guillotine's blade had been set loose and that's exactly the sound I imagined when I heard Tim Gray's unholy name. How long could it be till even more weird things came scurrying out of that brain of his? Things like the finer details of the 'communion' he found near our fire that night over at Alexander's.

"Look at this, Izzy," Mom said, as if she'd come upon a chunk of semiprecious stone, "I forgot we still had this. Let's have this tonight, too."

Coming back out, posthole digger and shovel in one hand, Dad asked, "What time shall we eat, Ma?"

"What suits?"

"We should be through with the fence and have the chores done by six, don'tcheh reckon, young'ns?"

Cambell, carrying a bucket with staples, pliers, hammer, crowbar and other stuff, said, "Easy. We have Boyd on our side." Z cackled in the background. I ignored her, giving the cat's belly one final, nervous buffing.

"Okay. Six. That's official. Please don't be late."

"Never."

So, a week before this, before Tim Gray's revelation, Ben had said to me: *Bet he didn't.* And, reflexively, because it was Ben, I guess, I said: *Bet he did.* I knew I would regret this bet. Even at this moment on the cellar steps with my chances greatly improved all of the sudden, I knew I would.

"How much?" he had demanded.

"I don't know. How 'bout three bucks?" I suggested peaceably.

Ben Dudley's eyes lit up with a sudden (and rare) message from his brain. "Three bucks? Is that what you got for getting third..." he hesitated, his jaw and head swooping forward, "Out of *two* with that mangy heifer—*Maple Syrup!*"

He roared. Oh, he was happy.

"Maple Leaf, Dudley. And yes that's what we won, not that it's any of your stupid business."

"You're on, Robison. Three big ones... you call me Dudley again I'm gon'neh clock you."

Old Dud was going to *clock* me? Somebody must've been reading to him again. This *was* about the time, though, when his surly take on the world around him—native habitat, let's say, in Ben's case—began to lope on ahead of his growth spurt. He wasn't just like a paper cut anymore. He was more like a big chigger. Maturing quite nicely, old Ben was.

So there I was, thanks to him, hoping against hope that Bobby Morgan—one of *our* guys, a Perth Hill guy, a Presbyterian, not a New Starling Catholic—was a murderer. For three bucks.

An extra three bucks would be dandy. But I did still feel bad for Mrs. Morgan. And for myself, too. Jimmy's bonfire jagged at me again and again. Tim Gray, *thief*, knew that Perth Hill was filthy with juvenile drunkards. If he could only remember it. If? *When*, when would this unsanitary fact pop out of him?

Out in the pasture I worried the digger down through rock after rock and the rock-like earth they were buried in and worried. And then when we were done with the fence and I was on my own little personal trip down through the woods searching high and low for a missing sow, I continued to worry, only more intensely. We had started the chores right on schedule when the unexcused absence was discovered. We'd been counting them at every feeding because lots of them were on the verge of farrowing and ready to make a break for "the waters and the wilds," which they sure like to do.

"We" was actually "me," theoretically, since lately I'd been feeding this particular batch of hogs. Then—suddenly!—Dad double-checked my count!

When he was done, he climbed back over the gate to where I was standing with my crossed fingers and said, "You better take a saunter down through the lower woods, Boyd, because I'm coming up one short."

I had two empty feed buckets with me to gather up the little survivors if she'd already farrowed. I prayed she hadn't. The deer flies and horse flies were absolutely horrendous down here, which was normal. Buzzing and biting any bare skin and even dive bombing to get at some nice sweaty scalp.

The horse flies were the actual size of horses. Not draft horses, but at least big ponies.

Rev. Stone did a sermon in the spring, before all our troubles, which I must've actually paid attention to because now, unfortunately, it came to mind. It was about the brothers Phinehas and Hophni. They were in Samuel in the Old Testament one door down from our nun who was still biding her time in Judges. They were priests, bad ones. Evil activities aside, the baddest thing about them was that they *pretended* to be good. Rev. Stone said God wanted their father, Eli, to kill them because they obviously deserved it. Eli wouldn't do it so God went ahead and killed the whole lot of them. Just like that. Clean as a whistle. And then to kind of keep the whole thing fresh put a never-ending curse on their descendants.

The lesson: Unless you want God to kill you and turn all your future relatives into pitiful begging lepers you better keep your house in order. This run I followed, which I thought of as ours, but never heard a name for, eventually meets up with Wallace Run. But there aren't any caves or anything weird like that up this far. Just trees and weeds. Traipsing along it I kept praying the sow hadn't farrowed yet. And I kept—I couldn't help it—I kept wondering about little Bobby and the Morgans. They seemed as cursed as Eli's family and I couldn't help but entertain the possibility that they too had done something, maybe hundreds of years ago, to deserve it.

This, of course, seemed unfair and I figured somehow there was a way to crawl out from under a curse like that.

But then Rev. Stone got off on some New Testament business and I couldn't quite follow him anymore. There just didn't seem to really be anything in there to help old Eli.

Before too long after crossing the fence you get to a bendy level place where three or four immense willows grow along the creek. It was right here that a tiny grunt startled me and I saw my prayer scamper away unanswered through the underbrush. We had startled each other, the piglet and me. But it was the most startled because it had never seen the likes of me before.

Her mother was a dozen yards off in a grass nest. She'd rooted a good-sized divot twice her size in the soft floor under the trees and was lying there with four little pigs plus the returned scout standing by her udder. These piglets had been down here for a couple weeks, easy. They had that crazy, alert attitude and cant to their heads that gets switched on if they're born out here, away. They were robust and strong and the skin on the crests of their necks was cracked and scabbed from getting sun burnt. Their stout little faces were also scabbed in bloody streaks from battling each other with their needle teeth. They were simply wild. They'd "gone native" as military expert Greg Pulaski would say.

The sow had her beady eye on me from the second I wandered into sight. She watched me from under the shade of her big ear, ready to bolt upright and defend her little homestead. I decided to retreat for reinforcements. The pigs were not new born and, therefore, not in danger for their lives. The weak had been culled long before. What we had here was the fittest of the fit—so I left them for the return trip. Once we caught them they'd be about the only thing that might lure their mother away from the nest.

As Jake and Cambell continued with the chores Dad and I got a just-vacated farrowing crate ready for the prodigal one. He wasn't unreasonably mad. About all he said was, "You boys will have to be more careful counting, even if it means taking off your shoes and socks."

All of this made us late for supper, naturally, and the pork chops were on the overly burned side. Mom was a bit curt with us for a few minutes.

The note on the kitchen table to call Ben, she had written and then amended '—*after* supper'. Washing my hands in the kitchen sink I asked her what he wanted.

"He said you two had a bet and that you lost," she said, plunking raw scones into a frying pan. She didn't ask what the bet was on—she believed in a certain amount of privacy—but did wonder, "How much were you betting, may I ask?"

I tried to be nonchalant. "Oh... a couple bucks... two bucks. Three. That's all," I drawled, as if it were trivial.

"Three bucks wasted," she replied softly without turning from her work.

Hard to argue with that. I bolted upstairs on a fact-finding mission.

CHAPTER XXXVI

Isabelle was in her room on the bed with the door open. I screeched to a halt just before it.

"Zeebee," I said, poking my head in meekly, "Is there some new news on Bobby Morgan?"

She looked up from a magazine. "Uh, *yes*, Boyd." She squinted, like I was out of focus or something. "Oh. You were out playing in the woods, I guess—"

"I wasn't playing—"

Just then Jake flew out of the bathroom where he'd been washing his hands and cried, "Little Bobby didn't chop the head off our nun!" He sliced his hands down through the air, like the blade of a guillotine, water droplets spraying.

"Calm down, Jake," Isabelle said, "The headhunter might be coming for you next."

"I'm not afraid of him. I'll get his head!" Up went the hands.

"With what?" she laughed, underestimating our little brother terribly.

He got serious. "With my bow and arrow, Zeezie. I killed a starling today."

"Really?" I said, startled and somewhat excited. We had made that bow and arrow out of binder twine and box elder twigs.

"You shouldn't kill birds," Z said, squinting again. "Should he, Boyd?"

Confronting a skeptical little face, I said, "That's true, Jake. Don't ask me why. Because they're small maybe."

"So what was your bet?" Z inquired. "With young Benjamin?"

"Oh," I started, off guard now. "That, well, I can't tell you really. Nothing important."

"Then you can tell us. Right, Jake?"

"Tell us!"

"I can't. You'll think less of me."

She produced a rude laugh.

"You'll tell Mom," I said, but she was actually getting better about this nasty habit.

"No I won't. I promise." She sounded sincere.

"Cross your heart?"

She did.

I took a breath. "I bet he did it."

"Little Bobby Morgan? You bet on a man's life, Boyd?"

"Nohhh-wuh... not his life. On his...." I searched for the right word.

"Morbidous impulses," provided Jake, suddenly bird-killer serious again.

Z and I both gazed at him for a moment appreciating his word choice. He was experiencing a nanosecond of remorse, I think, about the starling.

"Thank you, Jake. That was it exactly."

"Well, you lost."

"How do they know he didn't do it?" I asked.

"He had an alibi."

"Really? Just out of the blue?" I waited, expecting her to tell me what it was. But she dropped her eyes back to her magazine. "What was it?"

"What was what?" She didn't look up.

"The alibi you... nice person."

"I'm not saying."

"Why not, for Pete's sake?"

"I'm just not."

"What's wrong with you?" I pleaded. "What was it? Come on."

She shook her head.

"Twit," I harrumphed and slid by Jake hurrying down the short hall to find a better sibling.

Cambell's door was half-closed so I knocked on it softly but with enough force to drift it open. He was putting clean pants on.

"Aren't you forgetting something?" I asked.

"Nope," he said, grinning moronically. Then he cocked his bristly head authoritatively. "Thursdays have been declared underwear-free days."

"Really?"

"Of course."

"Hmmm... I didn't get the memo. Interesting. What's Bobby Morgan's alibi? Why didn't you tell me about him outside?"

"He was on a date," he said matter-of-factly.

"A date?"

"A date."

"Honest? With who?"

"Whom. Sue Kurncich."

"Hah!" I blurted, hopping into the air. "I knew he wasn't really mixed up with our nun. That was way too weird a thing." I felt bizarrely territorial, like our nun was now all mine.

"Weird all right." He opened a dresser drawer for a t-shirt.

"Who's this Sue girl?"

"Oh. Just some other nun," he said.

I laughed. "That would be hilarious."

"Oh yeah."

"So who is she?"

"A nun. I'm not kidding. Former nun, actually."

I sensed my eyeballs stretching away from their sockets. "You're not kidding?"

"I wouldn't kid about something as important as a date. Would I?"

I shook my head. "Bobby Morgan didn't kill our nun because he was with another nun?"

"That's about the size of it."

I laughed cautiously. "This is a joke."

"'Fraid not, Boydoh. Neat, huh?" His head popped out of the t-shirt and he tugged it down smiling extra sunnily.

I looked past him out the window, my brain slipping around.

"That is incredible. That guy is incredible."

"You can say that again. A real inspiration."

"Holy mackerel."

"Yessirreebob."

I pulled my stare back to him as he tucked the shirt into his pants. "Who killed our nun?"

"That's the question all right. Lookin' more and more like God maybe did it," he said, shrugging.

"Cambell," I whispered, shooting an anxious, guilty look back to the hall. It seemed like a bad thing to say. "Why God?"

He puffed out, then deflated, his cheeks. "He's the only one with a motive. Now *this* is the tricky part." He tugged the zipper of his shorts away from himself and upwards. "You can't be too careful on Underwear Free Days. 'UFD's' to fundamentalists."

"Fun-DEMENTED."

"Don't be mean. Don't judge."

"Can you tell me, please, what God's motive would be to kill our nun?"

"No. I cannot."

"Then what are you talking about? Not having underwear on is doing something to your brain."

"No, Boyd. Who knows what His motive was. But He had to have one, right? Like that little island that burned up in the middle of the ocean last week and all the people drowned trying to cool off. Or like in Africa when an entire nation starves to death right down to the rats. Or like when a heifer gets third place out of two. Who knows what His motive was. But He must have a reason. Right? And He's the only one without an alibi."

I looked out the window again without answering as Mom yelled up.

"Supper is ready. Again. Come down here. Please."

"Come on," Cambell said, a finger going in a twirling motion to get me to turn around and clear out.

I did and said, "UFD's, huh?"

"I'm a trendsetter, Boyd. I'm tearing down barriers."

"Of personal hygiene."

CHAPTER XXXVII

I said that, but for the life of me I couldn't think of what underwear actually did for a person.

Pork chops, French-fried eggplant, scones with blackberry preserves Mom had made that day, cooked carrots made sweet somehow, and wilted lettuce: supper.

Mom and Iz summed it up about as good as you could.

"I don't understand that boy. Think of all the nice girls at Perth Hill. Or even Grangefield. What could possess him to get mixed up with those... nuns?"

"Satan, for one," answered Iz. "Zero competition, for two."

We had peach pie for dessert.

Then I called The Chigger.

"Hey, Robison, you owe me three bucks," he said, dispensing with ridiculous words like "hello."

"So I hear."

"I'm real sorry."

I heard a little click on the other end but ignored it, saying, "Me, too. It's sad. Our Sunday School teacher isn't a murderist after all."

Ben, nonsensically, said, "Yep. Just dipping the old pen in the old company ink, that's all. *Heh-heh-heh.*"

"What're you talking about?"

"You know. The company ink."

"Okay." I laughed a little but I was laughing at him, nothing else. This was when I heard the phone slam down on the other end. It wasn't the one Ben was on.

He said, "Uh-oh... my stupid sist—"

At this moment, the other phone was picked back up. Janie was there.

"You two are perverts," she sputtered. "And you, Boyd Robison, are a scumball. A real scumball."

The phone slammed down again.

Ben was laughing. "She's not very nice. See! I've been trying to *tell* people that."

"Why am I a scumball, Ben?"

"You're a scumball because you hoped Morgan killed our nun."

"I did not! For crying out loud! I was just betting, not hoping..."

"Oh yeaaaaah. I have to go beat somebody up. Three dollars: remember."

He hung up. I said goodbye.

I went outside and put on my manure-y, blown-out ten-nies. The lowering sun was burning up the high-tension towers that cut across the Birr and MacRae places. I felt crummy.

How crummy? Well... I did have peach pie burps so I wasn't going to kill myself or anything but *still....*

So I went to the barn and with a *very* fast approach threw myself off the barn floor out the hay chute plummeting to the ground below. It was a good 15-foot drop and Jake and I were the only ones who ever did it anymore. It could make you feel on top of the world and heroic and in control of your pathetic destiny if you could get the courage up to do it and pull it off without hurting yourself too bad. On top of the world.

It didn't work. It hadn't been working for about a month. I noticed that. Even with an incredibly fast approach.

CHAPTER XXXVIII

Couple days later Mom drug Jacob and me into town to get new tennis shoes for gym class. Our old ones had been through too much woods and swamp and manure and were not "presentable." The sides were all ripped out and goofy and the soles were almost gone, even the nice neat parallel grill marks melted into them from when she tried to dry them too fast before the church picnic. And here they were, just getting comfortable.

This wasn't a planned trip or anything. The store had called and said they needed more eggs before the normal delivery day, which was Monday, so we loaded up the seven and half crates we had and away we went.

Jake was placing the legs of a bug in his shirt pocket—*for later*—when we got to the viaduct. The viaduct is the divider between New Sterling and the rest of the world. It's not Roman or stone or arched or anything. It's just a rusty old bridge, over a slow muddy river that has a scrap metal salvage yard on one bank. On the other side is New Sterling, its South Side first, where our nun volunteered, an area aspiring to be a big city slum. Black people and Lebanese people live there mostly.

It was very hard but we tried not to look very much at the black people because they were *just like us only... blacker*—and it wasn't nice to stare. For similar reasons we weren't allowed to look at the Amish at the auction. So when we were over the viaduct we glanced—*it's okay to glance and smile*—at the blacks walking along the sidewalks and sitting on the porches of the few grim, mangled bungalows still setting on weird, isolated spaces too small to build a grim, mangled tenement building. Sometimes I'd spot a particularly attractive girl who, contrary to Mom's opinion on the subject, looked very, very different from Jane Graham and *boy* would I glance at her and make some great plans for us.

Today, though, my eyes were fixed on the spires of the Catholic church, and my mind on our nun and on Bobby Morgan. This was where it all started, I guess. Right here in New Sterling, little Bobby coming in from Perth Hill to fiddle around with the little numbers at the convent. And there she was, our nun. Who could resist?

We dropped the eggs off at Zane's Super Market, South Side's grocery store. It was funny that the people here and we, that is, *us*, had something in common. This had never before occurred to me. Maybe our nun had eaten our eggs.

Mom negotiated through the center of town, which was less mangled than South Side but still gray and grimy even on a sunny day and even though pollution was going down because the factories were in the middle throes of being shut down permanently due to the Japanese who had secretly gone from slapping together clapping monkey toys and snapping dentures to creating genuinely splendid motor vehicles that made no noise whatsoever. No rattles? Car doors that went "thud"? New Sterling didn't make complete autos but they did supply some of the rattles and hollow door sounds so this was kind of a low blow. As the mill guys would tell you, though, it wasn't the worst thing they ever did to us.

Hamilton got steep as it ascended out of downtown, then, as it gradually leveled out, ran through all the tire and muffler places and the McDonald's, which I'd been to with the Lanes once, and a few other places like an air conditioner repair shop and a light fixture store and places like that. They were all open, I guess, but had a way of looking not very happy or inviting. You'd only go in if you really needed something. In a break in all this we came to a sign made out of two clay-colored brick pillars, about four feet high, and a piece of wood hung between them. It read, "St. Joachim's Convent."

Mom said, "This is it, boys. She lived in there." Having scouted it out earlier in the summer, she told us we'd be going by. It was kind of underwhelming at first.

Set back off the road 50 yards or so, it was a one story building made out of the same bricks as the pillars. Low with a flat roof and resting on the ground very meekly, not like the churches downtown in the least, it could've been an elementary school or a motel right off the turnpike. As we got by it, though, you could see it was bigger than it looked. It was shaped like a square, the side, maybe all the sides, identical to the front and there must've been a courtyard in the middle because some trees showed above the roof, pine trees.

I craned around out the window and gave the place as long a look as possible. Then car dealerships were going by. Ford, Chevrolet, Lucky's.

Lucky's.... This camp counselor tried to explain to us once at a Sunday School retreat why superstition was evil. It was sort of like you were trying to trick God... or something. I wasn't paying attention too great. He was some college guy, really nice and all—well, to tell the truth, he was kind of overly born again, if you know what I mean. Actually listening to him could've led to unkind thoughts.. And it didn't help things that this was right at the time Jody Dyson's northern hemispheres started to demand as much attention as you could get away with.

"She's an early riser," Jimmy noted, "Prodigious—breastigious."

He really liked that one. Anyway, it was Jody's pal Janie who summed up superstition better than anybody. If something really nice happened to her, she said, like, say, she shot a groundhog, she'd say a thank you prayer to God for her good luck. And if she also noticed that she had happened to tie her shoelaces in a funny, weird knot by mistake on that particular day she would thank God for that, too, and then, from then on, every time she went hunting, she'd be sure and tie her laces in the same funny, weird knot by mistake. Better safe than sorry.

"The Lord works in mysterious ways," she said. "You shouldn't ignore signs. I'd just be trying to help Him. Not trick Him."

This was back when she would talk to me and stuff, back before I had become a scumball.

We got our new, embarrassingly white tennies and left town. I thought of Janie's funny, weird knot and I thought of the strange things which must go on within the walls of St. Joachim's and of my arrowhead and of that pickled bishop and of other things and I wondered why Mom and Izzy weren't allowed to have communion at our nun's funeral. I mean, give or take a pope, what was the difference between us?

And when we got back into familiar territory again, fields, woods, cows and pigs the scenery, Eli's sons again jaggered at me. I wondered what other strange things had gone on at St. Joachim's, when little Bobby was there, and I thought of our poor nun and how she was dead. And I also thought of all the other sad things that had happened to the odd Morgan clan. Bad luck. Bad luck, it seemed to me, forever and a day. Bad luck till the cows came home.

CHAPTER XXXIX

Jake and I went to the pond for a dip that night after supper (braised steak, lima beans, blueberry pie... that pie made the rest of supper look like a set-up job) and after doing the last chores in the barn. The rush of cool water would wash away the day's grime. City grime, barn grime— we had a lot of grime.

The pond was the best thing about that miserably hot summer. Not that it had much competition from any other things. You'd dive through the muggy, buggy air off the board, a rough-cut oak plank (courtesy of Mr. Bell) covered at the end with a burlap sack for traction, and splash down through the miraculous water, through the top warm layer into the cool, growing cooler as you went, through them all and then come back up to see if you'd survived the jolt, and if you had then you had a whole new lease on life. Then you'd breath all the air out of your lungs and drop to the bottom feet first and wiggle them through the creamy mud, the coolest layer of all, and then you'd kick back up to the dark, still surface and float around for awhile on your back and try to find the first thin stars twinkling down at you through the dusk and haze. The days left for doing this were dwindling. Not that anybody in their right mind would've wanted to prolong that summer.

We crunched out the gravel lane in our unpresentable tennies, towels in hand. We were at the dock, where the dive was, kicking them off and yanking our shirts off when a tractor slowed out on Forbes and turned down the lane. Jake ignored it and dove in, legs scissored, yelling an excited, strangled *ahhh-eeee!* in anticipation of the pleasant shock. But it looked like one of Lane's tractors so I stood there and waited to see if it was Charlie.

It was. The old Oliver pulled over, even with the dam, and stopped. Charlie climbed off and walked across it. He knew Dad didn't want people driving on it and tracking up the fescue and vetch and making it look like a nice inviting parking area for unknown, uninvited types.

I hollered as he came, "Where's yer suit, McChain Lane?"

"You're lookin' at it." He had barn clothes on. "Are there still leeches in there?"

"Not really," I answered, hopping back to the dam from the dock.

"No thanks."

"Wimp. Hey—nice hat. Where'd you get one like that?"

He took it off and studied Bessemer-Jackson International's red and black logo.

"Mark," he said. "It is nice, isn't it? Wouldn't think they'd be wasting their money on ball caps when they're laying off half the planet, would'jyeh?"

"Advertisement, Charles. Rule uno-"

"Dos-tres-Ochohhh!... Fat lot o' good it'll do 'em on my head."

He pointed. "Looks like Jacob-the-Father-of-Israel found a new friend."

Jake had gotten a small snapping turtle, size of a salad plate, to chomp onto the end of a stick and he'd hauled it up onto the dock for an inspection. He was squatted down holding the stick nearly vertical, at arms length, the turtle dangling from the end.

"I taught him that. So, you were coming from Mark's right now? Is his Dad getting laid-off this time?"

"Not yet. They're still whacking the peons. I was takin' his telescope back to him."

He jabbed his thumb up at the sky and made a resigned spitting noise with his lips, looking off to Jake and the turtle.

"Thanks," I said. "I didn't know what telescopes were for. 'Jeh see anything cool? Up there in the—do they call that... the sky?"

"Eahhh... the moon and... and," he paused, an impure grin waxing across his face, "You really don't know what a telescope is for, do you, Red? You know our barn, how you can get up into the cupola and see out where the slats are missing?" A grin of full-blown deviancy was all over his big head.

"I'll take your word for it."

"Well, Boyd, m'boy, from up there you can actually see the Graham's house down in the hollow."

"'Zat a fact, Charles?" I said, warily.

"Ohhh yes. Fact. Would you like to know anything about a certain someone's evening attire?"

"You are kidding me? You pervert!"

He laughed deliriously, his head nodding in the affirmative. "So are *you*! I was just smart enough to borrow a telescope."

"You didn't... I don't believe it."

"Want'eh bet?"

"No!"

"Oh, yeah. Your betting record ain't too prosperous these days."

"Not too... Wehlll...."

"Well what?"

"What... you know... what'jeh see?" I tried to say it in a boring style, like I was just trying to keep the conversation up.

"Who's a pervert?" He hit me with his hat. Then he smiled with something approaching genuine fondness. "Boyd, Boyd, Boyd... you wouldn't believe it. I wish you could have seen it—you know... what she was wearing."

"What?"

"Have you ever seen a bacon strip?"

"Whuh'duh'yeh—wait—"

"I mean a Bacon Strip—strip!"

An idiotic fit of imagination seized ahold of me and then an idiotic fit of laughter seized ahold of Charlie.

"Ohhh," I said, coming around, "You didn't see anything, did you?"

"Some trees were in the way."

"But you tried."

"No way. I'm afraid of heights. I wouldn't go up there if my life depended on it. But, I had'jyeh going, yeh knuckle-head, didn't I!" He lapsed again into several miniature, hair-ball convulsions and then sighed at great, satisfied length.

I tried to imitate Jody Dyson's voice and occasional insights into our behaviors. "You are so childish, Charlie. *So* childish. A childish, childish boy who will never grow up." I planted my hands on my hips.

"I will, too! You'll see!"

"If you live that long."

"Hmmm, that will be the tricky part, won't it?" He shook his head and snapped the hat back on. "You should'eh seen your face... and you don't even like Janie Graham. 'Member?"

"Ohhh... is that who you were talking about? I thought—"

"That I meant her Grandma? That wouldn't surprise me. Or her Grandpa—that's what you were really hoping for, huh, Red?"

"Charlie—" I shivered. "You are... diseased."

"I take that as a compliment," he said, hitching his pants up with a proud little cock of his stupid noggin.

"That's how I meant it. Can we change the subject? Not to be rude or anything..."

"Okay. Have you talked to Stanley lately?"

Shaking my head, I pulled a seed head from a tall piece of timothy, its stem telescoping neatly out from the rest of the plant, and chewed the soft, pulpy end. "Sunday is all."

"He told his folks about his new di-version, little Just Jen."

"Uh-oh. What happened?"

"They laughed." Charlie wagged his head in amused disbelief.

"They did?"

"Yep."

"Why'd they do that?"

"Beats me."

"That's weird."

He nodded.

"Did they say anything, or just laugh?" I asked.

"They said they didn't care as long as she was nice and good and all that garbage. I think that means they didn't care as long as they're still both a couple'eh twerp teenagers."

"Right."

"Plenty'eh time for sonny boy to grow up and think righter."

"Righter, right. Like little Bobby."

"Speaking of bets."

"You heard about that, huh?"

"Who hasn't?"

"Man alive, it was only three bucks. I'm glad it made him so happy."

"He said five. And that he hadn't hoped and prayed that little Bobby Morgan was a murderer."

"I did not. For Pete's sake.... I just figured he was. I don't want anybody to be the killer."

"I'm afraid that's not going to be possible. A head doesn't just pop off its body like a seed, Boyd. I'm not even actually the best doctor in the world and I know that."

"You're not?"

Just then the rumble of a car approached up the lane with Cambell's speed. We turned to see him in the car. He beeped once and waved.

"He thinks God did it," I said.

"Well, God gets blamed for everything."

"Never has a very good alibi."

"Well, if Y're always gon'neh insist on being everywhere, whuh'cheh expect?"

I chuckled. "Right.... We were over at Mr. Bell's yesterday picking up boards—he thinks Berylie did it. But... he reminds me of a leprechaun."

"Hey, that's funny. Me, too. A tiny leprechaun."

"Don'tcheh want'eh know why he thinks Berylie did it?"

"Already know, Red."

"That the Morgans were about half-Catholic once upon a dark, dark time in the long ago? That Morgan cattle killed Cress Wells? "

"Actually, lightning killed Cress Wells but since Morgan cattle back then were kind'uh like God they got the blame. So Berylie finally got revenge by lopping off little Bobby's lopsided noggin. What she thought was little Bobby's lopsided noggin, Red, er, wait, uh, Timothy, is that you?" He squinted at me like Mrs. McHenry had in the Farm Show bleachers. "Then she dumped him off on old Cress' grave, right next to his old pal Mawson like a trophy."

"Old Berylie, the avenging angel. A bit tardy."

"Better late than never... The old, blind avenging angel. They should make you take an eye test for that job, don'tcheh think, Red?"

We chuckled a little. Not big or hearty chuckles, just smaller ones, cautious, proportioned, and we skipped glances at each other.

"Leprechauns." Charlie's face was shiny with sweat. It was still hot. "Y're startin' to sound like yer from around here, know that, Red?"

We watched Jacob for some seconds still messing with the snapper. Out of the blue, Charlie said, "You still trying to figure out who that O'Shanter guy is?"

An involuntary sound went through my nose. "Ho... what made you think of *that*?"

"Beats me."

"How'd you find out about him?"

"Dictionary."

"Dictionary?"

"Yep. That ratty one on the stand. In our living room? Real old one?" I nodded. "He was in the back. He's not a hat. He was a farmer. In some old story. He got all drunk at the auction and gets home late. On the way, though, some witches and warlocks try to get him. His horse gets her tail ripped off but they get away. Him... and his gray mare Meg."

"Tam O'Shanter's mare." I considered this for a moment. "Why should I remember her? What's that supposed to mean?"

"Beats hell out of me. Don't go to the auction?" He shrugged. "Don't play with witches? Watch your big fat be-hind? Who knows?"

"Why me?"

"'Cause you were there probbly. It's his job. He can't help it. Giving out warnings."

"I was where?"

"In front of him. Like a criminal. Maybe you remind him of a criminal." Charlie looked to the ground stubbing his toe against the ground like he was working a pebble to the front of his shoe.

"Great."

Suddenly, he juked backwards, one arm flying up to protect his head. "Yo! Bats!"

"Yep," I said. They'd been out for a few minutes. "Suppertime."

"I don't like bats. They're weird."

We watched them then for a little spell, Charlie's shoulders heaped up involuntarily to protect himself. They were out picking up where the barn swallows had left off that afternoon. Everyday like clockwork. Today, they were a pleasant, if fleeting, distraction. Swooping and fluttering, one moment just off the surface of the pond, the next, higher, over the trees on the bank, then back again skimming above the water. Their flights, scattered out in front of us like curly windblown graffiti, sinewy and liquid and whipped by sudden sharp arcs. They were just pretty dang marvelous the way they handled themselves.

Our reveries ended with Jacob shouting to us.

"Hey, guys, lookee!" He hoisted the turtle, jaws still locked onto the end of the stick, into the air and began spinning around with it in circles on the dock.

"Good work, Jake!" Charlie called down enthusiastically.

"Ohhh, yes. The Father of Israel, make no mistake about that."

"Righto. Plain 'z day. D'you ever eat those?" he asked.

"Couple times. In soup."

"Taste like chicken?"

"Of course."

A train whistle drifted in from down in the valley and a car went by with headlights on out on the main road and suddenly, though there was still color in the lower west, it seemed like night.

"The Oliver doesn't have lights does it?"

"Sure. But they only go off. I better get out o' here. Mom will be sending the dogs out," he said, wincing. Then he grabbed his hat, said, "And I still have to pick up her dishes from Zahnhisers. Dang it!" and hit me with it one final time.

"Regular delivery boy, aint'cheh? Tractor's the best equipment for the job, too, isn't it?"

"Red, I can not wait till I get my real license."

"I can't wait till you get your real license either."

"You really gon'neh swim in there? Bats, snapping turtles, leeches..."

"Yep. Right at home."

With a bewildered laugh, he walked back along the dam to the road and tractor.

"See yeh."

"Yep. See yeh."

Going back down the lane after swimming and pestering various wildlives, the turtle, frogs, a muskrat, Jake asked, "Boyd? Do you think we have to still take a bath?"

"Neah."

He held his ruminations for a few steps then said, "Snapping turtles are cool, huh?" His voice was small and wistful; his world was perfect.

"Sort of. They eat a lot of fish and baby ducks, though."

"I know."

"Oh."

We crunched slowly along enjoying the luxury of that damp interval when the bugs left you alone. An idea came to me and I latched onto it while it still seemed good.

"Hey, Jake?"

"Yeah?"

"Do you want to borrow my arrowhead for a while?"

"The lucky yellow one? Don't you need it anymore?"

"Oh... who knows. I'd just be lending it to you. You know, you'd have to give it back when I wanted it. Okay?"

"Oh sure. I will. I promise." He hesitated. "Did you do something to it?"

"No. Whuh'duh'yeh mean?"

"Did you pee on it?"

"No, Jake. I didn't pee on it."

"An Indian? It's pee-color."

"It's a rock. It's that color 'cause God pee'd on it. It's in perfect shape. I'm just takin' a break from it for a while, that's all. Just tired of luggin' it around and everything. Do you want it or not?"

"Yeah! I love that arrowhead."

I handed it over to him, dropping it into the palms of his hands. "Here yeh go. Don't lose it."

We were at the edge of the yard and he stopped and held it up to the last pale glow in the west. It was still wet from my shorts and pretty even in that much light.

"Boyd, do you see... how this is the same color as the moon?"

I looked past the stone between his fingers. It was setting, a brand new sickle moon.

"Pretty huh?"

"Yep."

It was and they stick in my mind, at the front of it, that moon and that arrowhead and I seriously doubt if they will ever unstick.

CHAPTER XL

Bits of their discussion were floating upstairs through our bedroom window. Dad and Mr. Birr had settled themselves below it on the stone steps to the porch. They were talking about Mr. Birr borrowing our boar, Festus, and then, about Bobby Morgan.

Their voices rose and fell away and shot past indecipherably as if carried on swirling thermals like a small version of the ones the turkey vultures ride when looking for something untoward and corrupted on the ground. Aaron Birr's voice was never quiet but that evening it was and there were occasional low, unnerving chuckles and the Reverend was mentioned and though I couldn't even make out the gist of it there was plenty enough to imagine, all sorts of exciting things. The *Intelligencer* had said that with every passing day the trail was growing colder and colder.

But as Mr. Birr had observed earlier the trails around here could never really grow cold, they were very long, they stretched back and ahead, sometimes hidden in the underbrush and jaggers—"the twilight shade of tangled thickets" (per Mr. Birr quoting some spooky old something)—but they were still there and they were still warm. Still warm. They were still being used.

In the wee hours of that night Jacob talked in his sleep again. It was mostly muzzy nonsense except for one word that punctuated through the soft gibberish quite clearly by spells—"*weeds*." It was a nightmare. He was haunted by his nemesis, the garden. But his bondage to it would soon end. Next week, school.

Then, in the even wee-er hours, I was startled upright by the creaking of a door. I thought someone was creeping into our room until I remembered our door was always left wide open. This relieved me for a split second until I thought maybe our door was creaking because someone or thing was *closing* it behind them as they entered. But... the door stood open. I lay back down, eyes open. They were just getting heavy when the sound came again.

I hoisted onto my elbows. Could it be that Cambell was sneaking in this late and that he had lost his mind and forgotten the riddle of the floor boards in the hallway, the location of the creaks, constantly shifting with the seasons and the humidity like living, breathing landmines? Ludicrous. His experience was formidable. Suddenly, the worst, most demented scenarios gripped me. My heart raced and I got extremely stiff—like *that* would deflect the decapitating blow of the razor-sharp broadsword making its way through our house. No more sounds came, though—maybe it was the wind, or maybe just my own sinful past stumbling around inside my thickened skull—and eventually I went to sleep.

CHAPTER XLI

Mr. Paden went by in the Township dump truck as I coasted the tractor down onto Orchard Road. from Kendall Road. He gave me his classic two-fingered wave, his black-tanned hand making the cigarette look very, very white. I was on my way over to Spoets's to get this contraption old Van Spoets had contrived for splitting black locust logs lengthwise. It was mounted on the remains of an old manure spreader and ran off your PTO so you could just hook it up to your tractor and supposedly it actually worked if you didn't mind taking the middling chance that it would also split you lengthwise in the process. Normally I would've gone left and by the church but I hadn't been this other way for a long time and I thought it would be shadier.

I popped the Massey into 5th High for the mile and a half of Orchard Road. before me and rolled. It was fun not pulling anything, zipping along without a care, high in the saddle and looking down on the fencerows and thistles and everything. Wind in your hair and all that junk. Easy Rider-type thing.

At the old Amish place Glen's older brother bought I turned left onto Oliver Road. I missed seeing their laundry out, all black and blue, sensible and serious, against the fancy colors in their garden beds. Most of the Amish were down around the Mud Bridge neck of the woods so I suppose these ones felt a little out of place against all of Perth Hill's progressiveness.

A half a mile up this gravel road was the Oliver place and Mr. Oliver was out sitting on an upturned bucket at the top of his barn bridge working on something in his lap. For all I knew he could've been petting a kitty. We waved. He thought I was a pinhead. It was *great* not to have to talk to him.

He was a nice enough old bird, it wasn't that. The problem was that I could only understand about every fifth word that came out of him. He had a tremendous overbite which seemed to work as a word scrambler. It was harrowing trying to talk to him. He had taken me to the Wool Pool that past spring to stomp wool bags. Three long, harrowing days helping pack up the county's wool, load it onto rail cars and comprehend what Mr. Oliver was saying to me. Actually, I don't truly know if he was a nice enough old bird, or not. All I can say for sure is that he never hit me.

Seeing him now, though, made me think of then, pre-nun, and not overwhelmingly of wool. At the time, summer was seeping through the school walls and I thought I had caught Janie Graham looking at me on a couple of occasions at the very instant I was stealing a gander at her. I was certain, well, hopeful, that we would find ourselves alone in a remote corner of the graveyard, the sound and blaze of the year-end youth group cookout gargling in the distance, and we would hold hands and... kiss. Possibly. I did know there were more things you could do but I was trying to be practical. Well, that cookout was to have been held on the night of the morning our nun happened into our lives among those same gravestones and iron markers in that same remote corner of the graveyard.

Near its end Oliver Road. made a couple of twists on the final modest rise drawing up to Duff Road. The old wild cherry trees on either side of me met overhead to carve the sun up into slabs and blobs and speckles of light, which with the curves, made for a pleasingly dizzying stretch of driving. Easing to a stop at the T-intersection I throttled down and reached into my shirt pocket for the German prune plum I had scrounged from under the tree by the driveway.

I bit into it and let my eyes adjust to the full sunlight and black macadam of the main road. It had been long enough that I needed a few seconds to get my bearings as I could not remember exactly where Oliver dumped out. The road to Spoets's was on down Duff to the left but I was curious to figure how far down. That didn't take long because the solo silo, Sager's, was down and across the road just a little ways, standing alone, anchoring only a pile of rubble hidden beneath a welt of briars and sumac. To my right,

100 yards off, was McHenry's road and further on, though you couldn't see the buildings, was the Alexander place. I pried the pit out and popped the remaining plum half in. My goodness, what a sweet one.

Slipping the clutch I crackled out onto smooth, hot tar and angled across. My left foot was yet halfway down on the pedal when a loud boom went off in front of me. I mean it split the air in front of me like a bolt of thunder. At the instant it happened I thought: flat tire. But the shock of it threw my foot clear off the clutch pedal all at once and the bucking lurch cantilevered my back way over the low seat twisting my spine very unfamiliarly and the ensuing swerving and the spasm in my shoulders informed me that contrary to my original thought what had actually happened was that someone had shot me with an extremely large-caliber deer rifle.

After some more heaving tractor bucks that you couldn't actually blame on the blowout, after I got stopped and catapulted myself to the ground and hid behind the big rear wheel, I saw it and thought: *Heyyy, a flat tire....* I thanked God for this wonderful miracle. The bullet hole had healed over completely, no scar even, and I had an excuse for being stopped like this in the middle of the nowhere.

But just for the record, so you know, a flat tire is no laughing matter either. The good thing was that it was the front tire, that was a blessing, too. Mitchie could fix that. A rear tire, huge and filled with mag water, would've taken a guy from some big garage in town with a special truck.

Mitchie could do this at his garage, today still, probably. He could, that is, if we could get it to him. That would take a jack and some blocks and wrenches and... a ride.

The last one there was a problem and it crossed my mind to just walk home because I loathed the thought of having to use someone's phone. Berylie McHenry was the closest probably and she, of course, wouldn't mind one bit. But I just hated to. She would probably offer to take me over home herself, blind as a bat—but the roads around here were hardwired into her somehow so that she seemed to navigate... like a *bat*, in fact—or wait inside and have a cookie and a chat, I mean, Berylie and me, just us, chatting and ha-ha'ing—how nerve-wracking would that be?

I kicked the tire and spaketh a mild swear word or two and headed off towards her lane. My nerves were coming back to me, stiffening up and regaining some spinal-like shape. A good swear word would often help with that. I felt strangely fortified by them. Soon my pace quickened and grasshoppers, energized by the heat, clacked and whirred before me, a little troop of advance cavalry. Bring on that chat, Berylie—and a cookie.

CHAPTER XLII

Every Christmas the Youth Group went around to all the old people's places to inflict a few carols on them, trying to get some of our youthful innocence and wonder to rub off on them and all. Some of them seemed to genuinely pretend to enjoy it. Others endured stoically, curtain pushed reluctantly to one side, head peering out the window, or standing on the porch, grimly, while we sped through one verse of "Silent Night" zipping directly into "We Wish You A Merry Christmas," our rousing closer. Mrs. McHenry was one of the grim stoics.

She had a really fine, long lane, straight, smooth, swooping gently down through expansive pastures then up past the house and barn, which, from the road, looked distant, unreal even, like they were in a movie. The last 50 yards were lined with huge, *towering* sugar maples and red oaks. Berylie had herself a showplace in the Fall.

The pastures, though, honestly, didn't look the best. They hadn't been grazed in a good long time and were overgrown with all manner of weeds, notably jimsonweed, pokeberry and burdock. Her nephews were too busy with their own stuff to get the fences in shape and their places weren't close enough by to make using them too awful convenient. Still, big pastures like that, it was a waste somebody wasn't.

The house and barn were both in nice shape, however, and didn't look at all like what Dad would've described as a typical widow's place, that being, kind of tattered and coming apart at the seams from lack of being kept up enough. They were both white and sat on the same side of the lane but were offset from each other at an angle on their own little knolls. The same date, 1859, was lain into each roof using darker, nearly black slate.

I turned and walked backwards for a few steps to see what everything looked like from the other direction. Different. The Oliver woods had disappeared and the tractor, too, though the top half of the silo was still there. I finished the turn and plucked the flower head from a Queen Anne's Lace, running my hand, palm up, fingers straddling the stem, upward to pop it off. It was pretty. The single tiny purple floweret floating in the big cloud of white ones. I bet our friends the Catholics had a legend about weedy old Queen Anne's Lace, Jesus floating around in Heaven or something.

When I got to the trees I was surprised that they didn't provide much relief from the sun. A pocket of heat seemed to move with me, every step. Cutting up between the great trunks onto the sweeping yard, the low, aspirated whistle of a mourning dove pushed through the air above me. I scanned around but saw only a few starlings taking a rest in a dusty lilac clump. Their feathers were roughened and they watched me as if I was up to something. I was *not*.

I considered going to the front door. The porch there, fronting the whole side of the house facing the lane, south, was neatly arranged—two old green wicker chairs at either end of an oval, braided rug made out of some rope-y material, a couple of hanging plants, ferns and a flowery one, and a swing near the west end, pointed west, strung by chains anchored in the wainscot-like ceiling. It seemed like it didn't want to be disturbed.

I strayed wide on a course to the back door at the side of her house, then stopped. Going back there meant intruding even further onto her place unannounced. But... Mom always seemed slightly perturbed when someone used the front door, and the back door was where we always caroled at Berylie, so I proceeded on, hoping I had chosen the lesser of two evils. I rehearsed some lines: Hi, Mrs. McHenry, etc.

The back steps were wooden with no handrail and led up to the stoop and the door. I went up. A shelf on the right wall of the stoop displayed an old gourd and a yellow, well-fed cat stretched out flicking its tail. I whispered hello to it and knocked on the screen door. The proper door was swung in, already open, but I heard no one and no one came. I knocked again, a little harder, but still she didn't answer.

I did not linger. I did not peek my eyes inside to her kitchen to see how she kept things. I whispered adios to the enormous feline presence and headed for the barn.

This made me feel a bit braver. Barns, machine sheds, gardens, didn't seem as personal.

The doves called again. Then stopped. The McHenry place was a very quiet place. Very quiet. At home, during the sudden lull of sundown or even in winter, there was still *some* kind of little racket going on, a bug or a bird or a frog or *something*. But... not here. I stopped dead, in mid-stride, to make sure I was right about that.

I was almost. There was something, a very distant something. A very soft and slow and steady... *whisking* sound, almost like a piece of sandpaper being drawn across a piece of wood. I couldn't pinpoint the direction it came from. Maybe *that* was a bug. Rasping its spiny little legs against each other, a come-hither little mating rasp. But that was really it. Otherwise, the place was—I hate to say it—a tomb. Maybe that's how widow's places were.

Berylie must keep a couple pigs around here *some* place, I thought. Maybe a goat or two. Some fancy ducks? Cornered up and safe from the coons and foxes?

I went past the milk house without looking in and pulled on the adjacent door to the bottom of the barn. It swung open easily with almost no sound, like it had been oiled. I stepped in with the light and then to one side out of its swath, waiting for my eyes to catch up. The stanchions, two long rows, stood open, expectant. I found myself tip toeing up the steps near the door I had come in, up to the barn floor. My hand slid along the flat wooden rail worn smooth by a century and more of McHenry hands hustling up and down, working, working, and I emerged into the closed vault of huge space upstairs. It was radiant with a dusky and almost unearthly glow.

The long, narrow, slatted windows, high and vertical, fed a very low brightness across the black walls in a stained glass way, churchly or ghostly or a combination. An ancient grain drill sat at the backside of the floor. One mow was a tenth full, the other empty. I walked across the empty one testing the spongy duff of straw and hay for missing floorboards with each slow step. Stopping, I peered up and around mildly in awe. The barn was perfectly quiet and perfectly huge. And I was small, imperfectly so, you might say.

How long I stood there motionless I don't know, a while. The spell was not easily broken—even by the first light tap I received on the top of my head. No, still transfixed, I craned my neck further back and, rather stupidly, looked straight up into the steepest pitch of the roof. Momentarily, another tap came, on my cheek now. A wet drop of something. I wiped it away, squinting to locate the source in the ascending dark recess. My feet stayed planted and yet another drip smatted my forehead. Again I wiped it. Warm and viscousy, its complete identity uncertain in the confusing light. Then... motion.

A dark form moved against the darker underside of the slate. I followed it away from the gable toward the interior of the barn, traveling along under the peak. It was on the hay rail, the steel track they used in the old days before bales to roll great iron clawfuls of loose hay into the mow from either end. High in the very center of the roofline, the lone cupola funneled a spot of light onto the rail and my eyes focused there anticipating the arrival of this shifty, drippy thing.

When it got to the spot it hesitated and peered around. Two narrowly set, beady eyes candled in the cupola's light... a possum. Its snake-like tail was coiled loosely around the rail and its pointed snout held a bird. Probably a squab snatched from an unguarded nest in the rafters. The unbecoming mammal was drooling around the soft chick's body—I'd seen it once before under fuller light in *our* barn, the drooling of a possum. The taps and the drops and the smats which were on my head and on my face: saliva.

My hands flew up and wiped hard, praying the thing wasn't rabid. I spit. And spit again and wiped. When I looked back it had scurried on, away into the blackness over the other mow.

That did it. Back down the steps I went, running. The hot, hard sun hit me and I felt delivered. I fired off a clip of spitting and shook my head like a wet dog. Squinting and focusing I moved away from the barn, one hand against the warm cement blocks of the milk house, and then I saw my hand and the relief and deliverance that had just been sweeping over me vanished.

My hand, the hand I had wiped my face with, was lightly smeared with blood not saliva. The squab's bones must've sliced into the possum's gums.... I rasped my face and forehead against the frayed short sleeve of my shirt. Possums made me crazy. Charlie didn't like bats; I didn't like possums. They played with my mind.

Then I heard the whisking sound again.

Whisssht-whisssht-whisssht....

This time it seemed to be coming from a direction, a particular direction. And that was from behind the house, clear behind the house and the small sheds there. Berylie, it had to be her.

Two wheel tracks in the grass between the house and the barn folded down from the barn bridge and I took one of them and then veered off toward the end post of a clothesline showing past the back corner of her house. Old Berylie had some nice glads and lilies planted in an island on this side and some irises right close to the house but these last, of course, had bloomed long ago and were just bladed foliage now. The sound got louder so I figured she was back here, where you'd expect her garden to be. Of course.

The feeling of trespass fussed at me again but I kept going. I reached into my pocket and worked my fingers through the emptiness that used to be my arrowhead until I dislodged a lint ball and then I worked that around.

At the back now, Berylie's sheets swaying gently on the lines in front of me, I stopped. *Whisssht-whisssht-whisssht....*

It was very close and seemed to be coming from the *house.* I looked over my shoulder and up. That summer should've been the backside's turn for paint, I saw, up and down, side to side, the white was peeling away in spalls big and small showing patches of some dull grayer time. The sound was being reflected off of the house, not coming from it.

I went down the clothesline slowly, stopping about halfway. The sound fell away and a breeze stiffened, moving the sheets, both rust-stained and miraculously white, in greater waves until I could see her intermittently through their swells and tumbles. She was in a faded, calf-length, short-sleeved shift-thing, a work dress, hair bound in a disintegrating knot at the back of her head and she was on her knees leaning against the snathe of a scythe. She had been cutting weeds from around a small shed, an old chicken coop. But now she was inspecting something and mumbling softly.

I stepped through the parallel shifting lines and hesitated midway. They rustled against my arms and legs and face. I listened closely. Berylie's voice was melodic and sorrowful, tender, soft, but there was also the faintest steely-edged undertone. A sorrowful yet somehow accusing or scolding undertone hardly there at all but there. She cradled something in her right hand.

Not wanting to disturb her—afraid to disturb her—I found myself frozen for a moment in the drying linens, until one hand came free of my pocket, let the lint ball drop to the ground, and slowly eased a sheet aside.

Blood was trickling down her hand and I could see now what she was holding there, a small rabbit, splayed open by a stroke from her scythe, wounded while hiding. Wounded *because* it had been hiding.

Almost without moving, it seemed, I faded back out of the sheets and around the house and headed back out Mrs. McHenry's long lane. I didn't really know I was back on Duff Road. until a car appeared at my side and Mr. Birr was offering me a ride home.

CHAPTER XLIII

My wits slowly unscrambled and came right. It was hard. Just as they got untangled from Berylie's clothesline they found themselves face to face with Tam O'Shanter's mare. There was nothing to worry about. Mr. Birr was excited about something and it had nothing to do with me. He had some news. Did I mind if he waited till we got over home and found my father before spilling it, he asked. Of course I didn't. The less he talked the less likely it was that I'd be accused of something.

So he drove on, speechless but giving off some weird invisible energy. I caught a quick glance or two at him as we rounded bends. His crew cut, freshly mowed, was bristling. It was sharp and shiny and seemed to defy the hot wind blowing in the windows.

We turned down the lane just ahead of Cambell who was coming home from Wendts. He'd gone over to help Bob Wendt trade out crop heads on their old combine. Such a neighborly fellow, my brother. Yes, *of course* Jo Wendt was back from her camp counselor job. Mr. Birr pulled over next to the fence just shy of the barn bridge where Cambell whipped in with the pickup.

"Mr. Birr," Cambell called loudly as we climbed out and hustled toward the front yard. "You must have some juicy information—judging by what I just heard from Bob Wendt."

"Hah! Figured it wouldn't take long to get around. What did Bob have to say?"

"Some nut named Lewis Grant killed our nun!" said Cambell, his voice ringing and joyful, like he was announcing the winner of a raffle or something.

"That's a generous description," replied Mr. Birr in a similar tone. "Where's your father, do you think?"

"In the garden with Jake maybe?" Cambell said, steering us in that direction.

We took about two strides when Dad called to us from behind, from the corncrib down beyond Mr. Birr's car and the fence. He and Jake had been filling sacks to take to the mill. They quit that and came quickly to join us. Jake took two or three little strides then jumped, two or three little strides then jumped, repeatedly, and swung a big ear of corn that was as much blue as it was yellow, probably from a plant at the edge of the field that had gotten crossed up with the Indian corn in the garden. It was fairly weird—he'd be saving it to show people.

Mr. Birr gave it a warm but brisk remark while register-
ing the unusual expression on my father's face. I had not
seen this expression since that amazing, horrifying day at
the beginning of summer, the expression of befuddled, wary
relief when he discovered the body stretched out there on
the ground was not Bobby Morgan's but a woman's.

"Rose got the word from Lucy MacRae half an hour ago,"
he said. "No details, just a name."

"As Cambell aptly puts it, some nut named Lewis Grant,"
said Mr. Birr, looking directly at me as if he owed me his
official report first after withholding it in the car. Then refo-
cusing on Dad, he let out an unusually high-pitched snort,
and continued, "Waltzed in on his own proud 'z a peacock
and confessed. Robert Morgan was evidently not Sister
Anna's only consort. This deranged fellow followed her out
and dispatched her with a sword from the Civil War, a family heirloom he says, right there in Perth Hill's cemetery. He
was miffed that she would chase all the way back out here,
to the cemetery, to meet little Bobby again—to say goodbye
before going to her mission."

"Again?" said a voice coming down the front porch steps.
It was Mom. We turned and faced her now as she got close.

With no hesitation Mr. Birr replied, "They had met
there before."

Mom pinched her eyes shut as if in pain, "Little
Bobby... where ever did his wits go?"

A very brief silence led, of course, to no conjectures.

Dad shook his head slowly and said, "Blest'f I know."

"This Grant character had been pestering her pretty

good, following her around whenever she left the convent. The sheriff's crowd thinks maybe the little Bobby getup was a way to sneak by him. It didn't work."

"It surely didn't," agreed Dad, almost whispering. Then in a bigger voice, he said, "But... this is jolly good news for our neck of the woods, isn't it, Aaron?"

"You can say that again. Keep yer fingers crossed this is the end of it."

"Mercy yes."

"A Civil War sword?" Jake said. His eyes sparkled.

"Maybe Santie will bring you one next Christmas," Cambell said, giving Jake's head a mild scuffing.

So Sheriff Donrett got his wish. One of his guys had done it. If Lewis Grant was telling the truth that is. His story had not yet stood the test of time, or any of the tests the experts from the boobyhatch would soon be giving him. It did not surprise me, though, that our nun had had more than one "consort." She was so pretty and excellent, if you looked at her, that is, like she was just a girl, which it was sounding to me she had been. She was just a picture now.

While the others, and Izzy now, too, worked over Lewis Grant and picked Mr. Birr clean of every detail I found myself not listening but watching them and becoming something like sad, or, actually, something somewhere between sad and mad. I had worked it out for myself how our nun's end had come and it was way more appropriate and chilling than Mr. Birr's story. I don't mean appropriate as in she deserved it or some stupid thing like that, just appropriate to the tangled little world she stumbled into. My version

involved the Morgans and the McHenrys and a very old trespass—a trespass being set right, being forgiven as it were. It
involved a very dark night and the most unfortunate dis-
guise you could imagine and a curse like Eli's being lifted,
violently. It was perfect.

I watched them. Jake was flipping his ear of corn end
over end in one hand. I felt cheated. I felt our nun was being
cheated, too. She had not become one of ours, her blood
becoming our soil, thanks to some demented loser from New
Sterling, in a trashed out El Camino, no doubt. She just
could not have. It was too simple. It was too... human.

Finally, Mr. Birr offered to take me back with the jack
and the tools and help with the tire as he was a nice guy and
he had some time and he was hoping to borrow the Massey
that evening to try and yank out an old willow stump.

He went the direct route, left down Orchard Road.
toward Perth Road., not the shady way up by Mr. Oliver's.
The peach trees went by on either side of us. They were just
trees. The peaches were long over. Duff knew how to grow a
peach. I never stole one, but it'd be easy. I did take an apple
once. It had rolled out onto the road. Cider season wasn't far
off, then winter. Eight feet of snow would be nice. Ten feet.
Snow would be the best.

Bending onto Perth Rd. then we saw cars at the church
and Mr. Birr slowed down. It was the Wilsons finally bury-
ing old Hugh's ashes. They had been waiting for a favorite
nephew to make it back from some weird job in
Newfoundland. The whole family had nice clothes on but
not suits.

They were all down in the Old Cemetery by the Ben Franklin trees where no one was allowed to be buried anymore. Except for really old people who got grandfathered in, whose people were all down there, whose plots had been spoken for years, decades ago. The preacher faced out towards the road and they were in a semi circle facing him and the big willow at the corner of the woods. A breeze swayed it.

As we were almost by, little Dougie Wilson heard us passing and turned his little head. It was nicely wetted down. He was holding his Mom's hand. He hesitated, just watching us, then with his free hand gave us a wave.

I waved back but we were too far past then and I doubted if he saw me. I'd be sure and tell him on Sunday that I had waved back. As we went down through the cherry orchard, Mr. Birr remarked, "That cemetery's been a lively place this summer."

He didn't laugh. I glanced quickly over at him and he was in a thought. It wasn't any old plot of earth, that cemetery. It was Perth Hill's.

A tractor pulled onto the road from the field below the trees and came towards us. Untwiggy, not bacon-y, getting hamburger-y, Jody Dyson on their old Farmall, a trike. She was pulling a hay tedder. She was wearing a halter-top and the road was pretty bouncy right there. I waved. Idiotically, I think.

THE END

ABOUT THE AUTHOR

Rob Laughner is a former petroleum engineer who quit to write. He started with a humor column for *The Helena Independent Record*, then articles about natural history for *Montana Magazine*, before turning to fiction that drew on his upbringing on a farm in Western Pennsylvania—where, he says, he had a "Currier and Ives childhood of playing in the creek and pitching manure." A direct descendent of one of Pennyslvania's most famous historic figures, Johnny Appleseed, Laughner is now one of his forebear's more far-flung sprouts: He currently resides in Helena, Montana.